MARIANA PINEDA

Lorca's drawing of Mariana

HISPANIC CLASSICS

Federico García Lorca

MARIANA PINEDA

Translated with an Introduction & Commentary
by

Robert G. Havard

ARIS & PHILLIPS - WARMINSTER

ISBN   0 85668 333 7 (cloth)
       0 85668 334 5 (limp)

3rd impression 1993

British Library Cataloguing in Publication Data

García Lorca, Federico
  Mariana Pineda. – (Hispanic classics)
  I. Title II. Havard, Robert III. Series
  862'.62 PQ6613.A763

Printed and bound by CPI Group (UK) Ltd, Croydon, CR0 4YY

CONTENTS

List of Illustrations

SELECT BIBLIOGRAPHY

The following list consists largely of works in English on Lorca. It includes critical material on *Mariana Pineda* and the play's historical background, studies of other related works by Lorca and texts from the Spanish tradition which influenced Lorca and which I have referred to in the Commentary.

Adams, Mildred, *García Lorca: The Playwright and Poet* (New York: Braziller, 1977).

Aguirre, J.M., 'El sonambulismo de Federico García Lorca', *Bulletin of Hispanic Studies*, 44 (1967), 267-85.

—   'Apostillas a "El sonambulismo de Federico García Lorca"', *Bulletin of Hispanic Studies*, 53 (1976), 127-32.

Allen, Rupert C., *Psyche and Symbol in the Theater of Federico García Lorca* (Austin: University of Texas Press, 1974).

Alonso, Dámaso and Blecua, José Manuel, *Antología de la poesía española: lírica de tipo tradicional* (Madrid: Gredos, 1969).

Anderson, Reed, *Federico García Lorca* (London: MacMillan, 1984).

Barea, Arturo, *The Poet and His People* (London: Faber and Faber, 1944).

Carr, Raymond, *Spain 1808-1975* (Oxford: Clarendon Press, second edition, 1982).

Cobb, Carl, *Federico García Lorca* (New York: Twayne, 1967).

Couffon, Claude, *Granada y García Lorca* (Buenos Aires: Losada, 1967).

Durán, Manuel, (ed.), *Lorca* (Englewood Cliffs: Prentice-Hall, 1962).

Edwards, Gwynne, *Lorca: The Theatre Beneath the Sand* (London: Marion Boyars, 1980).

Ford, Richard, *A Hand-Book for Travellers in Spain* (London: John Murray, 1845; republished London: Centaur Press, 1966).

García Lorca, Francisco, *Federico y su mundo* (Madrid: Alianza, 1980).

—   *Three Tragedies of Federico García Lorca*, (New York: New Directions, 1955).

Gibson, Ian, *The Death of Lorca* (London: W.H. Allen, 1973).

—   *Federico García Lorca. I. De Fuente vaqueros a Nueva York, 1898-1929* (Barcelona: Grijalbo, 1985).

Gil, Ildefonso-Manuel (ed.), *Federico García Lorca: El escritor y la crítica* (Madrid: Taurus, 1973).

Havard, Robert, 'The Symbolic Ambivalence of 'Green' in García Lorca and Dylan Thomas', *The Modern Language Review*, 67 (1972), 810-819.

- 'The Hidden Parts of Bernarda Alba', *Romance Notes*, forthcoming, 1986-7.

Hemingway, Ernest, *Death in the Afternoon* (London: Jonathan Cape, 1932, republished 1966).

Honig, Edwin, *Federico García Lorca* (London: Jonathan Cape, 1968).

Lima, Robert, *The Theater of García Lorca* (New York: Las Américas, 1963).

Morris, C.B., *García Lorca: 'Bodas de Sangre'*, Critical Guides to Spanish texts (London: Grant and Cutler, 1981).

Ramsden, Herbert (ed.), *F.G. Lorca: 'La casa de Bernarda Alba'*, (Manchester: Manchester University Press, 1983).

Reckert, Stephen, *Lyra Minima. Structure and Symbol in Iberian Traditional Verse* (Portsmouth: Eyre and Spottiswoode, 1970).

Rodrigo, Antonina, *Mariana de Pineda, heroína de la libertad* (Barcelona: Plaza & Janes, 1984).

- *García Lorca, el amigo de Cataluña* (Barcelona: Edhasa, 1984).

Zardoya, Concha, 'Mariana Pineda, romance trágico de la libertad', *Revista Hispánica Moderna*, 34 (1968), 471-497.

Portrait of Lorca by Anthony Stones, 1985

INTRODUCTION

Mariana Pineda was the first theatrical success for Spain's most celebrated poet and dramatist of modern times, Federico García Lorca (1898-1936). Reasons for its lasting appeal are not hard to find: it is Lorca's most overtly political play, being based on the historical event of a liberal uprising in the 19th century; it evokes all the colour and Romanticism of Andalusia and of Lorca's own Granada; it illustrates more starkly than perhaps any other of his plays that magical fusion of drama and lyricism which is Lorca's special genius. Written in 1925 and first performed in Barcelona's Teatro Goya in June 1927, *Mariana Pineda* is the work of a young, impassioned and as yet largely unrecognised literary talent; but though it shows occasional signs of immaturity in its stagecraft what faults it has pale into insignificance beside the powerful mood it generates through song, symbolism, scenography and dramatic tension. Here we have in precocious profile the playwright who was to write the great tragedies, whose theme was already fixing on the notion of fatalistic passion and whose creative art sprang so spontaneously from popular culture that in this his only historical drama he takes as his subject the folk heroine of Granada, the executed martyr, Mariana Pineda.

The historical topic might well have seemed safe water to an author who had seen his first theatrical venture, *The Butterfly's Evil Spell*, booed off the Madrid stage in 1920. That play of Lorca's student days had insects for characters and was far too avant-garde for the bourgeois theatre-going public of Madrid. But while in its topic *Mariana Pineda* was an act of compromise by one who had learnt a painful lesson from the commercial theatre, in practice the play was quite unlike the vacuous and evasive costume dramas which theatre impresarios had for so long fed to an unthinking public. Nor is it in any way a betrayal of Lorca's artistic integrity. Three points can be mentioned here. First, the play was written and staged during the dictatorship of Primo de Rivera (1923-30), a dictatorship reactionary enough to close Madrid University and, in 1929, to stop the curtain going up on Lorca's later play, *The Love of Don Perlimplin*. Clearly, *Mariana Pineda's* depiction of a liberal struggle against the repressive regime of Ferdinand VII in the 1820s was directly relevant to the situation Lorca's audience was experiencing under the anachronistic Primo in the 1920s. Second, *Mariana Pineda* makes

1

no concessions in terms of its language. The base is popular, certainly, but so shot through with Lorca's inventiveness of imagery that, according to one eye-witness of 1927, it had a startling effect upon its unsuspecting audience. Torrente Ballester observed that many of his fellow spectators were disorientated on hearing, as early as the play's fourth line, that a thread of cotton could hang 'like a knife-wound upon the air', and some left muttering about new-fangled poets when the bullfight ballad recounted that 'the very sky would turn/a chestnut brown' to match the matador's head. The success, then, of *Mariana Pineda* was by no means cosy, nor indeed was it resounding in commercial terms; rather, as Ballester says, it was a minority who took to it and they did so with an awareness that they were witnessing the beginning of a new type of theatre.[1]

A last point to be made about Lorca's choice of subject is simply that it was one close to his heart. Far from using history to distance and impersonalise, Lorca turned naturally and inevitably to Mariana Pineda as the figure through which he could best express his intense love of Andalusia and Granada. Her tragic tale was something he had grown up with:

'Mariana Pineda was one of the most moving things of my childhood. Children of my age, myself included, used to hold hands and form circles that would open and close rhythmically as we sang in melancholy and, what seemed to me, tragic voice:

How sad was that day in Granada,
when all the stones were made to cry,
when on the scaffold stood Mariana
who would not talk and had to die!

Marianita alone in her room
could never let her thoughts be free:
"What if Pedrosa should see me
sewing this flag of Liberty".

Poor Mariana, the flag of Liberty and Pedrosa all acquired in my eyes such a magical and immaterial shape that they seemed like a cloud, a sudden shower, white mist in the tree-tops that came upon us from the Sierra Nevada and enveloped our small village in a whiteness of silence and cotton'. (Lorca is speaking of his native village of Fuentevaqueros which is a few miles outside Granada).

'One day, holding my mother's hand, I went to Granada: once again I heard the popular ballad, and once again it was sung by children, though their voices were even more heavy and solemn than those which had filled the streets of my village, and then, deeply stirred, I began to ask, dig, hunt things down, and I came to the conclusion that Mariana Pineda was a woman, a marvellous woman, and that the meaning of her life, what essentially drove her, was her love for liberty'.

When Lorca grew up and went to study in Granada the history and legend of Mariana Pineda impressed itself even more strongly:

'In Granada her statue faced my window, and I looked at it all the time. How could I not feel duty bound, as a homage to her and to Granada, to sing of her gallantry?'

Mariana and Granada, the heroine and the city, two ideals of incomparable beauty that were irresistibly one in the poet's mind:

'Mariana Pineda struck me as a fabulous being of stunning beauty whose mysterious eyes traced all the city's movements with indescribable sweetness. As that ideal figure materialised in my mind it seemed to me that the Alhambra was a moon that adorned the heroine's heart, her skirt the fertile plain sewn in a thousand shades of green, her white petticoat the snow from the mountain indented against the blue sky, an edging of lace finely worked in the golden flame of a copper oil-lamp'.[2]

For Lorca, then, Mariana Pineda was nothing less than the personification of the lyrical beauty of Granada, a city which, with its Moorish towers, gypsy quarters, lush orchards, playing fountains and, above all, its breathtaking snowcapped mountains, is perhaps the most lyrical of all Spain's historic cities. But Mariana does not simply represent beauty; she is beauty brutalised, violated and mangled by one of the most chilling and barbaric forms of capital punishment, the garrote. In this synthesis of extremes, so typical of the baroque mentality of Spain, we have the key to her fascination: inlaid upon her exquisite feminine tenderness is the presentiment of the horror that is done to her. Throughout the play the fine line of her neck is at once the focal point of feminine gracefulness and the site that awaits the fatal thrust of iron. Mariana thus conjoins those two universal sentiments which Spaniards seem to experience with unusual physical vigour: the beauty of life and the terror of death. And yet in the last analysis Mariana's beauty transcends the physical. Her inner motivation, as Lorca noted, was her love for liberty, and on this basis she gives her life rather than betray her fellow conspirators to the police. Here Lorca skillfully interweaves another indispensable theme, that of love, for one of the conspirators is the man in whom Mariana has placed all her hopes for joy, Don Pedro de Sotomayor, and when

3

he prefers to seek his own safety rather than try to save Mariana from execution her martyrdom is put in even more poignant relief. Thus Mariana's beauty is an emblem of the highest ideals: those of liberty, love and, at the very end, of a spiritual transcendence which borders on mysticism. All these themes spring from the same historical source, though Lorca has needed to adapt history to achieve such a synthesis:

> 'I also said to myself that to create this fabulous being it was absolutely necessary to falsify history, history being an incontrovertible fact which allows the imagination no other escape than that of dressing it in the poetry of words, in the emotion of silence, and in the things there around it' (*ibid.*, 1738).

In a moment we shall look at the way Lorca uses poetry and the 'things' of Mariana's circumstance to invest his play with atmosphere and meaning. But let us begin with the historical situation, for this will show us both what Lorca took from history and what he added of his own, and it should thus provide a base for appreciating what his dramatic intentions were.

MARIANA PINEDA IN HISTORY

Mariana Pineda was executed at the age of twenty-seven in Granada on May 26, 1831. She had been charged and found guilty of embroidering a liberal flag, this being regarded as evidence of her complicity in an abortive anti-royalist conspiracy. Ramón Pedrosa, the Chief of Police who had been sent by the Crown to Granada to stamp out political subversion, offered her a pardon on condition she gave the names of the other conspirators. This Mariana resolutely refused to do, choosing instead to die by garrote. That the ultimate penalty could be exacted from one who, as her defence argued, was at worst guilty of criminal intent rather than criminal act, is a measure of the oppression which operated under Ferdinand VII, especially in the last ten years of his life, 1823-33, a period Spaniards refer to as 'the ominous decade'. To appreciate why Ferdinand's regime was oppressive and why provincial capitals like Granada were then teeming with revolutionary activity we must see this decade in its historical context.

At the beginning of the 19th century Spain was a shadow of the imperial power it had once been. The glorious Hapsburg era was now a remote childhood dream and a hundred years of Bourbons had witnessed irreversible decline in the shape of humiliating defeats by Britain and France, the loss of colonies, the loss even of Gibraltar and, for the first time since the days of the Moors, invasions of mainland Spain itself by foreign

4

troops. The result was a weakened economy and a weakened sense of national pride, the latter having been exacerbated by the fact that successive Bourbons, through family connexions, had invariably preferred things in the French or Italian style rather than the Spanish. Charles IV, who reigned from 1788-1808, was an amiable but dull king, and his extremely plain wife, María Luisa of Parma, had distracted herself with a lover half her own age, Godoy, whom she saw rise from the horse guards to be prime minister and virtual ruler of Spain by the age of twenty-five. Nicknamed 'the Prince of Peace' in pointed contrast to another soldier whose star had risen on the other side of the Pyrenees, Godoy had all Napoleon's ambition but none of his qualities. Having no care for Spain Godoy intrigued endlessly, at one time hoping to secure southern Portugal as a principality for himself while Napoleon carved up the rest of the Peninsula. So incensed were Spaniards that a mob stormed Godoy's mansion in Aranjuez in March 1808, the first major display of popular patriotism. Charles abdicated, his son Ferdinand went to Madrid expecting to be proclaimed king only to find that French soldiers occupied the city. There followed the sorriest chapter in Spanish history when Ferdinand, Godoy and a repentant Charles each went to plead their rival suits with Napoleon at Bayonne. The Emperor made dupes of them all by detaining them in France and putting his brother Joseph Bonaparte on the Spanish throne. But the departure of Ferdinand, the people's choice, had sparked off a riot in Madrid. In defiance of the brutality of Murat's soldiers the common people rose in the streets on May 2, 1808, *el dos de mayo*, the proudest date in the Spanish calendar. The events of that day and the carnage of the reprisals which followed on the next have been immortalised in paintings by Goya. They were also to inspire a mood of fervent political idealism which characterises the age in which Mariana Pineda lived.

There followed in 1808-1814 the Peninsular War, which Spaniards call the War of Independence. While Joseph presided for Napoleon in Madrid, Wellington defended and then countered from Portugal, and Spanish patriots formed juntas in the provinces. The key liberals withdrew to the walled city of Cadiz in western Andalusia where in 1812 they proclaimed their momentous Constitution, the most contentious document in Spanish history, which had as its cornerstone the notion of a monarch's constitutional as opposed to absolute sovereignty, his will being subject to that of an elected Cortes on certain issues. With Napoleon's defeat in 1814 the way was at last clear for the return of Ferdinand, *el deseado*, or 'desired one', but it was anybody's guess whether he would accept the Constitution. His answer was a prompt and resounding no. Perceiving that the masses wanted him simply because he was Spanish and not for any political niceties, Ferdinand abolished the Constitution and set about a vindictive persecution of its liberal perpetrators. The common people who had risen in the streets against Murat were now happy to shout '¡Vivan las cadenas!', 'Long live chains!', for they were at least their old familiar chains. Such euphoria was not likely to last in a bankrupt nation whose Latin-American trade or extractive policies had collapsed during the war. When in 1820 Ferdinand sent some 22,000 soldiers to Cadiz for the purpose of sailing to Buenos Aires and bringing the colonies to heel, their commander, Riego, as though inspired by the liberal associations of that city, made what was in fact the first Spanish *pronunciamento* and declared in favour of the Constitution. Riego instantly found support in other parts of Spain and the wily Ferdinand conceded with the words: 'Let us march honestly forward, and I the first, along the constitutional path'. But Riego's liberal triennium, 1820-23, was doomed to failure: the economic problems would not go away; the colonies had had their taste of freedom and wanted more; the idealistic Constitution proved impractical in many ways; the common people were not easily converted from regalism to an ideology inspired by the French Revolution; finally, while Ferdinand continued to scheme, Riego's parliament was bitterly divided between the *doceañistas*, the now more tempered men of 1812, and the *exaltados* or new radicals whose strength lay in the provincial capitals. Riego himself was of the extremist type and his over-hasty appropriation of Church wealth caused bitter antagonism. With the country in a state of virtual civil war, Ferdinand engineered the invasion of the 'hundred thousand sons of St Louis' from monarchist France who restored him to his absolute throne. For his three years and nine months of 'most ignominious slavery' he exacted full revenge. Riego was among the first to be hung, but hundreds followed suit and thousands more fled into exile. The 'ominous decade' had begun.

From Ferdinand's point of view an authoritarian rule was imperative after Riego's period of revolutionary anarchy. He adopted a system of ministerial despotism, investing enormous power in trusted supporters such as his minister of justice, Calomarde, whose name is writ large on the decade. It was Calomarde who carried out the purging of liberals, who saw to it that there were no newspapers but official gazettes and who closed the universities in the last years of Ferdinand's reign. The army which had brought Riego to power was cut to the bone; all officers who had links with secret societies were discharged, while 35,000 French troops stayed to keep an eye on things until 1828, mostly in the north and Catalonia. If Ferdinand's measures showed signs of easing up there was always the ultra-conservative clerical backlash to keep him on course. In the face of this oppression the near destitute class of ex-officers and other factions in the liberal support went underground and plotted in a mostly uncoordinated manner with the exiles. Between Valdés's landing at Tarifa in August 1824 and Torrijos's similar venture near Malaga in December 1831 there were several calamitous attempts at invasion and insurrection in the south, where masonic lodges were strongest and where British Gibraltar was a useful transit point for exiles. They all failed, for lack of organization and because the liberals were hopelessly optimistic in calculating the support their *grito* or cry of liberty would muster. It is this kind of utopian and ill-fated idealism which *Mariana Pineda* illustrates.

Turning now to the historical figure of Mariana Pineda, we are fortunate to have at our disposal Antonina Rodrigo's excellent biography on which the following summary is based.[3] Mariana was born in Granada on September 1, 1804, the second and only surviving child of María de los Dolores Muñoz y Bueno from Lucena (Cordova) and Mariano de Pineda y Ramírez, a retired naval captain. Mariana's father, a man of good stock, had been born in Guatemala City, where his father had presided as judge, but came to Granada at the age of two when his father was appointed judge there. After a distinguished naval career Mariano de Pineda was forced by ill health to retire at the age of forty-eight. Five years later, in 1800, he met the young woman of humble origin who would bear his children and he brought her from the village of Lucena to live with him in Granada. Soon after Mariana's birth, however, her mother left the family home and, in 1806, her father died, leaving the infant in the care of an uncle, José Pineda. Within another year her uncle would marry and pass Mariana on to the neighbouring Mesa family whom she would thereafter consider as her own, but the complications of her infancy were such that she was never legally able to claim her father's full inheritance.

At fourteen Mariana was engaged to Manuel de Peralta y Valte who at twenty-five was still only a cadet after eight years' service in the light infantry. A year later in 1819 they were married and in the next two years Mariana gave birth to first a boy, José María, and then a girl, Ursula María, who was named after Mariana's adopted mother, Ursula de la Presa. Tragedy struck in 1822 when Mariana's husband died at the age of twenty-eight, leaving his wife a widow, and a strikingly beautiful widow by all accounts, at just eighteen years of age. In September 1822, barely four months after her husband's death, Mariana would have witnessed the joyful scenes of Riego's visit to Granada when the citizens regaled their hero by singing the hymn of liberty to him. It was from about this time that Mariana began to get seriously involved in politics and, when Riego fell, her house became a centre for liberal meetings and an asylum for fugitives. Very likely it was liberal policy to enlist women in their secret army as a means of extending cover, but Mariana ran great risks and had already been charged and placed under house arrest by the time Ramón Pedrosa was sent to Granada in 1825. With its population of 65,000 Granada was then a hotbed of revolutionary activity, its walls still bearing slogans which dated back to the liberal triennium.

While Mariana's unfortunate husband no doubt first instilled liberal thoughts in her, it was a second and more successful soldier, Casimiro Brodett, who fully politicised her. It is likely that Brodett's legal petition to marry Mariana was turned down because of his known liberal affiliations, and further likely that the two years which show no trace of Mariana in Granada, 1825–27, were years she spent with Brodett, a Maltese, in northern Spain. Brodett, a fervent conspirator, was to be deported in 1830, and Mariana may well have thought it more prudent to return in 1827 to Granada where she continued as before to use her house for clandestine meetings. There she won an admirer in the young idealist José de Salamanca who, twenty years later, would be a powerful politician and the subject of a biography by Count Romanones, but who then, with his ardent unrequited love for Mariana, seems to have been the model for the abashed Fernando in Lorca's play. A last conspirator who needs to be mentioned here is Fernando Alvarez de Sotomayor, the character upon whom Lorca's Pedro de Sotomayor is based. Historically speaking, Sotomayor was Mariana's cousin and he hailed from Lucena, her mother's native village. He was a pedigree liberal, having served under Riego at Cadiz and having been taken prisoner in Navarre by the invading French in 1823. He had later been charged with acts of treachery to the Crown and, in 1828, when the authorities had intercepted a conspiratorial letter of his to an exile in Gibraltar, Sotomayor found himself in Granada prison under sentence of death. While his wife went off to plead on his behalf in Madrid, Mariana looked after his young son and visited Sotomayor each day in prison. Noting that the prison was visited by monks who cared for those condemned to die, Mariana conceived a plan of escape. Day by day, surreptitiously, she brought Sotomayor a Capuchin habit, a black hood, a rosary, a belt and even a false beard as a disguise. Then, on October 25, 1928, when the Brothers of Charity were going out to attend the execution of a man condemned for stealing sacred vessels from a church, Sotomayor made his daring escape. He joined in undetected with the brotherly throng and, once on the outside, made straightaway for Mariana's house from where, according to his own detailed account, he again promptly left only minutes before the police arrived. It is certain that Pedrosa suspected Mariana's complicity in the escape and, having been tricked in this way, he would no doubt have kept her house under close watch thereafter.

Mariana was now installed in 6, Calle del Aguila (Eagle Street) where she was joined in 1829 by her adopted mother, Ursula de la Presa, herself recently widowed. In the same year Mariana gave birth to a daughter, Luisa, the father being a politically ambitious twenty-eight-year-old law graduate, José de la Peña y Aguayo, who, though apparently having nothing to do with Mariana for the two remaining years of her life, later took responsibility for his daughter, and in 1836 published the first biography of Mariana Pineda which is the primary source for Antonina Rodrigo's recent biography.[4]

Moving on to the fatal year of 1831, the rest of Mariana's story is quickly told. In January Torrijos made his first unsuccessful attempt at invasion. Landing with 200 men at Tarifa near Algeciras, he was attacked by royalist troops and quickly took to his boats and sailed back to Gibraltar. In March General Manzanares, a hero of the war against Napoleon, led another small band of revolutionaries out of Gibraltar, expecting to gather support on the way to Granada. Trapped in the mountains near Ronda and his force reduced to barely twenty men, Manzanares was betrayed by a poor goatherd who had promised to guide him to a ship on the coast, and on March 6 the General took his own life after first shooting his guide. With this kind of activity now so common, the authorities stepped up their vigilance in the cities. Indeed, it was only a few days later, on March 14, that the flag of liberty which Mariana had been embroidering was discovered in the Albaicín district of Granada. The very next day Ferdinand began publishing a series of royal decrees in the *Madrid Gazette* which informed his subjects that, owing to the high level of activity of nefarious sects, he was empowering military bodies in the provincial cities to deal summarily with political criminals.

Mariana had sent the unfinished flag to two sister dressmakers in the Albaicín. Probably she thought the flag safer there, while the disappointment of recent events meant there was no urgency to finish it. As it happened, one of the sisters was involved with a young cleric who in turn was the son of an arch-royalist. The cleric, convinced that a revolution was imminent, warned his father to temper his political comments, mentioning the flag he had seen. The father, however, went straight to the police and they soon extracted all necessary information from the dressmakers, rewarding them for their help. Next Pedrosa and his men paid Mariana a visit and, no doubt with a view to simplifying court proceedings, later claimed that they had found the flag in her house. Mariana was immediately arrested, but, on grounds of ill health, a ploy she had used once before, was allowed to stay at home under house arrest. Within a week she had tried to escape by the balcony terrace, but her disguise as an old lady proved less effective than Sotomayor's and she was intercepted in the street below. On March 27 she was moved to the convent of Saint Mary of Egypt, which served as a prison and correction centre for Granada's fallen women. There, with Ursula de la Presa who had also been arrested, she was to spend the next two months, her sentence of death being confirmed by Calomarde on May 6, 1831. On May 24 the deputy mayor, Rafael Ansaldo, came to the convent to take Mariana by carriage to the Cárcel Baja (Low Prison) where, attended by the Brothers of Charity, she would spend her last three days preparing herself spiritually for her execution. The brothers and her own priest, Juan de la Hinojosa, implored Mariana to accept Pedrosa's offer of a pardon by giving the names of her accomplices, but Mariana remained serenely indifferent, saying only that she had no intention of dishonouring her family name. She ate no food in her spartan cell and her only concern was for the care of her two surviving children, José María, her first born, and the two-year-old Luisa.

On the morning of May 26 Mariana took Holy Communion in a brief service and was then dressed in sackcloth and led out of the prison. She was placed on a mule and went with a procession of guards and priests through the city to the Campo del Triunfo, an open space outside the old Arabic gateway of Elvira, the procession stopping every so often for the crier to read out her crimes and her punishment. It is reported that the streets were deserted and all shutters were drawn throughout her itinerary, also that there was thunder in the air and that it began to rain when the sentence was carried out. If there had been a plot to free Mariana there was no evidence of it that morning. After being garrotted she was buried in a common grave in Almengor cemetery where her body remained until it was exhumed in 1836. Then, with the inauguration of an annual festival in her honour on May 24-26, the liberal martyr's remains were borne through the streets of Granada each year in a processional hearse. Finally in 1856 she was given a permanent burial place in Granada cathedral.

LORCA'S TREATMENT OF HISTORY

By and large Lorca's treatment is faithful to history and there are signs of his having consulted Peña y Aguayo's original biography (see, for instance, my commentary on lines 183-4 of the third act), a text which, though now missing from Madrid's Biblioteca Nacional, was no doubt there in Lorca's student days in Madrid. An authentic sense of history is created in the play by references to figures such as Calomarde and Torrijos and to places like Cadiz, Gibraltar and Valençay, while Sotomayor's letter in the first act which relates his escape from prison conforms in precise detail to the escapee's own account as recorded by Peña y Aguayo and later republished by Antonina Rodrigo. On the other hand it is equally clear that history only serves Lorca as a base for a subject he wished to realise poetically and dramatically, and that to this end the playwright has taken some liberties both with events and the characters involved, notably in the cases of Torrijos and Sotomayor.

Looking first at Mariana herself, we find minor alterations and omissions on Lorca's part which have bearing on her characterization. Not surprisingly, no mention is made of her illegitimacy nor of her third child, the playwright preferring to untangle the web of her life both for the sake of clearer dramatic definition and to save spoiling the sense of honour and purity central to her character. Naturally, it was also more practical to have two children of acting age on stage. As regards Mariana's own age, Lorca indicates in line 52 of the First Engraving that she is over thirty as opposed to the twenty-seven-year-old who died in history, a slight but significant increment which tends rather to deepen her character and add more poignancy to her aspirations in love. Also noteworthy is the absence of any reference to her previous involvement in politics, such as her having been under house arrest in the early 1820s, and in general it could be said that Lorca depoliticises his heroine considerably. As to the final stages of Mariana's life, Lorca takes full advantage of her incarceration in a convent to develop the theme of religious transcendence in the Third Engraving. Evidently it was more fitting as well as simpler to have her go straight from the convent to her execution, omitting her days at the *Cárcel Baja*, and it was similarly more in keeping with the play's lyrical and nocturnal mood to have her leave at dusk rather than in the morning.

Turning to the men in Mariana's life who appear in the play, we have already suggested a model for Fernando in the historical person of José de Salamanca, who would have been just twenty years old in 1831. Secondly, Ramón Pedrosa appears as himself, his characterization being consistent with eye-witness accounts of his correct but steely Castilian manner. His lecherous interest in Mariana reflects the popular view of the villain of the piece as he appears in ballads, but this aspect of his personality, though not at all unlikely, remains unsubstantiated. Next, in Pedro de Sotomayor we have Lorca's main departure from history, there being no grounds to suspect that Mariana loved the historical Fernando Álvarez de Sotomayor, a married man and a father. Essentially Lorca seems to have conflated two historical characters

11

in the one dramatic persona of Don Pedro, namely Casimiro Brodett, her true lover, and Sotomayor, the escapee. The time of Don Pedro's escape is also brought forward from 1828 to a point much closer to Mariana's death, for the play indicates that the event took place in the autumn of 1830, a temporal compression which results in greater dramatic intensity. No doubt it was for the same reason that Lorca inverted historical chronology by having Torrijos's second disastrous invasion take place before Mariana's death. In fact, as we know, Torrijos was executed in Malaga in December of 1831, some six months after Mariana's execution, but clearly it was again more incisive to conflate the Tarifa and Malaga invasions and make the liberal hero's death ominously germane to Mariana's.

In all, then, Lorca's play is a synthetic reconstruction of certain events which took place between 1828 and late 1831, compressing these into what seems no more than a matter of a few months. Such foreshortening meets the requirements for plot momentum, while, in a more general sense, Lorca's concentrative technique leads to a synthesis of themes. In making Don Pedro at once lover and conspirator, Lorca unifies the play's two most prominent themes; similarly, he exploits the convent-prison setting of the Third Engraving to juxtapose the notions of spiritual and worldly freedom, or, more starkly, life and death. Clearly, the function of such powerful themes as liberty, love and spiritual transcendence had priority over historical veracity; moreover, it is precisely in this sense of fusion that Lorca's poetic conception of his subject is revealed. The poetic image, an agent which integrates different and often contradictory notions, is the crucial unifying element in the play. As such it is the point on which any consideration of the play's technical merits must begin.

ANALYSIS OF THE PLAY

True to its original inspiration, which came from ballads rather than the hard facts of history, *Mariana Pineda* is a play of exceptional poetic orientation. Written wholly in verse, apart from the eighteen lines of Don Pedro's letter in the First Engraving, the play gives prominence to poetry from the first lines of the Prologue where Lorca acknowledges the source of his inspiration by having the traditional ballad sung on stage. When the same lines are repeated at the play's end the effect is to frame the entire piece in what the subtitle calls *A Popular Ballad*. As to the body of the play, there are plentiful instances of what might be termed 'set pieces' of poetry, songs, recitations, narrative ballads, chorus-like incantations and frequent lyrical bursts in popular vein. The song of 'The Smuggler' in the Second Engraving, and, in the Third, those of 'the pirate ship' (from line 245) and the haunting lyric of 'the cool water side' sung off-stage (from line 165) are obvious set pieces. Only slightly less formal is the recitation of the Duke of Lucena ballad which so delights the children at the beginning of the Second Engraving, and from here it is a short step to the two full-blooded *romances* or traditional ballads on the Ronda bullfight in the First (lines 98-149) and Torrijos's disaster in the Second Engraving (331-378), ballads which spring naturally from the play's dialogue and plot. Next we note that the play contains several long speeches which are poetic in both manner and substance, ranging from Mariana's anguished soliloquies (for instance, from line 168 in the First Engraving and from line 89 in the Second Engraving) to Don Pedro's declamations on liberty in the Second. The latter are cast in long and cultured lines of verse as befits their weighty topic, but elsewhere Lorca catches our attention with abrupt flashes of imagery which come straight from the popular Andalusian tradition of the *cante jondo* or 'deep song' of flamenco whose boldness can take one's breath away:

> If my heart were glass
> you could look inside
> and see the silent
> drops of blood sobbing.
> (First Engraving, lines 435-438)

And here we come to the basic unit of poetry, the image, which is found in all parts of the play down to the most functional snippets of conversation. The cotton thread which, as we have already noted, 'hung like a knife-wound upon the air' (First Engraving, line 4), is one such example of the way images illuminate ordinary conversation. Ultimately it is the pervasiveness of the image which abolishes any sense of division between dialogue and what we have called 'set pieces', especially since the same images appear in both. The Novice Nuns' rhythmic and image-stocked litany on Mariana's imminent death in the Third Engraving is at once song, poetry and dialogue, but much the same holds true for the rest of the play which, in this sense, is akin to opera, its arias being the purple patches of verse which are tonally woven into the whole by the systematic repetition of motifs. On this basis we can say to those who suggest that the poetic sequences dilute or retard the play that they are simply missing the point, just as an opera-goer would be missing the point if he wished the arias could be shorter so as to hurry along the plot, for the point surely is that the play's mood, sensibility and theme, indeed its whole meaning, lies in the poetry. At the same time it would be wrong to see *Mariana Pineda* as merely a poet's virtuoso performance, and to avoid this we need to appreciate the organic function of poetry in the play.

13

To begin with the set pieces mentioned above, their most telling characteristic is that they all develop motifs germane to the play's principal themes. The songs of the smuggler (Second Engraving, lines 423-440) and the pirate ship (Third Engraving, 245-263) are typically Romantic evocations of freedom set against a backdrop of danger and struggle, freedom being implicitly hard-earned and even outside the law. The smuggler's song ends with a premonition of death, in which sense it links with the play's major ballads. The Duke of Lucena ballad (Second Engraving, 21-70), dealing with a young seamstress who embroiders a flag for a noble who intended going to war, fuses love and death, while no less relevant to Mariana is the depiction of death in the Torrijos ballad in the context of betrayal. Finally, in the ballad on the bullfight at Ronda, which at first glance seems no more than a poetic interlude, we have the most relevant theme of all to the heroine, sacrificial death. As in all cases death is beautified, here amid the colour and pageantry of the bullfight; what is more, the ritual act of killing the bull via its neck anticipates Mariana's own death by garrote. This introduces the play's most obsessive image, for shortly after recounting the ballad Amparo kisses Mariana's neck and says, 'this neck, this lovely neck /of yours... wasn't meant to suffer pain' (First Engraving, 156-7), and there follow numerous references to Mariana's neck by Don Pedro (Second Engraving, 200), Pedrosa (Second Engraving, 517-18), the First Novice (Third Engraving, 300-303) and Mariana herself (First Engraving, 365-67), culminating in her desperate defiance of Pedrosa:

> Can't you see that my neck is far too short
> for execution? Look! It can't be done.
> Besides, my neck is white and beautiful;
> and no one will want to harm it.
> (Third Engraving, 183-6).

Mariana's neck, the play's most synthetic and fatalistic motif, finds parallels and echoes in other patterns of imagery. Its most natural equivalent, in terms of the theme of violence done to innocence, is the suffering of Christ. This is evoked with typical Spanish physicality, for instance in the Third Engraving lines 70-1, and earlier when Mariana implores Christ's help:

> Oh Lord, think now of your bitter Passion,
> the wounds injustice hammered through your hands!
> (Second Engraving, 421-2).

Another and more frequent pattern is that of floral imagery which conjoins the notions of beauty and inevitable decay. Let us first note that this motif is sometimes integrated with those already mentioned, namely Christ's suffering:

Oh Lord! By the cruel wound in your side,
and by the sweet carnations of your blood...
(First Engraving, 310-11).

and, in one exquisite image, with Mariana's neck:

I saw her crying
and it seemed her neck fell
in petals to her lap.
(Third Engraving, 301-3).

The red carnation, so favoured in Andalusia, links visually with blood, for which purpose it is again used in the bullfight sequence (First Engraving, 137). By contrast, flowers also suggest the delicacy of female beauty, especially the soft texture of the skin. In Mariana's case the typical association is with a faded flower, for this suggests the time she has spent cooped up indoors embroidering as well as the anguish she suffers as a reluctant conspirator and forlorn lover. References to her waning complexion are found for instance in the First Engraving, 318-19, and at the play's opening:

The smile on her face has turned almost white,
like a delicate flower pressed on lace.

The persistent flower motif, then, is a virtual mirror-image of Mariana's neck, comparing figuratively with it by virtue of its slender stalk and conceptually through associations with beauty, tenderness, violence, decay and, implicitly, death. Moreover, the two images gain in plasticity, by being continually represented on stage. Mariana herself is seldom off-stage and it is not hard to imagine how the neckline of her dress as well as her deportment would focus attention on this part of her anatomy. Similarly, flowers are an ever-present prop. The initial scenic direction to the First Engraving indicates 'large bouquets of silk roses' on top of a sideboard; in the Second we find 'silk flowers in purple and green' in an urn on a console, and in the Third 'there is a large arch of paper roses in yellow and silver' above an image of Our Lady set in the convent wall (265+). In addition, the young women in the play wear flowers in their hair: Lucía and Amparo have 'a red carnation on each side' (First Engraving, 24+) and Mariana has 'a large red rose behind her ear' (First Engraving, 48+). When Mariana is about to be led from the convent to her death she exclaims 'Give me a spray of flowers!' (Third Engraving, 405) and the First Novice says:

Never again will your eyes see this orange light
that falls in blossoms on Granada's roofs at night.
(Third Engraving, 421-2).

15

When the departing Mariana is apostrophised as a 'springtime carnation' (Third Engraving, 420) her identification with flowers is so complete as to be in perfect accord with the anonymous lines of the original ballad:

> Like a lily they cut the lily,
> like a rose they cut the flower,
> like a lily they cut the lily,
> her heart more lovely by the hour.
> (Prologue, 12-15).

Finally, other images which might be briefly mentioned for their typically Lorquian fatalistic associations are: birds, fish, the wind, the horse and its rider, and that complex of nocturnal imagery which includes the moon, stars and planets.[5] The hint of fate in such images will almost always be apparent to the English reader, though it will occasionally be of help to know certain peculiarly Spanish derivations, as for instance in the case of the wind which, among other things, is what bullfighters fear most in the arena, wind being an unpredictable element which takes away their control of the cape. In any event, these and other images will be examined in the Commentary which is with the text and here it is simply their proliferation and interconnexion which we note and anticipate.

While the poetic element in *Mariana Pineda* has been universally acclaimed, critics have found fault with other features in the play. Shallow characterization, a melodramatic plot, lack of consistent tension, an anticlimactic third act, these are some of the charges levelled against the play.[6] The tendency has been to accept Lorca's own extremely harsh judgement expressed in May 1929:

> 'My play is the weak work of a beginner, and though it shows traces of my poetic temperament, in no way does it now reflect my concept of the theatre.'[7]

Certainly the play has faults and certainly Lorca's concept of the theatre had changed in the four years since he had written it, but this self-criticism seems far too severe. It may well have something to do with the time when the criticism was made, for, in the summer of 1929, with his life and work at a crossroads, Lorca was to leave Spain in a state of emotional distress for New York, where he would write his most avant-garde work. In other words, his above comments on *Mariana Pineda* were made at a time when he was turning his back on traditionalism and when, following the enormous success of *Gypsy Ballads* in 1928, he had grown tired of being labelled an Andalusian folk poet. But if 1929 was a year in which Lorca changed direction, we also know that he would return to his Andalusian topics for the great tragedies he wrote in the 1930s and that, not long before his death, he would write *Doña Rosita the Spinster*, or *The Language of Flowers*, a play which has a great deal in common with *Mariana Pineda* in terms of mood and poetic technique. Thus it may be unwise to accept Lorca's isolated damning remark, though, at the same time, one cannot ignore the issue of the play's possible failings, taking these in turn.

First, there is no denying that there are melodramatic, sentimental and self-consciously theatrical elements in the play. But is this necessarily a failing? The kind of unconvincing sequence critics have in mind includes Mariana's emotional manipulation of Fernando in the First Engraving, (lines 325-414), recalling him after he has departed, making him swear his love for her, then having him read aloud the letter from her true love Don Pedro, a man whom Fernando will then ironically be committed to save. Another theatrical cliché occurs in the Second Engraving (481+) when Mariana drops her ring on being interrogated by the loathsome Pedrosa, while modern audiences may be similarly unimpressed by that sequence in the Third (322+) when, having been told she has a visitor, Mariana excitedly arranges her hair in anticipation of Don Pedro's arrival only to find that it is the unfortunate Fernando who appears. These stylised moments of tension and pathos, just like Mariana's heart-rending speeches and the clandestine comings and goings of cloaked conspirators or of servants with candelabra, seem to belong to a different theatrical age and tradition. And indeed they do; they belong to the Romantic tradition. Here we encounter the real difficulty in assessing the play, for, before anything else, we must acknowledge that Lorca has deliberately cast it in the stylised vein of Romantic drama, a drama notorious for plundering its audience's emotional reserves by way of all kinds of theatrical trickery. Letters, rings, bereft lovers, plaintive speeches, villains and martyrs, convents and prisons, this is the very stuff of Romantic drama. Following the prescription meticulously, though without letting his play degenerate into pastiche, Lorca creates a package of theatrical signs which capture the flavour of the age in which Mariana lived. Ultimately everything is sacrificed for atmosphere, a stylised, period atmosphere, and frequently the scenic directions reveal how much the playwright delighted in this atmosphere: '*Mariana... looks at the time on one of those large gold clocks in which all the exquisite poetry of the age seems to be sleeping*' (First Engraving, 167+); '*Mariana sits down on a chair, her profile to the audience. Fernando is close by and a little in front of her. They compose a classical picture of the period*' (First Engraving, 328+), again, referring to the Conspirators, '*Some sit down while others remain standing, forming an attractive period picture*' (Second Engraving, 241+). Given this priority of 'atmosphere', a consciously artistic or

17

'staged' atmosphere, and given that Mariana's story is so deeply entwined with the Romantic ethos, it was both inevitable and logical that Lorca would immerse himself in the semiotics of Romantic drama and that, in short, he would use a theatrical language appropriate to his theme.

Much the same defence can be applied in the context of characterization, though other points may also be brought in here. Again we must begin by conceding that, outside Mariana, the play is not especially notable for characterization, which, given her dominant role, is hardly surprising. The three prominent males, Fernando, Pedrosa and Don Pedro, all serve to point up Mariana's emotional life and tragic situation. They all love or desire her in different ways; Fernando innocently, idealistically; Pedrosa sensuously and cynically; and Don Pedro, somewhere in between, begins as an idealistic gallant whose love seems inseparable from his political altruism and ends on the worst note of cowardly selfishness, his flight from Spain when Mariana awaits execution contrasting pointedly with her having risked her own life to help him escape from prison. Thus, while Fernando and Pedrosa are strictly stock types, though nonetheless well drawn for that, Don Pedro, by virtue of our changing conception of him, is an intriguing and ambiguous character. What is more, Lorca captures the ambiguity in the speeches he gives Don Pedro. The ardent conspirator is shown to be a man of great oratorical powers, his language having a fluency of rhythm, grandness of image and an exhortative emotional charge which is never less than impressive. But one cannot help suspecting as we listen to his fine words that much of what he says has been well practised in liberal meetings, and the manner in which he says it, especially when he has only an audience of one in Mariana, may strike us as excessively rhetorical. In short, there is what might be called an element of deconstructive bombast within Don Pedro's splendid lines, the result of which is that even his most ardent speeches have a disconcertingly hollow ring and we begin to anticipate cowardice in his daring, selfishness in his altruism. As it turns out, the revolutionary who was prepared to fight with 'hands and... nails' for Spain (Second Engraving, 190) gives up the woman whom he was betrothed to marry with no fight at all, a most provocative contradiction.

Before looking at the characterization and significance of Mariana herself it is worth making the point that many of the play's minor characters are well drawn. Lorca gives us a foretaste of his soon to be renowned skill at portraying females in, for instance, the servant Clavela and the motherly Doña Angustias, both of whom are humanised by their deep concern for Mariana and by their understandable disapproval of her involvement in political subversion. The brief appearances of Amparo and Lucía are also convincing, especially since Amparo's coquettish *joie de vivre* is all the more radiant in contrast to her sister's prim, bourgeois manners. Both sisters again worry for Mariana, a point which also applies to the sensitively drawn Mother· Carmen, who is not at all cowed or institutionalised, and to the First and Second Novices, whose spontaneity, innocence and uncomprehending sorrow at Mariana's fate makes a delightful mixture. Even the Second and Fourth Conspirators, in marked contrast to Don Pedro, express an honourable fear for their host's safety when Pedrosa unexpectedly arrives at her house. Indeed, all the characters, down to the reluctant bearer of bad tidings, Alegrito, grow in stature and human warmth by virtue of their relationship with the heroine, and they all point unerringly to her exceptional prominence in the play.

Fundamentally the play is structured around Mariana's mood and emotions. What little action there is occurs in the Second Engraving, while the First and Third are parallel in that they dwell on the introspective lyricism of her anguish. In both these acts the key note is suspenseful waiting: Mariana waits for news of Don Pedro in the first and for her own death in the third. The delicacy with which Lorca explores his heroine's changing moods, her conflicting hopes and responsibilities as lover, conspirator and mother, more than compensates for the lack of action in the First Engraving, while the beautifully caught theme of time's slow passing actualises and makes palpable the play's historical situation as we watch the steady movements of the gold clock. It is, however, the Third Engraving that I wish to turn to now, for this is where Lorca's powers of character portrayal, it seems to me, reach new heights. Here the theme of time's slow passing acquires new meaning, there being no time slow enough for the condemned prisoner, and the audience, just like Mariana, watches anxiously for every change of hue in the evening sky as the fatal moment draws inexorably closer. By this stage in the play, admittedly, the plot is as good as over: we are told as early as line 83 that Mariana's liberal friends have no intention of trying to save her, and, by line 105, that Don Pedro has departed Spain. But is the act – or the three-quarters of it which remain – anticlimactic? Far from sharing such a view, I suggest that in terms of its unsurpassable fatalism, its almost uninterrupted lyricism and, above all, its verbal and scenographic symbolism, the Third Engraving in *Mariana Pineda* ranks alongside Lorca's finest theatrical achievements.

The convent-prison setting is the key. Its white walls demarcate the bounds of Mariana's liberty in a way that looks forward to the claustrophobic use of space in Lorca's last play, *The House of Bernarda Alba*. At the same time the patio-garden in which Mariana is free to walk and meditate is softened by delightful Moorish features, as the scenic direction indicates: '*Archways, cypress trees, myrtles and small fountains*'. Thus the setting is a mixture of paradise and penitentiary, of heaven and hell, and this is the dialectical tension which frames Mariana's inner drama throughout the act. Having dismissed any thoughts of saving her own life by informing, Mariana faces the ultimate challenge of preparing herself for death by renouncing the world, a transcendental theme of stark proportions which is fully expressed by the physical setting. Victor Brombert has shown the importance of the prison symbol to Romanticism and to post-Romantic thinking, arguing that 'the link between enclosure and inner freedom is at the heart of the Romantic sensibility'.[8] In particular, Brombert describes two psychological projections which apply simultaneously in the prison symbol, 'the one toward an inner centre', since isolation forces the prisoner to look in upon himself, 'the other toward a transcending outside which corresponds to the joys of the imagination and the ecstacy of spiritual escape' (p.10). Both hold true in Lorca's play. Mariana looks inwards, chastising herself as 'a terrible sinner' (line 62), coming to accept such unpalatable truths as the realization that Don Pedro never really loved her (345-8), even renouncing her love for him (384), and declaring on two occasions 'I know full well how blind I was' (53, 73). At the same time she develops a new spiritual dimension:

> Sister, how sorely grieved I am
> by everything I find on earth! (68-9)

and, looking skywards:

> How well I understand the meaning of that light! (399)

Thus the prison walls are restrictive and help concentrate the mind, but they are also, in Brombert's happy phrase, 'an invitation to transcendence' (*ibid.*, 9), and it is this latter value which Lorca develops by giving remarkable prominence to stage lighting as the act progresses.

In prison Mariana discovers the peace of solitude, beautifully evoked in lines 55-9. She wishes, like an agoraphobic, that she could stay there 'for ever' (47), protected from the world. She begins to dream (59), but her dreams sometimes turn to morbid hallucinations (157-9) or else to extravagant fantasies about Don Pedro (112-133) in a futile attempt at justifying her worldly existence. These moments of madness are psychologically consistent with the stress of repression and the contradictions of her situation, one contradiction being that betwen prison time, arrested, atemporal and utopian, and the time which measures out the oncoming horror of her death. But madness and fantasy are,

20

it seems only transitional, escapist factors which attach to the process of renouncing the world, rejecting past values and discovering the spiritual self. Throughout the act Mariana lives in an intermediate, dissociated state – I'm already dead' she tells Mother Carmen (49) and again Fernando (371) – and the drama which Lorca now superbly captures is not that of her death but of her rebirth. In her 'splendid white costume', her complexion 'extremely pale' (43+), she epitomises spirituality. Attended by Novices, she sits ' in an other-worldly pose ' (313+) or else she moves ethereally between the skyward cypress trees while, intermittently, the air fills with the sounds of an organ, the choir, church bells and, constantly, the fountain's running water. Halfway through the act 'The light begins to take on the hue of dusk' (227+), and soon, more tangibly 'The cypress trees begin to take on a golden hue' (265+). Near the end this darkening process is reversed and there is a striking theatrical effect of new light which Lorca describes in meticulous and poetic detail:

'Right through to its end the whole scene increasingly acquires that strangely sharp light of a Granada sunset. A rose and green light comes in through the archways, while the cypress trees take on exquisitely subtle tones which make them seem almost like precious stones. A soft orange light comes down from above, which increases in intensity as the scene draws to a close' (392+).

That this is the flooding light of salvation is unambiguous in the final direction as Mariana departs:

'A splendrous, joyful light invades the scene' (432+).

Thus the play comes to an end with a moving synthesis of tragedy and triumph, but also with a synthesis of all the artifices of theatre. In this sense the final act brings to mind that much vaunted modern term 'total theatre', though we should also remember that Romantic dramatists such as Spain's Duque de Rivas and José de Zorrilla had excelled in blending poetic language with stagecraft. There is perhaps not such a great distance after all between the modern age and Romanticism; certainly Victor Brombert found a continuing thematic thread in his study of the prison symbol. We might add, by way of conclusion, that the theme which comes through most strongly in the last act of *Mariana Pineda* is also strikingly modern in its thinking. Shortly before departing Mariana says:

Now I know what the oak and the nightingale say:
Man is a prisoner who can never be free. (413-14)

This last line is the insight which links Romanticism and modern thought, uniting tortured poets like Espronceda, the Spanish Byron, with a film-maker like Luis Buñuel who also made man's futile struggle for freedom his central theme (see commentary on line 414). Lorca shares the pessimism of his friend Buñuel, while at the same time his heroine Mariana discovers the same truth Espronceda's Romantic archetype discovered in *The Student of Salamanca*, namely that death is the only passage to freedom. Mariana goes 'adorned and beautiful' (406) to the scaffold, a lace mantilla in her hair, a ring on her finger and a spray of flowers in her hand, just like a bride. Indeed, the final scene is nuptial, for Mariana, in death, is the bride of liberty, love and, ultimately, spiritual goodness. In going willingly to her death she incarnates freedom, the very thing Don Pedro loved; but while she is thus metaphorically reunited with her lover, she transcends the cares and ambitions of his world and stands on the threshold of a spiritual adventure. Effectively, then, the final act carries the play forward into new territory by exploring the heroine's projection towards a mythical, symbolical dimension. Its celebratory religious tone may be uncommonly orthodox for Lorca, but this in no way diminishes its merit.

The Spanish text which appears here is, with some minor variants, substantially that of the *Obras completas*, vol. 2 (Madrid: Aguilar, 19th edition, 1974). This is generally a more accurate text than that of the earlier editions, those published in Santiago de Chile, Editorial Moderna, 1927; Madrid, Rivadeneyra, 1928; Buenos Aires, Losada, 1943. In addition to containing some lines found neither in these nor in the annotated edition of R.M. Nadal and Janet H. Perry (London: Harrap, 1957), the *Obras completas* also provides on pp. 1410-14 a list of the variants in Rivadeneyra and Losada which is helpful to scholars. It does seem to me, however, that on a few occasions the variants of the earlier editions are more suitable. The reasons for this are given in the Commentary where every departure from the *Obras completas* is noted.

A word on the English translation: I would naturally like to claim that I have kept unwaveringly close to Lorca in both literal and poetic meaning. But while that was my original ideal, in practice I found that the literal and the poetic do not always make a match: either the poetic does not translate literally or the literal is not at all poetic. In a totally poetic play like *Mariana Pineda* compromises have to be made sometimes in translation if the poetic mood is to be sustained, especially if one has an English performance of the play in mind. One problem is the selection of roughly equivalent English verse patterns to render the Spanish versification. For the most part blank verse and iambic pentameters have replaced the Spanish forms and the Spanish preference for assonance has been ignored. In these sequences the translation is very often close to literal, though even here metrical constraints will sometimes determine word

22

selection. A case in point is the use of the more manageable verb 'sew' at times instead of the strictly correct 'embroider' to render *bordar*. The use of such variants is, I believe, preferable to the breaking of metric regularity, a view not entirely shared it seems by the previous translator, James Graham-Luján, *Mariana Pineda, Tulane Drama Review*, 7 (1962), 18-75. As for rhyme and assonance, my attempts have been largely confined to the 'set pieces'. It was important to highlight the formal, recitative tone of such sequences as the ballads on the Ronda bullfight and Torrijos's death. But rhyme of course makes its own demands, with the result that the English can become more a version than a translation, which is perhaps what has happened with the Torrijos ballad. In the main, however, I have tried to meet the exigencies of poetry and of literalness with a fairly even hand. Finally, it has not been my intention to tone down the colour and passion of Lorca's diction and imagery, extravagant as this may seem at times to English ears. Here we remember not only that the play is Andalusian in temperament, but also Romantic, and hence somewhat extreme even by Lorca's standards. To have compromised on this would have been to destroy the historical and poetic logic on which the play is based.

I would like to thank The British Academy for a grant which enabled me to spend time in Madrid in the summer of 1985 when the Introduction and Commentary of this book were completed. It is also proper that I single out two texts which have been especially helpful with regard to background information: the historical biography by Antonina Rodrigo, *Mariana Pineda, heroína de la libertad* (Barcelona: Plaza y Janes, 1984), and Richard Ford's eye-witness account of Andalusia and Granada in the 1830s, *A Hand-Book for Travellers in Spain* (originally published by John Murray, London, 1845, and republished by Centaur Press, London, 1966), which I have used extensively in the Commentary. I am grateful to Antonina Rodrigo and to the editors of Centaur Press for allowing me to make such plentiful use of the two texts. I would like to express my special thanks to Victor Dixon of Trinity College, Dublin, for his careful reading of my typescript and for the many useful suggestions he made. Finally, on a more personal note, I recall that *Mariana Pineda* was the first Spanish work I ever read and that my affection for it was much inspired by a man who was Spanish master for many years at Porth County Grammar School, Mr Georges Rochat, to whom I am greatly indebted.

NOTES TO THE INTRODUCTION

1. Gonzalo Torrente Ballester, 'Mariana Pineda, 1927', *Primer Acto*, 50 (Feb. 1963), 27.
2. F.G. Lorca, 'Entrevistas y Declaraciones', *Obras completas* vol. 2 (Madrid: Aguilar, 19th edition, 1974), pp. 945-6, 939, 94
3. Antonina Rodrigo, *Mariana de Pineda, heroína de la libertad* (Barcelona: Plaza & Janes, 1984).
4. José de la Peña y Aguayo, *Doña Mariana Pineda* (Madrid: 1836). For further details see Antonina Rodrigo, *op.cit.*, 295.
5. These and other images are briefly discussed by Concha Zardoy in her informative article '*Mariana Pineda*, romance trágico de la libertad', *Revista Hispánica Moderna*, 34 (1968), 471-497.
6. See Concha Zardoya's summary of critical appraisals, *ibid.*, 472.
7. F. García Lorca, *Obras completas*, vol. 1, 1154.
8. Victor Brombert, *The Romantic Prison. The French Tradition* (Princeton: Princeton University Press, 1978), 4.

MARIANA PINEDA

mance Popular en Tres Estampas   A Popular Ballad in Three Engravings
(1925)
Federico García Lorca

A la gran actriz
Margarita Xirgu

Personajes	Characters	
1ariana Pineda	Mariana Pineda	
sabel la Clavela	Isabel la Clavela	(her servant)
)oña Angustias	Doña Angustias	(her adopted mother)
mparo	Amparo	(daughters of the
ucía	Lucía	Chancery Judge)
1iño	Son	(of Mariana)
1iña	Daughter	(of Mariana)
or Carmen	Sister Carmen	
1ovicia 1	First Novice	
1ovicia 2	Second Novice	
1onja	Nun	
)on Pedro de Sotomayor	Don Pedro de Sotomayor	
ernando	Fernando	
edrosa	Pedrosa	
legrito	Alegrito	
:onspirador 1	First Conspirator	
:onspirador 2	Second Conspirator	
:onspirador 3	Third Conspirator	
:onspirador 4	Fourth Conspirator	
1ujer del Velón	Woman with an oil lamp	
1iñas, Monjas	Girls, Nuns	

PRÓLOGO

*Telón representando el desaparecido arco árabe de las Cucharas
y perspectiva de la plaza Bibarrambla, en Granada, encuadrado
en un margen amarillento, como una vieja estampa iluminada en
azul, verde, amarillo, rosa y celeste, sobre un fondo de paredes
negras. Una de las casas que se vean estará pintada con escenas
marinas y guirnaldas de frutas. Luz de luna. Al fondo, las niñas
cantarán con acompañamiento el romance popular.*

Three Engravings: the choice of the term 'engravings' (*estampas*)
rather than 'acts' (*actos*) in the subtitle and elsewhere is indicative not
only of the play's visual emphasis but also of its formal, almost excessively
conscious, artistry. The Spanish word *estampa* could in fact be translated
as 'print', 'plate' or 'engraving', and I have preferred the last of these
because of its unambiguous artistic reference and for the feel it gives of a
somewhat outmoded and even precious stylization which is in keeping with
the spirit and technique of Lorca's play.

Bibarrambla Square: a typical and picturesque square in the heart of
Granada near the Cathedral and Town Hall. It has also been known as
Constitution Square. Situated near a bend in the Darro, the river which
flows through the centre of Granada and which at this point is covered
over, the square takes its name from the Arabic *Bib Rambla*, meaning Sand
Gate, since the Darro used to deposit large quantities of sand at the
square's main gate. Richard Ford, who was in Granada in 1832, just one
year after Mariana Pineda's death, offers the following description of the
square and of the gateway of the Cucharas (literally 'spoons') which was
then standing:

'Walk up the *Carrera del Darro* (Darro Avenue), to the celebrated
Plaza de Vibarambla (sic), the 'gate of the river' (sic). This gate still
exists: the Moorish arch struggles amid modern additions, incongruous but
not unpicturesque. The quaint *Plaza* is now converted into a market-place:
one row of old Moorish houses, with square windows, yet remains on the
north side. This is the square so famous in ballad song for the *Cañas*, or
the Jereed, and the bull-fightings of Gazul. Here the pageantry of *Pasos*
and Corpus Christi are carried on to the joy of an illiterate community...
On market-days, sorts of booths and stalls are put up like an Arab *Douar*.
The fruit is very fine, especially the grapes, figs and melons... Keeping
along the left side, enter the Pescadería (fish-market); the old wooden
balconies will delight the artistical eye...' (Ford, *op.cit.*, 577).

an old engraving: the curtain which depicts the Bibarrambla is a
visual prop of conscious artistry designed to evoke the era of Mariana
Pineda. It thus links with the play's subtitle and prepares us for the
stylised period flavour of the work.

PROLOGUE

*A curtain depicts the now disappeared Moorish gateway of the
Cucharas and a view of the Bibarrambla Square in Granada. It is
framed in a yellowish border like an old engraving and it is lit up
with blues, greens, yellows, reds and sky-blues, against a background of black walls. One of the houses to be seen is painted over
in seascapes and garlands of fruit. There is moonlight. Offstage
girls sing a popular ballad to musical accompaniment.*

One of the houses... painted over in seascapes and garlands of fruit:
while the sea and fruit motifs evoke Bibarrambla's function as a
market-place described by Ford above, they have a more pressing symbolic
value. Lorca was highly practised as a poet in folklore and traditional
symbolism and often drew upon such motifs, especially when intending
emotional colouring. Here we might note that it is not merely a question of
the seascapes and fruit offering a seductive visual picture; the traditional
associations are more complex. In the context of the love theme it is
largely a question of the degree of sweetness or bitterness which the
motifs convey: thus the sea, salty and undrinkable, is traditionally in
Spain a bad omen for love, while fruit has a gamut of implications from the
sweet orange to the bitter lemon. Later the play will develop the negative
value of the sea in two specific instances: first, the hope of a liberal
uprising is dashed when Torrijos and his men are ambushed upon landing
on a beach near Malaga; second, at the play's end, Mariana's hope for love
and for her own freedom is ruined by the news that Pedro has set sail for
England.

Finally, it would seem that Lorca wished to suggest that the house
painted in seascapes and garlands of fruit was the house Mariana Pineda
once lived in, for when Fernando arrives at her house in the First
Engraving he remarks on its 'delightful exterior', 'with all those lovely
paintings / of sailing ships and flower garlands...!' (lines 197-9). The
historical fact, however, is that Mariana lived in Calle del Águila (Eagle
Street), which is set back a little from Bibarrambla Square. Later
references to the secluded location of the house, as when the Second
Conspirator speaks of 'this dark street' (line 233, Second Engraving), are
more consistent with history. Thus the parallel references to a decorated
house are clearly an example of Lorca using poetic licence to set up
reverberations and link the Prologue with the body of the play.

There is moonlight: the moon, or moonlight, is often used by Lorca for
symbolic effect. Throughout his work it is associated with death, usually
suggesting a violent death inflicted by silver or glinting daggers and the
like. The nocturnal atmosphere of the Prologue is continued through almost
the whole of the play.

a popular ballad: the ballad in Spanish literature is traditionally a

27

¡Oh, qué tan triste en Granada,
que a las piedras hacía llorar
al ver que Marianita se muere
en cadalso por no declarar!
Marianita sentada en su cuarto   5
no paraba de considerar:
"Si Pedrosa me viera bordando
la bandera de la Libertad."

[*Más lejos.*]

¡Oh, qué día tan triste en Granada,
las campanas doblar y doblar!   10

[*De una ventana se asoma una mujer con un velón encendido.
Cesa el coro.*]

MUJER: ¡Niña!   ¿No me oyes?
NIÑA [*Desde lejos*]:   ¡Ya voy!

[*Por debajo del arco aparece una Niña vestida según la moda
del año 1850, que canta*]:

Como lirio cortaron el lirio,
como rosa cortaron la flor,
como lirio cortaron el lirio,
mas hermosa su alma quedó.   15

[*Lentamente, entra en su casa. Al fondo, el coro continúa.*]

¡Oh, qué día tan triste en Granada,
que a las piedras hacía llorar!

[*Telón lento.*]

---

work composed collectively by the people, rather than by one author. It
frequently recounts the life and deeds of an historical figure, as in the
case of the earliest ballads which dealt with the Cid's exploits against the
Moors. The ballad is passed down from generation to generation by word
of mouth, an oral process which leads sometimes to legendary embellishment
and, almost always, to dramatic intensification as, literally, only the most
memorable parts are retained. Most typically the ballad has eight syllables
per line, but it is sometimes longer as is the case here. The rhyme is
always assonantal, that is, of vowels only, as in *Granada – Mariana* which
has assonance in *a – a*.

Lorca himself came to know of Mariana Pineda through hearing the
ballad of her life sung in the streets of Granada. Thus, as mentioned in
the Introduction, lines 1-10 of the Prologue are not Lorca's own but belong

How sad was that day in Granada,
when all the stones were made to cry,
when on the scaffold stood Mariana
who would not talk and had to die!
Marianita alone in her room   5
could never let her thoughts be free:
"What if Pedrosa should see me
sewing this flag of Liberty".

[*Further off.*]

How sad was that day in Granada
when all the bells rang through the sky!   10

[*A woman leans out of a window holding a burning brass oil
lamp. The chorus stops singing.*]

WOMAN: Child! Did you not hear me?
GIRL [*from a distance*]:   I'm coming!

[*Under the gateway arch a girl appears dressed in the style of
1850. She sings*]:

Like a lily they cut the lily,
like a rose they cut the flower,
like a lily they cut the lily,
her heart more lovely by the hour.   15

[*She goes into her house slowly. Offstage the choir continues.*]

How sad was that day in Granada,
when all the stones were made to cry!
The curtain falls slowly.

---

to the anonymous oral tradition. Other early poems on Mariana's life and
death are given by Antonina Rodrigo, *op.cit.*, 170-174, 201-207, 76.
7 Pedrosa: the Chief of Police in Granada, sent there by Ferdinand VII
to supress liberal or anti-royalist revolutionary activity (see Introduction).
11+ dressed in the style of 1850: given that Mariana was executed in 1831,
the Prologue postdates the body of the play by some twenty years. In
situating his Prologue at a point between his own day and Mariana's it was
presumably Lorca's intention to highlight the play's historical setting and
to suggest a sense of continuity and remembrance in accord with the
popular ballad tradition described above.
12-15 Like a lily they cut the lily...: these four lines also belong to the
oral tradition; see Antonina Rodrigo, *op.cit.*, 171.

*Casa de Mariana. Paredes blancas. Al fondo, balconcillos pintados
de oscuro. Sobre una mesa, un frutero de cristal lleno de membrillos.
Todo el techo estará lleno de esta misma fruta, colgada. Encima de
la cómoda, grandes ramos de rosas de seda. Tarde de otoño. Al
levantarse el telón aparece Doña Angustias, madre adoptiva de
Mariana, sentada, leyendo. Viste de oscuro. Tiene un aire frío,
pero es maternal al mismo tiempo. Isabel la Clavela viste de maja.
Tiene treinta y siete años.*

CLAVELA [*Entrando*]:
    ¿Y la niña?
ANGUSTIAS [*Dejando la lectura*]:
      Borda y borda lentamente.
    Yo lo he visto por el ojo de la llave.
    Parecía el hilo rojo, entre sus dedos,
    una herida de cuchillo sobre el aire.
CLAVELA: ¡Tengo un miedo!
ANGUSTIAS: ¡No me digas!
CLAVELA [*Intrigada*]:   ¿Se sabrá?   5
ANGUSTIAS: Desde luego, por Granada no se sabe.

White walls: the typical Spanish interior, simple and elegant.

small balconies: the room is on an upper floor, as we see later from
Mariana's instruction: 'Go down to the door' (line 81, Second Engraving).
Balconies played a significant role in Spanish life: religious and festive
processions were witnessed from them, and young ladies could allow
themselves to be courted and serenaded at their safe distance.

quinces: a fruit, yellow in colour, pear-like in shape, though rounder
and more lumpy. Extremely bitter, the quince's culinary use is primarily in
jams and marmalades. Its pleasant aromatic quality has given it the
traditional use, as here, of lending fragrance to a house's interior.

Doña Angustias, Mariana's adopted mother: Doña is a Spanish titular
convention used before Christian names of married women and widows; it
conveys respect, but not the official aristocratic ranking of 'Lady' in
English. Angustias, literally 'anguishes', is a common Spanish Christian
name which derives like most from religious concepts. The character's
name, invented by Lorca, is appropriate inasmuch as Angustias will suffer
great anguish in worrying about Mariana's destiny. In historical terms
Doña Angustias corresponds to Doña Úrsula de la Presa who took Mariana
into her care in 1805 when, at just one year of age, Mariana lost her
father. Doña Úrsula and her husband José de Mesa had no children of
their own. When José de Mesa died in 1829 Doña Úrsula joined Mariana
once again and lived with her at 6, Calle del Águila, Granada. When
Mariana received her death sentence Doña Úrsula was condemned for her
part in the conspiracy to ten year's imprisonment, though, by 1836, after
the death of Ferdinand VII, she was living as a free woman (see Antonina
Rodrigo, *op.cit.*, 141).

dressed in black: the black of mourning is still the standard dress of
Spanish women. Though it is not mentioned in the play, one would

FIRST ENGRAVING

*Mariana's house. White walls. Upstage small balconies darkly
painted. On a table a glass fruit bowl full of quinces. The entire
ceiling is hung with the same fruit. On top of a sideboard large
bouquets of silk roses. It is early evening, in Autumn. When the
curtain rises we see Doña Angustias, Mariana's adopted mother, who
sits reading. She is dressed in black and has a stiff though maternal
air. Isabel la Clavela, who is thirty-seven years old, is dressed in
the exhuberant maja style.*

CLAVELA [*entering*]:
    Where is she?
ANGUSTIAS [*stops reading*]:
        In her room, embroidering.   1
    I saw her through the keyhole sitting there.
    The crimson thread she held in her fingers
    seemed hung like a knife-wound upon the air.
CLAVELA: She worries me!
ANGUSTIAS: Be quiet!
CLAVELLA [*secretively*]:   If it got out.   5
ANGUSTIAS: Keep calm!   No one in all Granada knows.

---

naturally assume Doña Angustias to be a widow, as in fact was the case
with the historical figure described in the last note.

Isabel la Clavela: literally 'Elizabeth the Carnation'. Isabel was the
name of the queen who, with her husband Fernando, took Granada from
the Moors in 1492. Clavela is a common enough appellation, especially in
Andalusia. The character, a servant to Mariana, is invented by Lorca,
though in history Mariana had two female servants and one male servant at
the critical stage of her life (Antonina Rodrigo, *op.cit.*, 41).

maja: immortalised in Goya's paintings, the maja and her male
counterpart, the *majo*, were extremely colourful characters who originated
in the poor quarters of Spanish cities in the eighteenth century. On gala
occasions their dandy dress and gay songs expressed an intense patriotic
pride which purposefully contrasted with the Frenchified costume of the
upper classes under the Bourbon dynasty. Eventually the more comfortable
ladies of society took to copying the proud *maja* and dressed themselves
in the exuberantly fetching and distinctively Spanish manner, using lace,
ribbons, bows, usually a mantilla and almost always a flower in the hair.

1 embroidering: the activity for which Mariana will later be executed is
immediately brought to our attention.

4 like a knife-wound upon the air: a precise and highly evocative visual
image which, in its surprising linking of sewing and violence, has a
prophetic function so typical in Lorca. No doubt the mixture of tender
beauty and implicit violence in the person of Mariana attracted Lorca to the
topic, and certainly this is a consistent source of his images throughout
the play.

6 No one in all Granada knows: this and other remarks in the
conversation between Angustias and Clavela establish a mood of fearful
secrecy which is to prevail through the first two acts.

CLAVELA: | ¿Por qué borda esa bandera?
ANGUSTIAS: | Ella me dice

que la obligan sus amigos liberales.
[*Con intención.*]
Don Pedro, sobre todos; y por ellos
se expone... [*Con gesto doloroso.*]
        a lo que no quiero acordarme.   10

CLAVELA: Si pensara como antigua, le diría...
            embrujada.

ANGUSTIAS [*Rápida*]:
                Enamorada.

CLAVELA [*Rápida*]:   ¿Sí?

ANGUSTIAS [*Vaga*]:   ¿Quién sabe?
            [*Lírica*]
            Se le ha puesto la sonrisa casi blanca,
            como vieja flor abierta en un encaje.
            Ella debe dejar esas intrigas.   15
            ¿Qué le importan las cosas de la calle?
            Y si borda, que borde unos vestidos
            para su niña, cuando sea grande.
            Que si el rey no es buen rey, que no lo sea;
            las mujeres no deben preocuparse.   20

CLAVELA: Esta noche pasada no durmió.

ANGUSTIAS: ¡Si no vive! ¿Recuerdas?...Ayer tarde...
            [*Suena una campanilla alegremente.*]
            Son las hijas del Oidor. Guarda silencio.

[*Sale Clavela, rápida. Angustias se dirige a la puerta de la derecha y llama.*]
            Marianita, sal, que vienen a buscarte.

[*Entran dando carcajadas las hijas del Oidor de la Chancillería.*

8-9 she'd promised to for her liberal friends. / Don Pedro, most of all: the first political note, but one with the significant implication that Mariana made the flag less out of political conviction than as a favour obliged by friendship and amorous entanglement.

12 bewitched: Clavela suggests that Mariana's love for Don Pedro is excessive and irrational, thereby doomed to a tragic outcome.

13 The smile on her face...: the first of many lyrical sequences which give the play a conscious and even studied poetic mood. The simile which compares Mariana's face to a delicate flower pressed on lace is typical of the exquisite feminine sensitivity which Lorca evokes, at the same time its suggesticn of fragility and vulnerability relates to the foreboding, fatalistic atmosphere of the play.

15 ought not to meddle: this and line 20 voice Angustias's disapproval of women who meddle in politics, a traditional view which would still have had wide support in Lorca's own day. The tenor of the speech, however, is not simply that a woman's place is in the home, but that Mariana is neglecting her responsibilities as a mother.

19 the King: the despised Ferdinand VII who ruled with an iron hand from 1814 until 1833 (see Introduction).

CLAVELA: But why must she sew that flag?
ANGUSTIAS: She told me
             she'd promised to for her liberal friends.
             [*With emphasis.*]
             Don Pedro, most of all; and it's for them
             she risks... [*Disconsolately.*]
                          what I'd sooner forget about.   10
CLAVELA: In days gone by they would have said she was
             ... bewitched.
ANGUSTIAS [*quickly*]:   In love, that's all.
CLAVELA [*quickly*]:   Oh, yes?
ANGUSTIAS [*vaguely*]:   Who knows?
             [*Lyrically*]
             The smile on her face has turned almost white,
             like a delicate flower pressed on lace.
             She ought not to meddle in such plots and schemes,15
             nor bother her mind with things of the street.
             If sew she must, then why not make dresses?
             For one day her daughter will be a lady.
             And if the King's no good, then so be it;
             a woman's mind should turn to other things.   20
CLAVELA: Last night she hardly slept a wink.
ANGUSTIAS: Because
             she's so on edge. Remember, yesterday...?
             [*A little bell tinkles cheerfully.*]
             The Judge's daughters, I expect. Say nothing!
[*Clavela leaves quickly. Angustias goes towards the door on the
right and calls.*]
ANGUSTIAS: Marianita, the girls have come to visit
[*The daughters of the Chancery Judge enter, laughing gaily. They*

----

22 Remember, yesterday...?: Angustias was about to give an instance of
Mariana's nervousness, and, presumably, would have referred to her
meeting Pedrosa in the street the previous evening, a point recounted
later (lines 247-55, First Engraving) and the kind of detail or linking
which suggests careful composition on Lorca's part.
24+ The daughters of the Chancery Judge: typical of Lorca's synthetic
technique is that these two ladies should be associated with the law.
Though they come in friendship, their family connections cannot help but
foster the atmosphere of unease, while their visit also prefigures a less
friendly, official visitation by the law in the Second Engraving. Granada
was the seat of the southern Chancillería, Chancery or 'Supreme Court of
Appeal', as Richard Ford terms it (*op.cit.*, 550), and Mariana,
historically, was to be tried and sentenced at its *Audiencia* (Court of
Hearing). The Chancery Judge has no part in Lorca's play, a point which
accords with the historical fact that the Chief of Police, Ramón Pedrosa,
was given absolute legal power in Mariana's court case. Presumably Lorca
knew of Andrés Oller, a magistrate of liberal leanings and a friend of
Mariana's, who was forced to retire in order to make way for Pedrosa (see
Antonina Rodrigo, *op.cit.*, 130, 135), and this may be the source which

Visten enormes faldas de volantes y vienen con mantillas,
peinadas a la moda de la época, con un clavel en cada sien.
Lucía es rubia tostada, y Amparo, morenísima, de ojos profundos
y movimientos rápidos.]
ANGUSTIAS [*Dirigiéndose a besarlas, con los brazos abiertos*]:
               ¡Las dos bellas del Campillo   25
               por esta casa!
AMPARO [*Besa a Doña Angustias y dice a Clavela*]:
               ¡Clavela!
               ¿Qué tal tu esposo el clavel?
CLAVELA [*Marchándose, disgustada, y como temiendo más bromas*]:
               ¡Marchito!
LUCIA [*Llamando al orden*]:
               ¡Amparo!
             [*Besa a Angustias.*]
AMPARO [*Riéndose*]:
               ¡Paciencia!
               ¡Pero clavel que no huele,
               se corta de la maceta!   30
LUCIA: Doña Angustias, ¿qué os parece?
ANGUSTIAS [*Sonriendo*]:
               ¡Siempre tan graciosa!
AMPARO

                         Mientras
               que mi hermana lee y relee
               novelas y más novelas,
               o borda en el cañamazo   35
               rosas, pájaros y letras,

---

accounts for Mariana's friendship with a Judge's daughters in the play.

    flowing dresses: in their striking Andalusian dress these young ladies of fashion make a splash of colour on stage. No doubt they would hope to catch the eye of suitable males in Granada when coming to pay this visit.

    mantillas: the traditional head-dress of a high comb at the back of the head from which flows a veil of silk or lace. It owes much to Arabic custom which held that a lady's face and head should not be exposed. Richard Ford noted: 'There are three kinds of *Mantillas*... first is the white, which is used on grand occasions, birth-days, bull-fights and Easter Mondays... but it is not becoming to Spanish women, whose sallow olive complexion cannot stand the contrast. The second is black, and is made of *raso* or *alepin*, satin or bombezeen (*sic*), often edged with velvet, and finished off with deep lace fringe...' The third type he mentions is a *maja* mantilla of lace. He concludes: 'one of the great secrets of a Spanish woman's attraction is, that most of her charms are hidden' (*op.cit.*, 300–1).

    a red carnation on each side: Ford comments: 'The hair is another glory of the Spanish sex... The *Andaluza* places a real flower, generally a red pink, among her raven locks' (*op.cit.*, 302). In the play the red carnations serve not only as items of local colour but as symbolic motifs which again convey that mixture of fragile beauty and, by association with the colour of blood, death.

34

wear flowing dresses full of flounces, with mantillas on their heads
and their hair combed in the fashion of the day with a red carnation
on each side. Lucía is golden brown and Amparo very dark with deep
eyes and quick movements.]
ANGUSTIAS [*coming over to kiss them, her arms open*]:
              I never! The two Campillo beauties   25
              in our house!
AMPARO [*kissing Doña Angustias and speaking to Clavela*]:
              Clavela, old flower!
              And how's your young bud of a husband?
CLAVELA [*moving away, peeved and fearing more teasing*]:
              All withered up!
LUCIA [*telling her to behave*]:
              Amparo!
            [*She kisses Angustias.*]
AMPARO [*laughing*]:   Oh, hush!
              Carnations with no bouquet
              shouldn't be put on display!   30
LUCIA   Doña Angustias, what must you think!
ANGUSTIAS [*smiling*]:
              As witty as ever!
AMPARO: My sister,
              you see, spends all her time reading,
              novel after novel, and cover
              to cover; if not, she sews roses   35
              or birds on canvas, all nicely
              initialled. But I like to sing

Lucía is golden brown and Amparo very dark with deep eyes and quick
movements: Andalusians are the most dark-skinned Spaniards, both
because of the southerly climate and from the greater strain of Arabic
blood. The *morena*, or woman of dark hair and dark complexion, is a
traditional topic in lyric poetry and she is generally represented as the
most sensuous and vivacious kind of woman. Such women are famed for
their flashing provocative eyes, a communicative facility which again can
be linked to the Moorish mania for facial concealment. Lorca follows the
prescription by making the darker Amparo a more outgoing and flirtatious
girl than her sister Lucía.
25 Campillo: literally 'little field', the Campillo was an open area on the
other side of the Genil River from Mariana's house and the town centre. It
was to become, as Ford noted, 'the site of the monument to the
unfortunate Mariana Pineda' (*op.cit.*, 575).
26 Clavela, old flower: some light-hearted punning ensues, on the basis
that the name Clavela also means 'carnation'.
29 Carnations with no bouquet shouldn't be put on display!: Spaniards
delight in their *refranes* or rhyming proverbs, of which they have a great
stock. Here Amparo saucily suggests that a man who is past his prime is
no good to anyone.

```
                    yo canto y bailo el jaleo
                    de Jerez, con castañuelas:
                    el vito, el olé, el bolero,
                    y ojalá siempre tuviera                              40
                    ganas de cantar, señora.
ANGUSTIAS [Riendo]:
                    ¡Qué chiquilla!
                    [Amparo coge un membrillo y lo muerde.]
LUCIA [Enfadada]:
                                  ¡Estate quieta!
AMPARO [Habla con lo agrio de la fruta entre los dientes]:
                    ¡Buen membrillo!
                    [Le da un calofrío por lo fuerte del ácido, y guiña.]
ANGUSTIAS [Con las manos en la cara]:
                                         ¡Yo no puedo
                    mirar!
LUCIA [Un poco sofocada]:
                    ¿No te da vergüenza?
AMPARO:             Pero ¿no sale Mariana?                              45
                    Voy a llamar a su puerta.
                    [Va corriendo y llama.]
                    ¡Mariana, sal pronto, hijita!
LUCIA:              ¡Perdonad, señora!
ANGUSTIAS [Suave]:                    ¡Déjala!
[La puerta se abre y aparece Mariana, vestida de malva claro,
con un peinado de bucles, peineta y una gran rosa detrás de
la oreja.  No tiene más que una sortija de diamantes en su mano
siniestra.  Aparece preocupada, y da muestras, conforme avanza
el diálogo, de vivísima inquietud.  Al entrar Mariana en escena,
las dos muchachas corren a su encuentro.]
```

38-9 the vito, Jerez, the olé and bolero: these are all traditional dances
of Andalusia, each having a distinctive rhythm or special choreographic
feature. The vito - the subject of a drawing by Goya - is a very lively
dance, quicker than the olé which is danced to the accompaniment of a
guitar, while the Jerez is a vivacious solo dance from the town of that
name in western Andalusia famed for sherry. The bolero is the best known
of all flamenco dances and is characterised by its intermittent musical
pauses when the dancer strikes up dramatic poses. It certainly impressed
Richard Ford who described the bolero as 'matchless, unequalled, and
inimitable, and only to be performed by Andalucians' (sic). He goes on to
evoke its mood beautifully: 'What exercise displays the ever-varying
charms of female grace, and the contours of manly form, like this
fascinating dance? The accompaniment of the castanet gives employment to
their upraised arms. C'est le pantomime d'amour. The enamoured youth -
the coy coquettish maiden; who shall describe the advance - her timid
retreat, his eager pursuit? Now they gaze on each other, now on the
ground; now all is life, love, and action; now there is a pause - they stop
motionless at a moment, and grow into the earth. It carries all before it.
There is a truth which overpowers the fastidious judgement. Away, then,

<pre>
          and dance to castanets, the vito,
          Jerez, the olé and bolero,
          and truth be told, my Señora,   40
          I pray to God I always will.
</pre>

ANGUSTIAS [*laughing*]:
          That girl's a scamp!
          [*Amparo picks up a quince and bites it.*]
LUCIA [*annoyed*]:   Can't you behave?
AMPARO [*speaking with the bitter taste of the fruit in her mouth*]:
          What a juicy quince!
          [*She shudders and blinks from the acid taste.*]
ANGUSTIAS [*her hands over her face*]:
                              I can't bear
          to look!
LUCIA [*her voice choking*]:
                    Sister, have you no shame?
AMPARO: But when is Mariana coming?   45
          I'm going to knock on her door.
          [*She runs, calling.*]
          Mariana, come out quickly, girl!
LUCIA: I'm terribly sorry!
ANGUSTIAS [*softly*]:   Don't worry!
[*The door opens and Mariana appears dressed in a mauve colour,
her hair done in ringlets, with a high comb and a large red rose
behind her ear. She has a single diamond ring on her left hand.
She seems preoccupied and, as the dialogue proceeds, shows
increasing restlessness. When she comes on stage the two girls
run to meet her.*]

---

with the studied grace of the French *danseuse*, beautiful but artificial,
cold and selfish is the flicker of her love, compared to the real
impassioned *abandon* of the daughters of the South' (*op.cit.*, 284-5). The
Obras completas gives *sorongo* while the Rivadeneyra, Losada and Harrap
editions give *bolero*. Since the latter dance is much better known,
especially to English readers, I have chosen not to follow the *Obras
completas* in this instance.
42+ Amparo picks up a quince and bites it: quinces are never eaten raw,
and this devil-may-care gesture is clearly linked to her passion for the
rousing dances just mentioned. It also suggests one of the play's thematic
notions, that of suffering being associated with reckless love.
45 But when is Mariana coming?: with this and earlier remarks Lorca
skillfully creates an air of expectancy for his heroine's appearance on
stage.
48+ Mariana appears: renowned as she was for her beauty, Mariana's
entrance must necessarily be most striking. Her maturity, gracefulness and
sombre mood stand out by contrast with the gaiety of her young visitors,
Amparo especially. The mauve colour of her dress and the large red rose
behind her ear are prophetic allusions to her violent death. The single
diamond ring on her left hand is later said to be her wedding ring (line
483, Second Engraving), but in the course of the play it tends rather to
suggest her engagement to Don Pedro de Sotomayor.

AMPARO [*Besándola*]:
      ¡Cuánto has tardado!
MARIANA [*Cariñosa*]:   ¡Niñas!
LUCIA [*Besándola*]:   ¡Marianita!
AMPARO: ¡A mí otro beso!
LUCIA: ¡Y otro a mí!
MARIANA: ¡Preciosas!   **50**
      [*A Doña Angustias.*]
      ¿Trajeron una carta?
ANGUSTIAS: ¡No! [*Queda pensativa.*]
AMPARO [*Acariciándola*]:   Tú, siempre
      joven y guapa.
MARIANA [*Sonriendo con amargura*]:
          ¡Ya pasé los treinta!
AMPARO
      ¡Pues parece que tienes quince!
[*Se sientan en un amplio sofá, una a cada lado. Doña Angustias
recoge su libro y arregla una cómoda.*]
MARIANA [*Siempre con un dejo de melancolía*]:
          ¡Amparo!
      ¡Viudita y con dos niños!
LUCIA: ¿Cómo siguen?
MARIANA: Han llegado ahora mismo del colegio.   **55**
      Y estarán en el patio.
ANGUSTIAS: Voy a ver.
      No quiero que se mojen en la fuente.
      ¡Hasta luego, hijas mías!
LUCIA [*Fina siempre*]:
          ¡Hasta luego!
      [*Se va Doña Angustias.*]
MARIANA: Tu hermano Fernando, ¿cómo sigue?
LUCIA: Dijo
      que vendría a buscarnos, para saludarte.   **60**
      [*Ríe*]
      Se estaba poniendo su levita azul.
      Todo lo que tienes le parece bien.
      Quiere que vistamos como tú te vistes.
      Ayer...

---

51 <u>a letter</u>: Mariana is expecting news of her love, Don Pedro de Sotomayor, since, as we soon see, she is currently planning to help him escape from prison where he has been detained for anti-Royalist activity.

52 <u>I won't see thirty again!</u>: Lorca ages his heroine slightly, for in history Mariana was three months short of her twenty-seventh birthday when executed.

54 <u>widowed with two children:</u> Mariana's son and daughter, aged ten and nine respectively, will appear in the Second Engraving.

AMPARO [*kissing her*]:
      You've come at last!
MARIANA [*affectionately*]:   My precious!
LUCIA [*kissing her*]:   Marianita!
AMPARO: Another kiss for me!
LUCIA: And me!
MARIANA: My treasures!   50
      [*To Doña Angustias.*]
      Was there a letter?
ANGUSTIAS: No! [*She looks pensive.*]
AMPARO [*caressing her*]:   As young and lovely
      as ever!
MARIANA [*smiling wistfully*]:
      I won't see thirty again!
AMPARO: But really, I'd say you were just fifteen!
[*They sit down on a spacious sofa, one each side of her. Doña
Angustias picks up her book and tidies a chest.*]
MARIANA [*with her usual touch of sadness*]:
      And widowed with two children?
LUCIA: How are they?
MARIANA: They've only this minute come home from school.   55
      No doubt they're in the patio.
ANGUSTIAS: Let me see!
      I don't want them to splash about the fountain.
      I'll say goodbye, then, girls.
LUCIA [*polite as ever*]:   Goodbye, Señora!
      [*Doña Angustias leaves.*]
MARIANA: Your brother, Fernando, how is he keeping?
LUCIA: He said he'd fetch us and pay his respects.   60
      [*She laughs.*]
      We left him trying on his blue frock-coat.
      He thinks everything you wear is divine,
      and now he wants us to copy your clothes.
      Yesterday...

---

57 splash about the fountain: Mariana's house follows the typical
Andalusian design of Moorish influence which favours an interior patio on
the ground floor with a fountain of running water at its centre. This
offers cool in the heat of the day, while the plants which grow in pots
around the fountain perfume the house. 'Granada is a city of fountains',
says Richard Ford (*op.cit.*, 553) and indeed the two rivers Genil and
Darro provide abundant water from the melted snow of the Sierra Nevada.
61 blue frock-coat: the frock-coat was of non-Spanish origin and a
relatively recent feature in Spanish dress. Richard Ford lamented that city
Spaniards were slavishly following European fashion at this time (*op.cit.*,
302). But Fernando is a young man who would wish to impress Mariana by
dressing in the very latest style.

AMPARO [*Que tiene siempre que hablar, la interrumpe*]:
Ayer mismo nos dijo que tú
[*Lucía queda seria.*]
tenías en los ojos... ¿Qué dijo?
LUCIA [*Enfadada*]:   ¿Me dejas   65
hablar? [*Hace intención de hacerlo.*]
AMPARO [*Rápida*]:
¡Ya me acuerdo! Dijo que en tus ojos
había un constante desfile de pájaros.
[*Le coge la cabeza por la barbilla y le mira los ojos.*]
Un temblor divino, como de agua clara,
sorprendida siempre bajo el arrayán,
o temblor de luna sobre una pecera   70
donde un pez de plata finge rojo sueño.
LUCIA [*Sacudiendo a Mariana*]:
¡Mira! Lo segundo son inventos de ella.
[*Ríe.*]
AMPARO: ¡Lucía, eso dijo!
MARIANA: ¡Qué bien me causáis
con vuestra alegría de niñas pequeñas!
La misma alegría que debe sentir   75
el gran girasol, al amanecer,
cuando sobre el tallo de la noche vea
abrirse el dorado girasol del cielo.
[*Les coge las manos.*]
La misma alegría que la viejecilla
siente cuando el sol se duerme en sus manos   80
y ella lo acaricia creyendo que nunca
la noche y el frío cercarán su casa.
LUCIA: ¡Te encuentro muy triste!
AMPARO: ¿Qué tienes?
[*Entra Clavela.*]

65-71 eyes: the attention given to Mariana's eyes accords with the high
ranking of this female feature in Spanish culture generally and in
traditional lyric poetry especially. Numerous poems exist on the subject of
ojos morenos, dark eyes, the old cliché of the eyes being the windows of
the soul having more pertinence in a society which stressed the
concealment of facial features. Richard Ford refers to the Spanish woman's
'Moorish eyes, which never passed the Pyrennees... The finest are
"raised" in Andalucia; they are very full, and repose on a liquid somewhat
yellow bed, of an almond shape' (*op.cit.*, 302). Lorca's series of images is
highly evocative of this beauty: a flight of birds suggests the raised eye
with its hint of the Orient; the heavenly trembling, water that ripples and
goldfish tank stress the stunning liquid quality; finally, there are touches
of green (myrtle), gold and red, all illuminated by the pupil's sheen of
moonlight and silver fishes. In addition to suggesting the dark, mysterious
beauty of Mariana's eyes, Lorca's description also indicates personality
traits: notably, the flight of birds and heavenly trembling point towards

AMPARO [*as eager as ever to speak, interrupting her*]:
                 Yesterday he said that you
        [*Lucia turns serious.*]
        had eyes in which... oh, how did he put it?   65
LUCIA [*annoyed*]:
        May I continue?   [*She is about to speak.*]
AMPARO [*quickly*]:   I've got it! He said
        a flight of birds was always in your eyes!
        [*She takes hold of Mariana by the chin and looks
        into her eyes.*]
        A heavenly trembling, he said, like water
        that ripples suddenly under a myrtle tree,
        or moonlight that broods on a goldfish tank   70
        where silver fishes feign a deep red sleep.
LUCIA [*shaking Mariana*]:
        Don't listen! She made up the last bit herself.
        [*She laughs.*]
AMPARO: Lucia, that is what he said!
MARIANA: How good
        you two are for me, with your young girls' joy!
        You have the kind of joy a sun-flower feels   75
        when opening at dawn, so big to the world,
        when the sun itself, on the stem of night,
        burgeons its golden blossom in the sky;
        [*She takes their hands.*]
        the kind of joy a wizened woman feels
        when the sun lies sleeping between her hands,   80
        and, stroking it, she thinks for a moment
        her bones won't feel the cold of night again.
LUCIA: Why so sad, Mariana?
AMPARO: Yes, why?
        [*Clavela enters.*]

---

her excessive idealism, while <u>moonlight, silver, deep red sleep</u> and the
verb <u>broods</u> are all ominous in value, in which context the image of a
<u>goldfish tank</u> may well relate to her future confinement. The latter image
of enclosure is of a type frequently found in Lorca, for instance in his
poems '*La monja gitana*' (The Gypsy Nun) and '*Romance sonámbulo*'
(Sleep-walking Ballad) as well as virtually throughout his last play, *The
House of Bernarda Alba*.
75-82 <u>the kind of joy</u>...: this is one of those studied poetic sequences
which, though perhaps to be faulted in dramatic terms for slowing down
the action, nonetheless contributes effectively to the play's atmosphere.
Once again it is the fragile beauty of flowers in relation to female
vulnerability which justifies the sequence thematically. The imagery in
lines 75-78 is precious in its parallelling of flowers blooming at dawn with
the sun, another flower, opening on the stem of night. The next four
lines imply the hopelessness of a woman's illusion, with the concluding
negative note of <u>cold</u> and <u>night</u> providing an unfavourable prognosis.

MARIANA [*Levantándose rápidamente*]:   ¡Clavela!
    ¿Llegó? ¡Di!
CLAVELA [*Triste*]:   ¡Señora, no ha venido nadie!
    [*Cruza la escena y se va.*]
LUCIA: Si esperas visita, nos vamos.
AMPARO: Lo dices,   85
    y salimos.
MARIANA [*Nerviosa*]:   ¡Niñas, tendré que enfadarme!
AMPARO: No me has preguntado por mi estancia en Ronda.
MARIANA: Es verdad que fuiste; ¿y has vuelto contenta?
AMPARO: Mucho. Todo el día baila que te baila.
[*Mariana está inquieta, y, llena de angustia, mira a las puertas
y se distrae.*]
LUCIA [*Seria*]:
    Vámonos, Amparo.
MARIANA [*Inquieta por algo que ocurre fuera de la escena*]:
                   ¡Cuéntame! Si vieras   90
    cómo necesito de tu fresca risa,
    cómo necesito de tu gracia joven.
    Mi alma tiene el mismo color del vestido.
    [*Mariana sigue de pie.*]
AMPARO: Qué cosas tan lindas dices, Marianilla.
LUCIA: ¿Quieres que te traiga una novela?
AMPARO: Tráele   95
    la plaza de toros de la ilustre Ronda.

---

84 He's come, at last?: the cause of Mariana's acute nervousness is her
anguished waiting for Don Pedro. The theme of waiting is present
throughout the play, in which sense it compares closely with *Doña Rosita,
the Spinster*, and it reaches a peak in the final engraving.
87 Ronda: an Andalusian city in the sub-province of Malaga which, in the
1910 census, had a population of 22,000. It is perched on a mountain and
is divided in two by a spectacular ravine two hundred metres deep.
93 My mood inside is like my dress in colour: a line which shows not only
that Lorca's colour symbolism is intentional and explicit, but also that it is
natural to his characters and very much part of their way of thinking; it
is, in short, a popular, traditional symbolism. Here, however, Mariana's
dress is not a primary colour, but mauve, *malva* in Spanish - literally
'mallow', a plant whose colour is a delicate nuance of light blue and rosy
pink - and the symbolic implications are correspondingly subtle. The muted
colour presumably suggests Mariana's mixed emotions: the idealistic,
aspiring aspect of celestial blue being tempered and indeed overshadowed
by the rose's fatalism.
98-149 this fifty-two line *romance* or ballad - just four lines longer than
the ballad on Torrijos in the Second Engraving - is the longest poetic
sequence in the play. On the topic of a bullfight at Ronda, it shows Lorca
in his most traditional vein, for here he uses many of the age-old devices
which have made the ballad the supreme instrument for oral narrative in
Spain. Clean-cut definition, rhythmic continuity and colourful flashes of
imagery are all part of the ballad's perennial appeal, but so too is its
underlying patriotism, its sense of national heritage, which, as here, owes

MARIANA [*getting up quickly*]:   Clavela!...
        He's come, at last?
CLAVELA [*sadly*]:   No one has come, Señora!
        [*She crosses the stage and leaves.*]
LUCIA: If guests are coming, we'll go.
AMPARO: Say the word   85
        and we'll be off.
MARIANA [*nervously*]:   Would you upset me so?
AMPARO: You haven't asked about my trip to Ronda.
MARIANA: Of course, you went to Ronda. Was it fun?
AMPARO: Fantastic! I was dancing all day long.
[*Mariana is restless and she looks anxiously at the doors without paying attention.*]
LUCIA [*seriously*]:
        Best we go, Amparo.
MARIANA [*worried about something off-stage*]:
                Oh, tell me, please!   90
        If you could know how much I need your cheer,
        and what it means to me to hear your laughter.
        My mood inside is like my dress in colour.
        [*Mariana remains standing.*]
AMPARO: What pretty things you say, Marianita.
LUCIA: I have a tale to lift your spirits.
AMPARO: Tell her   95
        about the bullfights in Ronda the brave.

---

as much to the treatment as to the *costumbrista* or indigenously Spanish subject-matter. It was for these reasons that the ballad experienced a revival in the 1830s when, following the death of Ferdinand VII, the Romantics expressed a resurgence of national pride. Certainly the historical feel of the ballad, its sense of dealing with the people at large, fits in well with the liberal sympathies of *Mariana Pineda*. But there are further specific reasons for seeing this long sequence as something more than a pleasant poetic interlude: its bullfight topic is a celebration of death, an embellished ritual of sacrifice and violence, while it is also relevant that the bull dies in the arena from being pierced through the neck by a sword, a death which inevitably brings to mind Mariana's execution by garrote. The link is insinuated in the ballad by Amparo repeating that Mariana was always on her mind while she watched the bullfight. Thus the ballad is a crucial feature in Lorca's creation of a fatalistic aura around his heroine.

    True to its genre, Lorca's ballad bases itself on factual detail, in this case detail pertaining to the bullfight. Lorca was very knowledgeable on the bullfight, as this ballad shows, and in 1935 he wrote one of his most memorable poems on the death in the ring of a famous matador and personal friend, 'Llanto por Ignácio Sánchez Mejías' (Lament for Ignacio Sanchez Mejias), *Obras completas*, I, 551–58. Readers unfamiliar with the bullfight should find the following account by Richard Ford very informative, parallelling as it does many of the points Lorca makes:

    'The first thing to do is to secure a good place before hand, by sending for a *Boletín de Sombra*, a shade-ticket. The prices of the seats

43

[*Ríen. Se levanta y se dirige a Mariana.*]
¡Siéntate!
[*Mariana se sienta y la besa.*]
MARIANA [*Resignada*]
                    ¿Estuviste en los toros?
LUCIA: ¡Estuvo!
AMPARO: En la corrida más grande
          que se vio en Ronda la vieja.
          Cinco toros de azabache,   100
          con divisa verde y negra.
          Yo pensaba siempre en ti;
          yo pensaba; ¡si estuviera
          conmigo mi triste amiga,

---

vary according to position. The great object is to avoid the sun: the best places are on the northern side, which are in the shade. The transit of the sun over the Plaza, the zodiacal progress into Taurus, is decidedly the best calculated astronomical observation in Spain (*cf.* lines 115-117).

'Nothing can exceed the gaiety and sparkle of a Spanish public going, eager and full-dressed, to the *fight*. They could not move faster were they running away from a real one. All the streets or open spaces near the outside of the arena are a spectacle. The merry mob is everything. Their excitement under a burning sun, and their thirst for the blood of bulls, is fearful... The men go in all their best costume and *majo*-finery: the distinguished ladies wear on these occasions white lace mantillas...; a fan, *abanico*, is quite necessary... (*cf.* lines 106-113). Fine ladies and gentlemen go into the boxes, but the real sporting men, the *aficionados*, prefer the pit, the *tendido*, or *los andamios*, the lower range, in order, by being nearer, that they may not lose the nice traits of tauromaquia.'

'The spectacle is divided into three acts: the first is performed by the *picadores* on horseback; at the signal of the president, and sound of a trumpet, the second act commences with the *chulos*... Their duty is to draw off the bull from the *picador* when endangered, which they do with their coloured cloaks; their address and their agility are surprising; they skim over the sand like glittering humming birds (*cf.* line 139), scarcely touching the earth. They are dressed *a lo majo*, in short breeches, and without gaiters... Their hair is tied into a knot behind, *moño*, and enclosed in the once universal silk net, the *retecilla*... The *chulos*, in the second act, are the sole performers; their part is to place small barbed darts, *banderillas*, which are ornamented with cut paper of different colours, on each side of the neck of the bull. The *banderilleros* go right up to him, holding the arrows at the shaft, and pointing the barbs at the bull; just when the animal stoops to toss them, they dart them into his neck and slip aside.

'The last trumpet now sounds, the arena is cleared, the *matador*, the executioner, the man of death, stands before his victim alone (*cf.* line 118 *et seq.*); on entering, he addresses the president, and throws his *montera*, his cap, to the ground. In his right hand he holds a long straight Toledan blade, *la espada*; in his left he waves the *muleta*, the red flag, the *engaño*, the lure, which ought not (so Romero laid down in our

[*They laugh.   She gets up and goes towards
Mariana.*]
Won't you sit down?
[*Mariana sits and Angustias kisses her.*]

MARIANA [*resigned*]:   **You saw the bulls?**
LUCIA: **She did!**
AMPARO: **It was, they say, the grandest bullfight
                ancient Ronda had ever seen,
                with five brave bulls as black as jet   100
                all trailing ribbons dark and green.
                And every minute I thought of you;
                if only my sad friend, I thought,
                if only she could be here too,**

---

hearing) (*cf.* line 132) to be so large as the standard of a religious
brotherhood, or *cofradía*, nor so small as a lady's   pocket-handkerchief,
pañuelito de señorita; it should be about a yard square. The colour is red
because that best irritates the bull and conceals blood.

'The *matador, el diestro* (in olden books), advances to the bull, in
order to entice him towards him...; he next rapidly studies his character,
plays with him a little, allows him to run once or twice on the *muleta*, and
then prepares for the *coup de grace*... There are many *suertes*, or ways
of killing the bull; the principal is *la suerte de frente, o la verónica* - the
matador receives the charge on his sword... The sword enters just
between the left shoulder and the blade - *buen estoque*. In nothing is the
real fancy so fastidious as in the exact nicety of placing this death-wound;
when the thrust is true, death is instantaneous' (Ford, *op.cit.*, 273-78).

For a more detailed account the reader should consult the classic
English text on the bullfight: Ernest Hemingway, *Death in the Afternoon*
(London: Jonathan Cape, 1932, republished 1966). Goya's numerous
sketches of the bullfight are also very informative.

99 <u>ancient Ronda</u>: the city was known to the Romans, and its so-called
ancient quarter stands on one side of the ravine which divides the city in
two. Bullfighting centres 'were confined to four cities, *viz.*, Ronda,
Seville, Granada and Valencia, to which Zaragoza was added by Ferdinand
VII' (Ford, *op. cit.*, 272). From this we see that Andalusia was, as Ford
said, 'the *alma mater* of *toreros* for all the Peninsula' (*ibid.*, 270). Ronda
was regarded as the academy of *tauromaquia*, for the Romero brothers
taught its art there, and the present-day bullring in Ronda was built in
1784. Hemingway writes: 'Ronda school or the Ronda style of bullfighting,
(is) sober, limited in repertoire, simple, classic and tragic as against the
more varied, playful and gracious style of Sevilla' (*op.cit.*, 324).

101 <u>trailing ribbons:</u> Hemingway: 'the colours of the bull breeder which
are attached to a small harpoon-shaped iron and placed in the bull's
murillo (neck) as he enters the ring' (*op.cit.*, 285). Black and green later
became renowned as the colours of Miura who, from the middle of the
nineteenth century, bred bulls famous for their courage and ferocity. Ford
also notes: 'The bull bears on his neck a ribbon, *la divisa*; this is the
trophy which is most acceptable to the *querida* (lady love) of a *buen
torero*' (good bullfighter) (*op.cit.*, 276).

mi Marianita Pineda!   105
Las niñas venían gritando
sobre pintadas calesas
con abanicos redondos
bordados de lentejuelas.
Y los jóvenes de Ronda   110
sobre jacas pintureras,
los anchos sombreros grises
calados hasta las cejas.
La plaza, con el gentío
(calañés y altas peinetas)   115
giraba como un zodiaco
de risas blancas y negras.
Y cuando el gran Cayetano
cruzó la pajiza arena
con traje color manzana,   120
bordado de plata y seda,
destacándose gallardo
entre la gente de brega
frente a los toros zaínos
que España cría en su tierra, 125
parecía que la tarde
se ponía más morena.
¡Si hubieras visto con qué
gracia movía las piernas!
¡Qué gran equilibrio el suyo 130
con la capa y la muleta!
¡Mejor, ni Pedro Romero
toreando las estrellas!

---

108 their fans in circles all aflutter: fans were and still are not only a practical necessity due to the heat, but a very important accessory in a Spanish lady's seductive accoutrement; they epitomise the fine line between modest concealment and erotic enticement, as Ford neatly observed: 'the fan, *abanico*,... is part and parcel of every Spanish woman, whose nice conduct of it leaves nothing to be desired. No one understands the art and exercise of it like her. It is the index of her soul, the telegraph of her chamelion feelings... A handbook might be written to explain the code of signals' (*op.cit.*, 301). The lady with a fan has been a topic for many Spanish painters, including Velázquez and Goya.

112 grey hats so broad of rim: Cordovan felt hats with an extremely broad rim are traditionally associated with the bullfight, notably the Calaña hats, of line 116, from Calañas (Cordova), which are worn with one side of the rim turned up towards a low crown.

115 like a zodiac: with admirable economy the image captures the rippling play of light and shade which, as Ford remarked above, is such a feature of the bullring and its geometrically segregated spectators. At the same time the image suggests the horoscope and, by extension, fate.

118 Cayetano: Cayetano Sanz (1821-1891) was one of the most celebrated

my dearest Mariana Pineda!   105
The ladies came with gay abandon
in open coaches one by one,
their fans in circles all aflutter
with sequins gleaming in the sun.
The males of Ronda mounted came   110
showing off their elegant paces,
with grey hats so broad of rim
and cocked like this to hide their faces.
The bullring was so tightly thronged,
it spun about like a zodiac;   115
Calaña hats and tall mantillas
on smiles that flashed from white to black.
And when the matchless Cayetano
strode so manly on straw and sand,
his suit a fresh-cut apple colour   120
in finest silk and silver band,
among the troupe he stood apart
a truly handsome, brave gallant,
and when he faced the fiercest bulls
that ever Spain has reared and bred,   125
it seemed the very sky would turn
a chestnut brown to match his head.
You should have seen how gracefully
he spun his hips and turned his waist,
his perfect timing and his poise,   130
with cape and cloth there was no haste.
Not even Pedro Romero
polishes off the stars so clean;

---

toreros of the nineteenth century, though clearly Lorca is again
exercising poetic licence in having him slay bulls as early as 1831.
122 the troupe: consisting of the *picadores* and *banderilleros*, all under
the *matador*'s command.
127 a chestnut brown to match his head: the image has a superb focalising
effect, as all eyes bear down from the amphitheatre upon the isolated
matador in the bullfight's final act, the *faena*.
128-131 how gracefully...no haste: it is the *gracia* or elegance of the
matador which the bullfight enthusiast looks for. His movements should be
smooth and unhurried, and, when the bull charges, his feet should not
move, only his hips and torso, which spin as the bull's horns come past.
The cape, *capa*, is used by the *matador* for certain quicker passes before
he takes up the smaller cloth, the *muleta*, to prepare the bull for the kill.
132 Pedro Romero: one of the most famous of all bullfighters, Pedro
Romero (1754-1839) was born in Ronda and was a key figure in its school.
He was described as one of the 'first professors' of bullfighting by
Richard Ford (*op.cit.*, 272), who, as we saw above, heard Romero
pronounce on some of the finer points of his art. A famous portrait of
Pedro Romero was painted by Goya in 1801-2.

Cinco toros mató; cinco,
con divisa verde y negra.   135
En la punta de su estoque
cinco flores dejó abiertas.
y en cada instante rozaba
los hocicos de las fieras,
como una gran mariposa   140
de oro con alas bermejas.
La plaza, al par que la tarde,
vibraba fuerte, violenta,
y entre el olor de la sangre
iba el olor de la sierra.   145
Yo pensaba siempre en ti;
yo pensaba: ¡si estuviera
conmigo mi triste amiga,
mi Marianita Pineda!...

MARIANA [*Emocionada y levantándose*]:
¡Yo te querré siempre a ti   150
tanto como tú me quieras!

LUCIA [*Levantándose*]:
Nos retiramos; si sigues
escuchando a esta torera,
hay corrida para rato.

For lines 132-3 the *Obras completas* gives 'Ni Pepe-Hillo ni nadie/toreó como él torea' (Neither Pepe-Hillo nor anyone else/fought as he fights). But the Rivadeneyra, Losada and Harrap variant which I follow here is preferable both because of the greater renown of Pedro Romero and on account of the aptness of the image of <u>stars</u>. The latter links with the image of the <u>zodiac</u> (line 115) and thereby continues the theme of fate. It also evokes the bullfighter's sequined suit, known in Spanish as a *traje de luces*, suit of lights. If, however, Lorca was suggesting in this image that Pedro Romero was already dead, then this is yet another example of poetic licence.

135 <u>all trailing ribbons dark and green</u>: a repetition of line 101; the echo-line was a typical feature or the old ballad and of oral poetry generally, since such lines facilitated the memorisation of long poems.

137 <u>five red carnations</u>: again Lorca beautifies death and violence in this floral simile which evokes the blood pouring on the bull's neck. The simile is precise in form as well as colour since the hump of muscle on the bull's neck, which rises when he is angry, has been deeply contoured by the picador's lance and decorated by the banderillero's darts before the matador takes charge.

The insistence on number – <u>five</u> occuring here for the fourth time in the sequence – accords with the ancient ballad and its primitive story-telling art, since number always held enigmatic powers for the illiterate. Modern bullfights usually consist of six bulls, but the number five has a special meaning as Hemingway notes: '*No hay quinto malo*, the fifth one can't be bad' (*op.cit.*, 319), a traditional belief that the fifth bull was always the best. Five is also repeated with haunting effect in

five bulls he slew, five brave bulls,
all trailing ribbons dark and green.   135
So deftly did his sword unfold
five red carnations to the sky,
and spinning on vermillion wings,
as delicate as a butterfly,
with every pass he brushed his suit   140
on horn and snout of massive beast.
The bullring and the afternoon
vibrated to the violent feast,
and wafting on the smell of blood
I caught a breath of mountain air.   145
But every minute I thought of you:
if only my sad friend, I thought,
if only she could be here too,
my dearest Mariana Pineda...

MARIANA [*getting up, very moved*]:
    I'll always hold you dear to me,   150
    and trust your heart will feel the same.

LUCIA [*getting up*]:
    We'll leave you now. If you listen
    longer to this *aficionada*
    the bulls will gore inside your head.

Lorca's '*Lament for Ignacio Sánchez Mejías*', which begins: 'At five in the afternoon. / It was exactly five in the afternoon...', *Obras completas*, I, 551.

138-9 vermillion wings...butterfly: the image suggests the matador's graceful elusiveness, but the precise visual link centres on the matador's cape which moves with such bewildering speed around the bull's head that it seems to be two wings. In fact the *mariposa* or butterfly is a standard term in bull-fighting as Hemingway explains: 'butterfly; series of passes with cape over the man's shoulders and the man facing the bull, zigzagging slowly backwards, drawing the bull on, with a wave of first one side of the cape, then the other, supposedly imitating the flight of a butterfly. Invented by Marcial Lalanda, this *quite* (withdrawing manoeuvre) requires great knowledge of bulls to execute properly' (*op.cit.*, 299).

140 he brushed his suit: the matador's skill and courage is measured by how close he brings his body - particularly his chest and heart - to the bull's horns. In the *pase de pecho*, 'chest pass', 'emotion is given by the closeness... and it is prolonged by the slowness with which he can execute the pass'; 'if there is no blood on his belly afterwards you ought to get your money back' (Hemingway, *op.cit.*, between pages 262 and 263).

145 mountain air: since the city of Ronda is situated in the mountains, the *Serranía de Ronda* (1900 metres high), it enjoys the pure air of high altitudes. Here, however, the image also effectively suggests the sense of expiation which follows such blood-letting rituals as the bullfight, their primitive *raison d'être*.

AMPARO:	Y dime: ¿estás más contenta?;	155
	porque este cuello, ¡oh, qué cuello!,	
	[*La besa en el cuello.*]	
	no se hizo para la pena.	

LUCIA [*En la ventana*]:
Hay nubes por Parapanda.
Lloverá, aunque Dios no quiera.

AMPARO:	¡Este invierno va a ser de agua!	160
	¡No podré lucir!	
LUCIA:	¡Coqueta!	
AMPARO:	¡Adiós, Mariana!	
MARIANA:	¡Adiós, niñas!	
	[*Se besan.*]	
AMPARO:	¡Que te pongas más contenta!	
MARIANA:	Tardecillo es. ¿Queréis	
	que os acompañe Clavela?	165
AMPARO:	¡Gracias! Pronto volveremos.	
LUCIA:	¡No bajes, no!	
MARIANA:	¡Hasta la vuelta!	
	[*Salen.*]	

[*Mariana atraviesa rapidamente la escena y mira la hora en uno de esos grandes relojes dorados, donde sueña toda la poesía exquisita de la hora y el siglo. Se asoma a los cristales y ve la última luz de la tarde.*]

---

156 this neck, this lovely neck: the first of several references to the bodily part which symbolises Mariana's beauty, her vulnerability and her fate. It is all the more telling for coming so soon after the bullfight sequence.
158 Parapanda: a mountain, 1600 metres high, about thirty kilometres north-west of Granada. It is considered the barometer of the whole area, for, according to the proverb which Richard Ford gives (*op.cit.*, 555):

| Cuando Parapanda se pone la montera | When Parapanda puts its black hat on, |
| Llueve aunque Dios no lo quisiera. | It'll rain, whether God likes it or not. |

161 parading: Amparo, an eager, unattached young female, is not overjoyed at the prospect of being cooped up through a harsh Granada winter. Her favourite pleasure is to show off in fine clothes on one of the city's boulevards. Richard Ford: 'The Spaniards as a people are remarkably well dressed... The variety of costumes which appears on the Spanish public *alamedas* renders the scene far gayer than that of our dull uniform walks' (*op.cit.*, 308).
167-187 The lights of evening persist...: Mariana's first soliloquy gives vent to the deep anxiety she had been at pains to conceal from her young visitors. A cluster of inventive, typically Lorquian images conveys her sombre mood, her sense of danger and the well known topic of time's slow passing. The images of arrows (line 170) and spears - actually 'espadas', *swords*, in the Spanish - (187), which parenthesise her speech, continue

50

```
AMPARO:        But tell me, are you more cheerful?              155
               Because this neck, this lovely neck
               of yours...
               [She kisses her neck.]
                     wasn't meant to suffer pain.
LUCIA [at the window]:
               Big clouds lie on Parapanda.
               That means rain, God willing or not.
AMPARO:        A wet old winter lies in store!                  160
               And no parading for me!
LUCIA:                               Coquette!
AMPARO:        Goodbye, Mariana!
MARIANA:                         Goodbye girls!
               [They kiss one another.]
LUCIA:         I do hope you're feeling brighter.
MARIANA:       It's getting late. Would you prefer
               Clavela to accompany you?                        165
AMPARO:        Oh, thanks! We'll see you again soon.
LUCIA:         No need to see us out!
MARIANA:                         Goodbye, then!
               [They leave.]
```

[Mariana crosses the stage quickly and looks at the time on one of those large gold clocks in which all the exquisite poetry of the age seems to lie sleeping. She looks out of the window at the fading evening light.]

---

the theme of physical violence established in the bullfight sequence, while the stellar imagery, <u>planet</u> (174) and <u>stars</u> (176) keeps the idea of fate to the fore. Three images are especially effective in giving visible and tangible substance to such an abstract concept as time's slow passage: first, the comparison of evening light with a bird's hovering wings (lines 168-9) captures the tantalising interplay of flickering light and shadow at dusk; second, that of a planet trapped in her throat (174-5) has a choking, paralytic quality which again foreshadows Mariana's strangulation by garrote; finally, the idea of light caught up in trees and water (180-4) has a rare plasticity or three-dimensional, painterly effect.

In this latter connexion we might also recall the profound influence exerted on Lorca by popular song and especially the *cante jondo* or 'deep song' of Andalusia. In an essay on the topic Lorca remarked: 'But what impresses most in the admirable poetic reality of the "deep song" poems is the strange materialization of wind that is achieved in many songs' (*Obras completas*, I, 987). By the same token the sequence is remarkably effective in giving material substance to mood, a mood based on a sense of confinement and implosive claustrophobia which, for Lorca, was so typical of Granada: 'Granada cannot leave its own home. It is not like those cities which are on the coast or astride large rivers, cities that travel and return home enriched by what they have seen. Granada, solitary and pure, condenses and pulls in its extraordinary soul and has no other exit than by its own upward link with the stars' (*ibid.*, 936).

MARIANA: Si toda la tarde fuera
            como un gran pájaro, ¡cuántas
            duras flechas lanzaría   170
            para cerrarle las alas!
            Hora redonda y oscura
            que me pesa en las pestañas.
            Dolor de viejo lucero
            detenido en mi garganta.   175
            Ya debieran las estrellas
            asomarse a mi ventana
            y abrirse lentos los pasos
            por la calle solitaria.
            ¡Con qué trabajo tan grande   180
            deja la luz a Granada!
            Se enreda entre los cipreses
            o se esconde bajo el agua.
            ¡Y esta noche que no llega!
            [*Con angustia.*]
            ¡Noche temida y soñada;   185
            que me hieres ya de lejos
            con larguísimas espadas!
FERNANDO [*En la puerta*]:
            Buenas tardes.
MARIANA [*Asustada*]:   ¿Qué?
            [*Reponiéndose.*]   ¡Fernando!
FERNANDO: ¿Te asusto?
MARIANA: No te esperaba [*Sonriendo.*]
            y tu voz me sorprendió.   190
FERNANDO: ¿Se han ido ya mis hermanas?
MARIANA: Ahora mismo. Se olvidaron
            de que vendrías a buscarlas.
[*Fernando viste elegantemente la moda de la época. Mira y
habla apasionadamente. Tiene dieciocho años. A veces le
temblará la voz y se turbará a menudo.*]
FERNANDO: ¿Interrumpo?
MARIANA: Siéntate.
            [*Se sientan.*]
FERNANDO [*Lírico*]:
            ¡Cómo me gusta tu casa!   195
            Con este olor a membrillos.
            [*Aspira.*]

---

189 [smiling]: the *Obras completas* gives '[Reponiéndose.]', [*composing
herself*]. But since that had occurred only two lines before, the variant
from Rivadeneyra, Losada and Harrap seems preferable.
193+ Fernando: this character is an invention of Lorca's, though in fact
Mariana did have a young admirer of roughly the same age, a certain José

52

MARIANA: The lights of evening persist,
hovering like a great bird's wings,
and I wish a hail of arrows   170
would close them and darken the sky.
Oh time, so roundly measured,
you weigh heavy on my lids;
grief of an ancient planet
trapped in my throat like a sigh!   175
By now the stars should be here
twinkling at my window sill,
stepping down this gloomy street,
the night's only passers-by.
But with what painful effort   180
does daylight leave Granada,
tangled between cypress trees
and lost beneath the water.
Oh night that comes so slowly!
[*With anguish.*]
Night that brings my joy and fears,   185
how distantly you would me
with your long and countless spears!

FERNANDO [*at the door*]:
Good evening.
MARIANA [*startled*]:   What?
[*Composing herself.*]
                            Oh, Fernando!
FERNANDO: I startled you?
MARIANA: Oh, no. [*smiling.*]
                            Your voice,
that's all, it took me by surprise.   190
FERNANDO: And have my sisters left already?
MARIANA: A moment ago. They'd forgotten
that you were coming to fetch them.
[*Fernando is dressed elegantly in the style of the day. He speaks
passionately and moves his eyes ardently. He is eighteen years old.
At times his voice trembles and he frequently seems embarrassed.*]
FERNANDO: Am I interrupting?
MARIANA: Please, sit down.
[*They sit.*]
FERNANDO [*poetically*]:
How dearly do I love your house!...   195
So fragrant is its scent of quinces.
[*He breathes in.*]

---

de Salamanca y Mayor (Antonina Rodrigo, *op.cit.*, 69–71).
197–199 ... sailing ships and flower garlands: see note on the scenic
directions to the Prologue.

```
                    Y qué preciosa fachada
                    tienes..., llena de pinturas
                    de barcos y de guirnaldas.
MARIANA [Interrumpiéndole]:
                    ¿Hay mucha gente en la calle?                    200
                    [Inquieta.]
FERNANDO [Sonríe]:
                    ¿Por qué preguntas?
MARIANA [Turbada]:              Por nada.
FERNANDO:    Pues hay mucha gente.
MARIANA [Impaciente]:                    ¿Dices?
FERNANDO:    Al pasar por Bibarrambla
                    he visto dos o tres grupos
                    de gente envuelta en sus capas    205
                    que aguantando el airecillo
                    a pie firme comentaban
                    el suceso.
MARIANA [Ansiosamente]:
                    ¿Qué suceso?
FERNANDO:    ¿Sospechas de qué se trata?
MARIANA:    ¿Cosas de masonería?                    210
FERNANDO:    Un capitán que se llama,
                    [Mariana está como en vilo.]
                    no recuerdo..., liberal,
                    prisionero de importancia,
                    se ha fugado de la cárcel
                    de la Audiencia.
                    [Viendo a Mariana.]
                    ¿Qué te pasa?                    215
MARIANA:    Ruego a Dios por él. ¿Se sabe
                    si le buscan?
```

---

205 all wrapped up tightly in their cloaks: the picture of a man muffled up in a long cloak is again well known from Goya's paintings. For its sense of mystery and the clandestine it was a favourite image in Romantic literature. But it also had specific connexions with nationalism and anti-royalist subterfuge, as we can see from Richard Ford's comments: 'A genuine Spaniard would sooner part with his skin than his *capa* (cloak); so when Charles III (Ferdinand VII's Italianate grandfather) wanted to prohibit their use, the universal people rose in arms, and the Squillacci, or anti-cloak ministry, was turned out. The *capa* fits its wearer admirably, it favours habits of inactivity, ... conceals a knife and rags, and, when muffled around, offers a disguise for intrigues and robbery' (*op.cit.*, 304). The cloaked men in Bibarrambla Square are evidently of the patriotic, intriguing type.

210 freemasons: Freemasonry was a clandestine brotherhood of liberal sympathy which opposed the absolutism of Ferdinand VII and which was abolished by him in 1824. The King decreed 'That masons and society members should alike suffer the ultimate penalty'; also 'That those who

And what a delightful exterior
it has, with all those lovely paintings
of sailing ships and flower garlands...!
MARIANA [*interrupting him*]:
    Are there many people about?   200
    [*She moves restlessly.*]
FERNANDO [*smiling*]:
    Why do you ask?
MARIANA [*uneasily*]:   No special reason.
FERNANDO: In point of fact there are.
MARIANA [*impatiently*]:   Are there?
FERNANDO: On coming up Bibarrambla
    I saw several groups of men
    all wrapped up tightly in their cloaks;   205
    undaunted by the biting wind
    they were standing there discussing
    the latest news.
MARIANA [*anxiously*]:   What latest news?
FERNANDO: Have you not had word of it, then?
MARIANA: It must be about freemasons.   210
FERNANDO: A captain who goes by the name of...
    [*Mariana is left in suspense.*]
    Oh, I forget... A liberal,
    a prisoner of some importance,
    just broke out of Audiencia jail.
    [*Looking at Mariana.*]
    What is it that bothers you so?   215
MARIANA: I pray to God for him. And are
    they on his trail?

---

speak against royal sovereignty in public places, even when nothing comes of it... should be punished by four to ten years imprisonment' (Antonina Rodrigo, *op.cit.*, 60-1). Raymond Carr writes: 'Civilian revolution was organised in Masonic Lodges and it is the undoubted contribution of Freemasonary to the Revolution of 1820 that created the myth of its occult force. According to clerical conservatives, liberalism was nothing but a permanent Masonic conspiracy' (R. Carr, *Spain 1808-1975*, p.127).

214 <u>Audiencia jail:</u> a jail attached to the Audiencia, or place of 'hearing', that is, the Supreme Court, which was built about 1526 and stands between the Alhambra and the Albaicín quarters of Granada. Ford notes: 'The Audiencia has now a jurisdiction over 1,214,124 souls. The number tried in 1844 was 4434 (being about one in 273). The proceedings are carried out in a very slovenly and continental way according to English notions of justice' (*op.cit.*, 583). The jail itself is known as the *Antigua cárcel* (Old Prison) and is connected by stairways to the Audiencia, though it is no longer used as a prison. In this sequence Lorca maintains suspense by not revealing the identity of the escapee, though clearly we assume it to be Mariana's love, Don Pedro.

FERNANDO: Ya marchaban,
                 antes de venir yo aquí,
                 un grupo de tropas hacia
                 el Genil y sus puentes   220
                 para ver si lo encontraban,
                 y es fácil que lo detengan
                 camino de la Alpujarra.
                 ¡Qué triste es esto!
MARIANA [*Llena de angustia*]:   ¡Dios mío!
FERNANDO: Y las gentes cómo aguantan.   225
                 Señores, ya es demasiado.
                 El preso, como un fantasma,
                 se escapó; pero Pedrosa
                 ya buscará su garganta.
                 Pedrosa conoce el sitio   230
                 donde la vena es más ancha,
                 por donde brota la sangre
                 más caliente y encarnada.
                 ¡Qué chacal!   ¿Tú le conoces?
                 [*La luz se va retirando de la escena.*]
MARIANA: Desde que llegó a Granada.   235
FERNANDO [*Sonriendo*]:
                 ¡Bravo amigo, Marianita!
MARIANA: Le conocí por desgracia.
                 El está amable conmigo
                 y hasta viene por mi casa,
                 sin que yo pueda evitarlo.   240
                 ¿Quién le impediría la entrada?
FERNANDO: Ojo, que es un viejo verde.
MARIANA: Es un hombre que me espanta.
FERNANDO: ¡Qué gran alcalde del crimen!
MARIANA: ¡No puedo mirar su cara!   245
FERNANDO [*Serio*]:
                 ¿Te da mucho miedo?
MARIANA: ¡Mucho!
                 Ayer tarde yo bajaba
                 por el Zacatín. Volvía

---

220 <u>Genil</u>: the larger of the two Granada rivers, Genil and Darro, and the
river which separates the city from the mountainous regions to the south
and east of the city.
223 <u>Alpujarra</u>: the mountain region of the Alpujarras is on the other side
of the Sierra Nevada peaks facing the Mediterranean.
228 <u>has gone without trace</u>: Pedro's daring escape will shortly be
described in detail (lines 378–81). Pedrosa is the Chief of Police in Granada
and, effectively, Mariana's executioner (see Introduction).
231–32 <u>for the throat, for the jugular...</u>: Pedrosa is immediately linked
with rapaciousness and the idea of death inflicted through the neck.
244–5 <u>the Supreme Judge of criminals</u>: Fernando suggests that Mariana is

FERNANDO: Indeed they are.
                Before I came up here just now
                a band of troops was heading down
                towards the Genil, expecting   220
                to trap him on the bridges there.
                Otherwise they'll catch up with him
                on the road to Alpujarra.
                How sad this business is!
MARIANA [*full of anguish*]:   My God!
FERNANDO: The people have suffered endlessly,   225
                but surely now enough's enough.
                This prisoner, like some phantom being,
                has gone without trace; but Pedrosa
                can sniff out shadows at midnight.
                Pedrosa is a carnivore,   230
                he makes straight for the throat,
                for the jugular, where the flesh
                tears easy and the blood runs warm.
                More jackal than man! Do you know him?
                [*The light fades more quickly now.*]
MARIANA: Since first he came to Granada.   235
FERNANDO [*smiling*]:
                A good friend to have, Mariana!
MARIANA: Knowing him is my misfortune.
                He's always attentive to me,
                and sometimes he visits this house,
                without invitation, of course.   240
                But who can deny him entrance?
FERNANDO: Take care, for he's a lecherous type.
MARIANA: Truth be told, he terrifies me.
FERNANDO: Then you should be the Supreme Judge
                of criminals!
MARIANA: I can't look him   245
                in the face!
FERNANDO [*serious*]:   He scares you that much?
MARIANA: He does! Last evening, going down
                the Zacatín, on my way home

---

a good judge of character and that Pedrosa is the one who should be put
in the dock.
248 Zacatín: amongst the most delightful of Granada's streets, and one
which clearly intoxicated Richard Ford in the 1830s: 'The Moorish Zacatín
is as antique as the *Plaza Nueva* is modern. The Arabic word means an
"old clothes man", and is the diminutive of *Zok*, a market. In summer it is
covered with an awning, a *toldo*, which gives a cool and tenty look. At
the *respaldos* (sides), the Prout-like houses and toppling balconies are so
old that they seem only not to fall. Here is every form and colour of
picturesque poverty; vines clamber up the irregularities, while below
naiads dabble, washing their red and yellow garments in the all gilding

57

de la iglesia de Santa Ana·,
tranquila, pero de pronto   250
vi a Pedrosa. Se acercaba,
seguido de dos golillas,
entre un grupo de gitanas.
¡Con un aire y un silencio!
¡El notó que yo temblaba!   255
[*La escena está en una dulce penumbra.*]
FERNANDO: ¡Bien supo el rey lo que se hizo
al mandarlo aquí a Granada!
MARIANA [*Levantándose*]:
Ya es noche. ¡Clavela! ¡Luces!
FERNANDO: Ahora los ríos sobre España,
en vez de ser ríos son   260
largas cadenas de agua.
MARIANA: Por eso hay que mantener
la cabeza levantada.
CLAVELA [*Entrando con dos candelabros*]:
¡Señora, las luces!
MARIANA [*Palidísima y en acecho*]:
¡Déjalas!
[*Llaman fuertemente a la puerta.*]
CLAVELA: ¡Están llamando!
[*Coloca las luces.*]
FERNANDO [*Al ver a Mariana descompuesta*]:
¡Mariana!   265
¿Por qué tiemblas de ese modo?
MARIANA [*A Clavela, gritando en voz baja*]:
¡Abre pronto, por Dios, anda!
[*Sale Clavela corriendo, Mariana queda en actitud expectante
junto a la puerta, y Fernando, de pie.*]
FERNANDO: Sentiría en el alma ser molesto...
Marianita, ¿qué tienes?

---

glorious sunbeams. What a picture it is to all but the native, who sees
none of the wonders of lights and shadows, reflections, colours, and
outlines' (*op.cit.*, 576).
249 <u>Mass at Santa Ana</u>: situated in the square of that name, the church
has a fine portal, which, like its roof and tower, is in the Mudejar style.
The tower, built in 1561, caught Ford's eye: 'Passing the elegant tower of
Sa. Ana, we reach the Alameda del Darro' (*op.cit.*, 584). Lorca, in an
essay entitled 'Granada (A Closed Paradise for Many)', commented: 'The
improbable-looking little tower of Santa Ana... comes from the Renaissance
tradition: a tiny tower, built more for doves than bells, with all the fine
bearing and ancient elegance of Granada' (*Obras completas*, I, 937).
256 <u>The King...sent him to Granada</u>: Ramon Pedrosa y Andrade was

```
                    from Mass at Santa Ana, feeling
                    quite peaceful and at ease, suddenly          250
                    I saw Pedrosa.  He came up
                    with his two bodyguards in tow
                    and thronged by gypsies on all sides.
                    He had that steely air of silence...
                    No doubt he saw my hands were shaking.        255
                    [The stage is now softly shadowed.]
FERNANDO:           The King knew what he was doing
                    when he sent him to Granada!
MARIANA [getting up]:
                    It's dark.  Clavela!  Bring some lights!
FERNANDO:           The rivers that flow across Spain
                    no longer run a course that's free,           260
                    but are like endless liquid chains.
MARIANA:            And that's why it's so important
                    to keep our minds and spirits high.
CLAVELLA [entering with two candlesticks]:
                    The lights, Señora.
MARIANA [ever watchful and extremely pale]:
                                        Leave them there.
                    [A loud knocking is heard on the door.]
CLAVELA:            Someone's in a hurry!
                    [She puts the candlesticks down.]
FERNANDO [seeing Mariana's nervous state]:
                                        Mariana,                   265
                    what makes you shake so fearfully?
MARIANA [to Clavela, whispering urgently]
                    The door, go quickly, in God's name!
[Clavela runs off.  Mariana remains standing expectantly near
the door with Fernando close by.]
FERNANDO:           The last thing I want is to interfere...
                    But dear Mariana, what grieves you...?
```

---

appointed Chief of Police in Granada by Ferdinand VII in 1825, his main brief being to eradicate liberal conspirators in the city. After the death of the King in 1833 he was deposed from office and returned to live in Madrid. In any Spanish production of the play Pedrosa would stand out for his more correct Castilian speech, all the other characters being Andalusians who, especially Granadans, have a very colourful, aspirate speech which tends to drop intervocalic consonants.

259-61 The rivers...are like endless liquid chains: the image is effective in its transforming of water, normally associated with freedom, into a metaphor of bondage. It has visual precision too, inasmuch as Spain's four major rivers – the Duero, Ebro, Tagus and Guadalquivir – all cross the Peninsula in roughly west-east or latitudinal direction, thereby, on the map at least, suggesting fetters or chains.

MARIANA [*Angustiada exquisitamente*]:
                              Esperando,
          los segundos se alargan de manera   270
          irresistible.
FERNANDO [*Inquieto*]:   ¿Bajo yo?
MARIANA: Un caballo
          se aleja por la calle. ¿Tú lo sientes?
FERNANDO: Hacia la vega corre.
          [*Pausa.*]
MARIANA: Ya ha cerrado
          el postigo Clavela.
FERNANDO: ¿Quién será?
MARIANA [*Turbada y reprimiendo una honda angustia*]:
          ¡Yo no lo sé! [*Aparte.*] ¡Ni siquiera pensarlo!   275
CLAVELA [*Entrando*]:
          Una carta, señora.
          [*Mariana coge la carta ávidamente.*]
FERNANDO [*Aparte*]:   ¡Qué será!
CLAVELA: Me la entregó un jinete. Iba embozado
          hasta los ojos. Tuve mucho miedo.
          Soltó las bridas y se fue volando
          hacia lo oscuro de la plazoleta.   280
FERNANDO: Desde aquí lo sentimos.
MARIANA: ¿Le has hablado?
CLAVELA: Ni yo le dije nada, ni él a mí.
          Lo mejor es callar en estos casos.
[*Fernando cepilla el sombrero con su manga; tiene el semblante
inquieto.*]
MARIANA [*Con la carta*]:
          ¡No la quisiera abrir! ¡Ay, quién pudiera
          en esta realidad estar soñando!   285
          ¡Señor, no me quites lo que más quiero!
          [*Rasga la carta y lee.*]
FERNANDO [*A Clavela, ansiosamente*]:
          Estoy confuso. ¡Esto es tan extraño!
          Tú sabes lo que tiene. ¿Qué le ocurre?
CLAVELA: Ya le he dicho que no lo sé.
FERNANDO [*Discreto*]:   Me callo.
          Pero...
CLAVELA [*Continuando la frase*]:
          ¡Pobre doña Mariana mía!   290
MARIANA [*Agitada*]:
          ¡Acércame, Clavela, el candelabro!
[*Clavela se lo acerca corriendo Fernando cuelga lentamente la
capa sobre sus hombros.*]

---

274 **postern door:** a private, back-door entry which the messenger has
evidently used for greater secrecy.

MARIANA [*unbearably anxious*]:   This waiting,
       this endless waiting sets my nerves on edge.   270
FERNANDO [*uneasy*]:
       Shall I go down to see?
MARIANA: Was that a horse
       I heard? A horse that made off up the street?
FERNANDO: Yes, bound at great speed for the country.
       [*Pause.*]
MARIANA: Clavela
       has shut the postern door.
FERNANDO: Who could it be?
MARIANA [*agitated, but repressing a deep anguish*]:
       I've no idea! [*Aside.*] Nor can I bear to think! 275
CLAVELA [*entering*]:
       A letter, Señora.
       [*Mariana takes the letter eagerly.*]
FERNANDO [*aside*]:   From whom, I wonder?
CLAVELA: A horseman handed it to me. All cloaked
       he was up to the eyes, a frightening sight!
       He whipped his mare and went like the wind
       to vanish in the darkness of the square.   280
FERNANDO: We heard him gallop off.
MARIANA: He spoke to you?
CLAVELA: Nor I to him nor he to me exchanged
       a single word. It's better to say nothing
       at such times.
[*Fernando brushes his hat with his sleeve, his face anxious.*]
MARIANA [*with the letter*]: I hardly dare to read it!
       If only I were dreaming this nightmare!   285
       Lord, don't deprive me of my dearest love!
       [*She tears the letter open and reads.*]
FERNANDO [*to Clavela anxiously*]:
       I don't understand. Why all this mystery?
       If you know what's going on, please tell me.
CLAVELA: I've told you once, I know nothing at all.
FERNANDO [*discreetly*]:
       Well, then, I'll ask no more. . .
CLAVELA [*as though speaking for him*]:   My poor Mariana! 290
MARIANA [*nervously*]:
       Clavela, bring a candle over here!
[*Clavela brings it quickly while Fernando slowly puts his cloak
around his shoulders.*]

---

276 A letter: a device which seems calculated to capture the flavour of
Romantic drama, even its melodrama. Historically Mariana received the
escaped prisoner at her house, not merely his letter (Antonina Rodrigo,
op.cit., 91); but it was obviously better theatre to delay Don Pedro's
appearance in this way.

CLAVELA [A Mariana]:
        ¡Dios nos guarde, señora de mi vida!
FERNANDO [Azorado e inquieto]:
        Con tu permiso...
MARIANA [Queriendo reponerse]:
                ¿Ya te vas?
FERNANDO: Me marcho:
        voy al café de la Estrella.
MARIANA [Tierna y suplicante]:   Perdona
        estas inquietudes...
FERNANDO [Digno]:   ¿Necesitas algo?   295
MARIANA [Conteniéndose]:
        Gracias... Son asuntos familiares hondos,
        y tengo yo misma que solucionarlos.
FERNANDO: Yo quisiera verte contenta. Diré
        a mis hermanillas que vengan un rato,
        y ojalá pudiera prestarte mi ayuda.   300
        Adiós, que descanses.
        [Le estrecha la mano.]
MARIANA: Adiós.
FERNANDO [A Clavela]:
        Buenas noches.
CLAVELA: Salga, que yo le acompaño.
        [Se van.]
MARIANA [En el momento de salir Fernando, da rienda suelta
a su angustia]:
        ¡Pedro de mi vida! ¿Pero quién irá?
        Ya cercan mi casa los días amargos.
        Y este corazón, ¿adónde me lleva,   305
        que hasta de mis hijos me estoy olvidando?
        ¡Tiene que ser pronto y no tengo a nadie!
        ¡Yo misma me asombro de quererle tanto!
        ¿Y si le dijese... y él lo comprendiera?
        ¡Señor, por la llaga de vuestro costado!   310
        [Sollozando.]
        Por las clavelinas de su dulce sangre,
        enturbia la noche para los soldados.
        [En un arranque, viendo el reloj.]
        ¡Es preciso! ¡Tengo que atreverme a todo!
        [Sale corriendo hacia la puerta.]
        ¡Fernando!
CLAVELA [Que entra]: ¡En la calle, señora!
MARIANA [Asomándose rápidamente a la ventana]:
                        ¡Fernando!

---

306 to forget that I am a mother: Mariana cannot reconcile her love for
Pedro, the conspirator, with her responsibilities as a mother. As a widow

CLAVELA [to Mariana]:
        May God protect us, my precious Señora!
FERNANDO [upset and restless]:
        If you'll excuse me.
MARIANA [trying to be calm]:   You're leaving already?
FERNANDO: Yes, I'll be off to the Café Estrella.
MARIANA [tender and apologetic]:
        Excuse my sombre mood.
FERNANDO [dignified]:   If you should need me... 295
MARIANA [containing herself]:
        I'm grateful... but these are family matters,
        and I myself will have to sort them out.
FERNANDO: I only wish to see you smile. I'll tell
        my sisters to call again soon. But please,
        if ever you need help, just call on me.   300
        Goodbye, and try to rest a while.
        [He takes her hand.]
MARIANA: Goodbye.
FERNANDO [to Clavela]:
        Good night.
CLAVELA: Come on, I'll keep you company.
        [They leave.]
MARIANA [as soon as Fernando leaves, gives free rein to her anguish.]:
        Oh Pedro, my love! Who else can I send?
        Unhappy days have come upon this house.
        And my woman's heart, where does it lead me,   305
        except to forget that I am a mother?
        He needs help quick, yet I am all alone!
        It takes my breath that I should love him so.
        And if I told him... and he understood?
        Oh Lord! By the cruel wound in your side,   310
        [Sobbing.]
        and by the sweet carnations of your blood,
        please darken this night for the soldiers' posse!
        [With a start, seeing the clock.]
        There's no one else I can ask! I must act!
        [She runs towards the door.]
        Fernando!
CLAVELA [entering]: He's gone, Señora!
MARIANA [rushing to the window and leaning out]:
                   Fernando!

---

she is naturally fearful of leaving her children destitute.

310-11 Oh Lord! By the cruel wound...by the sweet carnations of your blood: the reference to Christ's Passion introduces another note of sacrifice and martyrdom. The image of carnations was used in the bullfight sequence, and the connexion is stronger if we recall that Christ had five wounds.

63

CLAVELA [Con las manos cruzadas]:
                   ¡Ay, doña Mariana, qué malita está!   315
                   Desde que usted puso sus preciosas manos
                   en esa bandera de los liberales,
                   aquellos colores de flor de granado
                   desaparecieron de su cara.
MARIANA [Reponiéndose]:   Abre,
                   y respeta y ama lo que estoy bordando.   320
CLAVELA [Saliendo]:
                   Dios dirá; los tiempos cambian con el tiempo.
                   Dios dirá: ¡Paciencia!
                   [Sale.]
MARIANA: Tengo, sin embargo,
                   que estar muy serena, muy serena, aunque
                   me siento vestida de temblor y llanto.
[Aparece en la puerta Fernando, con el alto sombrero de
cintas entre sus manos enguantadas. Le precede Clavela.]
FERNANDO [Entrando, apasionado]:
                   ¿Qué quieres?
MARIANA [Firme]:   Hablar contigo.   325
                   [A Clavela.]
                   Puedes irte.
CLAVELA [Marchándose, resignada]:
                   ¡Hasta mañana!
[Se va, turbada, mirando con ternura y tristeza a su señora.
Pausa.]
FERNANDO: Dime, pronto.
MARIANA: ¿Eres mi amigo?
FERNANDO: ¿Por qué preguntas, Mariana?
[Mariana se sienta en una silla, de perfil al público, y
Fernando junto a ella, un poco de frente, componiendo una
clásica estampa de la época.]
                   ¡Ya sabes que siempre fui!
MARIANA: ¿De corazón?
FERNANDO: ¡Soy sincero!   330

---

317 that unfortunate liberal flag: in Clavela's eyes the flag is cursed with
bad luck, and, in these superstitious terms, so is Mariana by touching it.
318 pomegranate flower: a further natural simile to stress Mariana's
beauty, which, like flowers and fruit, must wither and decay. This has an
additional reverberation in that pomegranate – granada in Spanish – takes
its name from Mariana's city, the shield of which has a pomegranate for its
motif.
323 trembling tears engulf my heart, I must: a bold image, particularly
Andalusian in flavour, which recalls the emotional intensity of the 'deep
song', cante jondo, on which Lorca wrote a critical essay (Obras
completas, I, 973–94).
327 Are you my friend?: in the sequence which now begins Mariana could
perhaps be faulted for the way she manipulates Fernando and takes

CLAVELA [*her hands across her chest*]:
        Oh, Doña Mariana, how troubled you are!   315
        The moment you put your delicate hands
        on that unfortunate liberal flag,
        your face, once fresh as pomegrante flower,
        shed all its blossom.
MARIANA [*resolved*]:   Go down to the door,
        and love and respect the flag that I sew.   320
CLAVELA [*leaving*]:
        God only knows where this will lead. But all
        things change in time, God knows.
        [*She leaves.*]
MARIANA: Yes, but
        even though inside of me trembling tears
        engulf my heart, I must try to keep calm.
[*Fernando appears at the door, holding his ribboned top hat between his gloved hands. Clavela enters before him.*]
FERNANDO [*entering in a state of passion*]:
        What do you want?
MARIANA [*firmly*]:   To speak with you.   325
        [*To Clavela.*]
        You can go now.
CLAVELA [*leaving, resigned*]:
                Good night, Señora.
[*She leaves, much disturbed, looking at her mistress with sad affection. Pause.*]
FERNANDO: What is it then?
MARIANA: Are you my friend?
FERNANDO: What need have you to ask, Mariana?
[*Mariana sits down on a chair, her profile to the audience, and, with Fernando close by and a little in front of her, together they compose an engraving typical of the period.*]
FERNANDO: You surely know I was and am!
MARIANA: But are you truly?
FERNANDO: Absolutely!   330

---

advantage of his innocent love; which possibly means to say that Lorca could be faulted for showing his heroine in a dubious light. However, Mariana's weakness is very human and the guile she uses very feminine, while the whole tenor of the dialogue again recalls Romantic drama which delighted in the ironies and paradoxes of love.

328+ They compose an engraving typical of the period: from such a line we see that one of Lorca's primary intentions was to recreate on stage in the most plastic and sensory terms the whole ambience of the Spain and the Granada in which Mariana lived. Each line of verse and each gesture or pose is thus slightly stylised to achieve this seductive effect. The current sequence is no doubt among the most difficult to carry off, since the line between recreation and pastiche is very fine.

MARIANA: ¡Ojalá que fuese así!
FERNANDO: Hablas con un caballero.
                [*Poniéndose la mano sobre la blanca pechera.*]
MARIANA [*Segura*]:
                ¡Lo sé!
FERNANDO: ¿Qué quieres de mí?
MARIANA: Quizá quiera demasiado
                y por eso no me atrevo.   335
FERNANDO: No quieras ver disgustado
                este corazón tan nuevo.
                Te sirvo con alegría.
MARIANA [*Temblorosa*]:
                Fernando, ¿y si fuera...?
FERNANDO [*Ansiosamente*]   ¿Qué?
MARIANA: Algo peligroso.
FERNANDO [*Decidido*]:   Iría.   340
                Con toda mi buena fe.
MARIANA: ¡No puedo pedirte nada!
                Pero esto no puede ser.
                Como dicen por Granada,
                ¡soy una loca mujer!   345
FERNANDO [*Tierno*]:
                Marianita.
MARIANA: ¡Yo no puedo!
FERNANDO: ¿Por qué me llamaste? Di.
MARIANA [*En un arranque trágico*]:
                Porque tengo mucho miedo,
                de morirme sola aquí.
FERNANDO: ¿De morirte?
MARIANA [*Tierna y desesperada*]:
                                Necesito,   350
                para seguir respirando
                que tú me ayudes, mocito.
FERNANDO [*Lleno de pasión*]:
                Mis ojos te están mirando,
                y no lo debes dudar.
MARIANA: Pero mi vida está fuera,   355
                por el aire, por la mar,
                por donde yo no quisiera.
FERNANDO: ¡Dichosa la sangre mía
                si puede calmar tu pena!
MARIANA: No; tu sangre aumentaría   360
                el grosor de mi cadena.
[*Se lleva decidida las manos al pecho para sacar la carta.*
Fernando tiene una actitud expectante y conmovida.]
                ¡Confío en tu corazón!
                [*Saca la carta. Duda.*]

MARIANA: If only I could believe you!
FERNANDO: Mariana, you offend my honour.
             [*Putting his hand on his white shirt front.*]
MARIANA [*decided*]:
             I know!
FERNANDO: What do you want of me?
MARIANA: Perhaps I want a lot too much,
             which makes it hard for me to say.   335
FERNANDO: And I know you don't wish to see
             this young heart of mine unhappy,
             so tell me how I best can serve.
MARIANA [*trembling*]:
             Fernando, and if it were...?
FERNANDO [*anxiously*]:   What?
MARIANA: Fraught with danger?
FERNANDO [*resolved*]:   No less I'd go,   340
             for you, without a second thought.
MARIANA: I have no right to ask you this!
             I cannot stoop so low! It's true
             what everyone in Granada says,
             I'm a woman whose brain has turned!   345
FERNANDO [*gently*]:
             Marianita.
MARIANA: I must not ask!
FERNANDO: Why did you call me back, then? Say!
MARIANA [*in an outburst of grief*]:
             Because I have a terrible dread
             of dying, all alone in here.
FERNANDO: Of dying, you say?
MARIANA [*with gentle desperation*]:
                              I need you,   350
             young friend; if I'm to go on breathing
             I desperately need your help.
FERNANDO [*passionately*]:
             When my eyes look straight at yours,
             is it possible you can doubt me?
MARIANA: But my heart has taken to wings,   355
             it flies through air and sails the sea,
             gone where I never intended.
FERNANDO: To shed my blood would be a joy
             if it could only ease your pain!
MARIANA: Oh no, your young blood must not weigh   360
             on my already heavy chains.
[*Her mind made up, she lifts her hands to her bosom to take out
the letter. Fernando, moved, waits expectantly.*]
             My whole faith is in your keeping!
             [*She takes out the letter, but hesitates.*]

67

                    ¡Qué silencio el de Granada!
                    Fija, detrás del balcón,
                    hay puesta en mí una mirada.   365
FERNANDO [*Extrañado*]:
                    ¿Qué estás hablando?
MARIANA: Me mira
                    [*Levantándose.*]
                    la garganta, que es hermosa,
                    y toda mi piel se estira.
                    ¿Podrás conmigo, Pedrosa?
                    [*En un arranque.*]
                    Toma esta carta, Fernando.   370
                    Lee despacio y entendiendo.
                    ¡Sálvame! Que estoy dudando
                    si podré seguir viviendo.
[*Fernando coge la carta y la desdobla. En este momento, el
reloj da las ocho lentamente. Las luces topacio y amatista de
las velas hacen temblar líricamente la habitación. Mariana
pasea la escena y mira angustiada al joven. Este lee el
comienzo de la carta y tiene un exquisito, pero contenido,
gesto de dolor y desaliento. Pausa, en la que se oye el reloj
y se siente la angustia de Marianita.*]
FERNANDO [*Leyendo la carta, con sorpresa, y mirando
asombrado y triste a Marianita*]:
                    "Adorada Marianita."
MARIANA: No interrumpas la lectura.   375
                    Un corazón necesita
                    lo que pide en la escritura.
FERNANDO [*Leyendo, desalentado, aunque sin afectación*]:
"Adorada Marianita: Gracias al traje de capuchino, que tan
diestramente hiciste llegar a mi poder, me he fugado de la
torre de Santa Catalina, confundido con otros frailes, que   380
salían de asistir a un reo de muerte. Esta noche, disfrazado
de contrabandista, tengo absoluta necesidad de salir para

364-5 And there...eyes that fall upon my neck: this near hallucination is
the first real sign of the extent of Mariana's distress. Again we note the
neck motif, repeated two lines later – his steely eyes upon my throat –
which virtually characterises Pedrosa as a vampire.
373+ a lyrical tremor: lighting is one of the most important features in the
play and its director would need to be expert to capture the flickering
play of candlelight on the variously coloured props, clothing, flowers,
fruit, gold clock and drapes, thereby to evoke the delicate lyricism Lorca
intended.
378-80 "My darling Mariana...": the letter's first sentence is an historically
accurate account of the conspirator's escape from prison, though, as
pointed out in the Introduction, the escapee's real name was not Pedro but
Fernando Alvarez de Sotomayor and he escaped some three years earlier

What stealthy silence in Granada!
And there, behind the balcony,
those eyes that fall upon my neck.   365
FERNANDO [*alarmed*]:
What are you saying?
MARIANA: There, staring,
[*getting up*]
his steely eyes upon my throat,
and all my flesh is tight with fear.
Pedrosa, can I be your match?
[*Resolved.*]
This letter, take it, Fernando.   370
Read it slowly and with great care.
Oh help me now to ease my mind
and find the strength to go on living!
[*Fernando takes the letter and unfolds it. Just then the clock
strikes eight very slowly. The candle lights of topaz and
amethyst give the room a lyrical tremor. Mariana crosses the
stage and looks anxiously at the young man. He reads the
first part of the letter and his face registers an exquisite but
controlled expression of disappointment. A pause in which the
clock is heard and one senses Mariana's anguish.*]
FERNANDO [*reading the letter with surprise, and looking at
Mariana with shock and sadness.*]
"My darling Mariana."
MARIANA: Don't stop,
for pity's sake, Fernando, please.   375
There is an honest heart in need
of what is written down in there.
FERNANDO [*reading with utter disappointment but without
affectation*]:
"My darling Mariana: Thanks to the Capuchin habit which
you so propitiously put into my hands, I have escaped from
Saint Catherine's Tower. I left unnoticed among a group of   380
monks who went out to comfort a condemned man. Tonight,
disguised as a smuggler, I have the most urgent need to make

---

than the play indicates, in 1828. A full account of his daring escape is
given by Antonina Rodrigo (*op.cit.*, 81-93).
382 disguised as a smuggler: that a fugitive from the law should choose such
a disguise is accounted for by the fact that Andalusia was literally teeming
with bandits at this time, especially the mountainous areas. The proximity
of Africa encouraged the smuggling of contraband, while the
preponderance of gypsies in Andalusia was another factor in the province's
lawlessness. The modern police force of the Civil Guard was originally
founded in 1844 for the specific purpose of suppressing banditry.

Válor y Cádiar, donde espero tener noticias de los amigos.
Necesito antes de las nueve el pasaporte que tienes en tu
poder y una persona de tu absoluta confianza que espere   385
con un caballo, más arriba de la presa del Genil, para, río
adelante, internarme en la sierra. Pedrosa estrechará el
cerco como él sabe, y si esta misma noche no parto, estoy
irremisiblemente perdido. Me encuentro en la casa del viejo
don Luis, que no lo sepa nadie de tu familia. No hagas por   390
verme, pues me consta que estás vigilada. Adiós, Mariana.
Todo sea por nuestra divina madre, la libertad. Dios me
salvará. Adiós, Mariana. Un abrazo y el alma de tu amante.
– Pedro de Sotomayor."

FERNANDO   [*Enamoradísimo.*]
            ¡Mariana!
MARIANA [*Rápida, llevándose una mano a los ojos*]:
                    ¡Me lo imagino!   395
            Pero silencio, Fernando.
FERNANDO [*Dramático*]:
            ¡Cómo has cortado el camino
            de lo que estaba soñando!
            [*Mariana protesta mímicamente*]
            No es tuya la culpa, no;
            ahora tengo que ayudar   400
            a un hombre que empiezo a odiar,
            y el que te quiere soy yo.
            El que de niño te amara
            lleno de amarga pasión.
            Mucho antes de que robara   405
            don Pedro tu corazón.
            ¡Pero quién te deja en esta
            triste angustia del momento!
            Y torcer mi sentimiento
            ¡ay qué trabajo me cuesta!   410
MARIANA [*Orgullosa*]:
            ¡Pues iré sola!
            [*Humilde.*]   ¡Dios mío,
            tiene que ser al instante!

---

383 <u>Válor and Cádiar</u>: two villages situated in the Alpujarra mountains on
the southern side of the Sierra Nevada. Cádiar, with nearly 2000
inhabitants in the 1910 census, is the bigger, and from it, as Ford noted,
'there is a chamois path over the heights to Granada' (*op.cit.*, 596).
384 <u>passport:</u> presumably for entering British Gibraltar, at that time a
refuge for liberal conspirators.
391 <u>I know for sure they are watching you</u>: given this information, we
might well wonder why Pedro and his fellow conspirators choose to meet at

for Válor and Cádiar, where I hope to have news of our
friends. Before nine o'clock I need the passport which you
have and a person of your absolute trust who will wait for   385
me with a horse just above the Genil dam from where I'll
make upstream and lose myself in the hills. Pedrosa knows
how to draw the net tighter, and if I don't break out this
very evening I'll be hopelessly trapped. I'm at the house of
old Don Luis, which no one in your family should know.   390
Don't try to see me since I know for sure they are
watching you. Goodbye, Mariana. Let all be risked for our
divine mother, Liberty. God will help me. Farewell. You
have my heart and soul - Your loving Pedro de Sotomayor."
FERNANDO [*moved with love*]:
        Mariana!
MARIANA [*speaking quickly, with one hand raised to her eyes*]:
        I should have known better!   395
        But not a word of this, Fernando.
FERNANDO [*intensely*]:
        How you have sealed the path
        that I once dreamed to tread!
        [*Mariana gestures her protestations.*]
        No, it is not your fault
        that I must help the man   400
        whom I've begun to hate.
        I, the one who loves you!
        The one who since a lad
        has felt this bitter passion,
        long before Don Pedro   405
        came and pillaged your heart.
        But who can leave you now
        alone with your anguish?
        And how it twists my heart
        to take this decision!   410
MARIANA [*proudly*]:
        I'll go alone, then!
        [*Meekly.*]   Oh my God!
        I'll have to leave immediately!

Mariana's house in the Second Engraving, a point which indicates not only
the liberals' foolhardiness but also, on Pedro's part, a disregard for
Mariana's safety.
400-1 <u>I must help the man whom I've begun to hate</u>: the chivalresque code
of honour requires absolute obedience and devotion to the lady, even
when, as here, it is against the gentleman's own interests. The irony of
Fernando's situation is a sub-theme which parallels Mariana's own situation,
for she too is obliged by love to take risks she would otherwise have
avoided.

71

FERNANDO: Yo iré en busca de tu amante
por la ribera del río.

MARIANA [*Orgullosa y corrigiendo la timidez y tristeza de
Fernando al decir "amante"*]:

Decirte cómo le quiero   415
no me produce rubor.
Me escuece dentro su amor
y relumbra todo entero.
El ama la libertad
y yo la quiero más que él.   420
Lo que dice es mi verdad
agria, que me sabe a miel.
Y no me importa que el día
con la noche se enturbiara,
que con la luz que emanara   425
su espíritu viviría.
Por este amor verdadero
que muerde mi alma sencilla
me estoy poniendo amarilla
como la flor del romero.   430

FERNANDO [*Fuerte*]:

Mariana, dejo que vuelen
tus quejas. Mas ¿no has oído
que el corazón tengo herido
y las heridas me duelen?

MARIANA [*Popular*]:

Pues si mi pecho tuviera   435
vidrieras de cristal,
te asomaras y lo vieras

---

419 His passion is for Liberty: even at this stage in the play Mariana seems to know that she comes second best to liberal idealism in Pedro's heart.

429-30 the bloom has left my face...: as mentioned, the floral imagery is almost as systematic in this play as it was to be in *Doña Rosita, the Spinster*, which was subtitled *The Language of Flowers*. In the course of the play Mariana's complexion will visibly wither, until, in the final act, it is described as ' extremely pale' and 'white'.

432-3 you will not hear/that my heart too is sorely wounded: Mariana's less than sympathetic attitude towards Fernando is indicative of the virulence of her own passion for Pedro. Though images like that of a *wounded heart* smack of a literary stylisation which goes back as far as the courtly tradition with its concept of love as a battle, the reckless, fatalistic nature of Mariana's passion also anticipates the powerful, instinctual treatment of love in Lorca's later plays, notably *Blood Wedding*.

434+ in popular vein: the four lines that follow are not in fact Lorca's own but were taken by him from the popular tradition of the *cante jondo* or 'deep song'. He quotes this gypsy *siguiriya* in his essay on the *cante jondo* and goes on to say: 'These poems have an unmistakable popular air

72

FERNANDO: No, it's for me to go and find
your lover by the river bank.
MARIANA [*proudly, picking up Fernando's sad irony in saying*
the word 'lover']:
To tell you that he is my love 415
brings me no shame nor makes me blush.
For I am burning in his love
and my whole being is aflame.
His passion is for Liberty
which I love even more than he. 420
And what he says, though bitter truth,
in my mouth has a honey taste.
It matters not that day and night
now seem all wrapped in confusion,
for morning will soon break again 425
and daylight's sparkling lamp shine free.
My simple heart has been ravaged
for this my one and only love;
the bloom has left my face and withered
like the yellow flower of rosemary. 430
FERNANDO [*forcefully*]:
You give full voice to your anguish,
Mariana, but will you not hear
that my heart too is sorely wounded?
Its pain beats out remorselessly.
MARIANA [*in popular vein*]:
If my heart were glass 435
you could look inside
and see the silent

---

and they are, in my view, the best expressions of the *cante jondo*'s melancholy pathos. Their melancholy is so irresistible and their emotive force so stark that they provoke in all genuine Andalusians an intimate sense of grief, a grief that cleanses the spirit and carries it away to the luminous lemon grove of Love' (*Obras completas*, I, 989).

The starkness and unashamedly naive directness of such images is found in other Andalusian poets too, for instance Manuel Altolaguirre, who could write:

Era mi dolor tan alto,	My grief was so big
que la puerta de la casa	that the doorway of the house
de donde salí llorando	through which I left crying
me llegaba a la cintura.	only came up to my waist.

Manuel Altolaguirre, *Poesías completas* (Mexico: Tezontle, 1960), 66.

This stripping down to the level of raw emotion, so typical of popular song, had the express purpose of capturing what Andalusians call *duende*, literally 'ghost', which is not unlike the American negro's concept of 'blues' or 'soul'. Lorca himself wrote an essay on the theory of the *duende* (*Obras completas*, I, 1067-1079).

                        gotas de sangre llorar.
FERNANDO: ¡Basta!   ¡Dame el documento!
                        [*Mariana va a una cómoda rápidamente.*]
                        ¿Y el caballo?
MARIANA [*Sacando los papeles*]:
                                En el jardín.   440
                        Si vas a marchar, al fin,
                        no hay que perder un momento.
FERNANDO [*Rápido y nervioso*]:
                        Ahora mismo.
                        [*Mariana le da los papeles.*]
FERNANDO: ¿Y aquí va?...
MARIANA [*Desazonada*]:
                        Todo.
FERNANDO [*Guardándose el documento en la levita*]:
                                ¡Bien!
MARIANA: ¡Perdón, amigo!
                        Que el Señor vaya contigo.   445
                        Yo espero que así sea.
FERNANDO [*Natural, digno y suave, poniéndose lentamente
la capa*]:
                        Yo espero que así será.
                        Está la noche cerrada.
                        No hay luna, y aunque la hubiera,
                        los chopos de la ribera   450
                        dan una sombra apretada.
                        Adiós.   [*Le besa la mano.*]
                                Y seca ese llanto,
                        pero quédate sabiendo
                        que nadie te querrá tanto
                        como yo te estoy queriendo.   455
                        Que voy con esta misión
                        para no verte sufrir,
                        torciendo el hondo sentir
                        de mi propio corazón.
                        [*Inicia el mutis.*]
MARIANA: Evita guarda o soldado...   460
FERNANDO [*Mirándola con ternura*]:
                        Por aquel sitio no hay gente.
                        Puedo marchar descuidado.
                        [*Amargamente irónico.*]
                        ¿Qué quieres más?

---

438 drops of blood sobbing: a favourite image in the *siguiriya*, or gypsy
'deep song'. Lorca quotes two further examples in his essay; here is one:
     comienzan mis pobres ojos   my poor eyes begin
     gotas de sangre a llorar   to weep tears of blood (*Obras completas*, I
                                                                      991)

74

```
                    drops of blood sobbing.
FERNANDO:    Enough!  Give me the document!
                    [Mariana goes quickly to a chest of drawers.]
                    And the horse?
MARIANA [taking out the papers]:
                              It's in the garden.                           440
                    If your mind is made up to go
                    there's not a moment you can spare.
FERNANDO [quickly and nervously]:
                    I'll leave straightaway.
                    [Mariana hands him the papers.]
                              And what's this?
MARIANA [disconcerted]:
                    Everything.
FERNANDO [putting the document inside the frock-coat]:
                              Good!
MARIANA:                      I'm so sorry,
                    my friend!  May the Lord go with you.         445
                    I trust that He will guide you safely.
FERNANDO [natural, dignified and polite, as he slowly puts
on his cloak]:
                    We'll put our trust in Providence.
                    At least the night is very dark.
                    There's no moon, and should it come out,
                    the poplars along the river                           450
                    will give a heavy cloak of shadow,
                    I'll say farewell.  [He kisses her hand.]
                              And dry your tears.
                    But know, at least, before I go,
                    that no one could compare his love
                    for you with mine at this sad hour.            455
                    And know, too, that I go on this mission
                    because I would not see you suffer;
                    that, doing this, I deeply wound
                    the dearest feelings in my heart.
                    [He starts to leave.]
MARIANA:    Avoid any guards and soldiers...                     460
FERNANDO [looking at her tenderly]:
                    It should be clear around those parts.
                    There'll be no mishaps on the way.
                    [Bitterly ironic.]
                    Was there anything else?
```

---

445 The *Obras completas* gives 'señor' while the other texts give 'Señor',
which is more customary in this context.

MARIANA [*Turbada y balbuciente*]:
                                      Sé prudente.
FERNANDO [*En la puerta, poniéndose el sombrero*]:
                        Ya tengo el alma cautiva;
                        desecha todo temor.   465
                        Prisionero soy de amor,
                        y lo seré mientras viva.
MARIANA:
                        Adiós.
                        [*Coge el candelero.*]
FERNANDO: No salgas, Mariana.
                        El tiempo corre, y yo quiero
                        pasar el puente primero   470
                        que don Pedro.   Hasta mañana.
                        [*Salen.*]
[*La escena queda solitaria medio segundo.   Apenas han salido
Mariana y Fernando por una puerta, cuando aparece Doña
Angustias por la de enfrente, con un candelabro.   El fino y
otoñal perfume de los membrillos invade el ambiente.*]
ANGUSTIAS: Niña, ¿dónde estás?   ¡Niña!
                        Pero señor, ¿qué es esto?
                        ¿Dónde estabas?
MARIANA [*Entrando con un candelabro*]:
                                      Salía
                        con Fernando...
ANGUSTIAS: ¡Qué juego   475
                        inventaron los niños!
                        Regáñales.
MARIANA [*Dejando el candelabro*]:
                                      ¿Qué hicieron?
ANGUSTIAS: ¡Mariana, la bandera
                        que bordas en secreto...
MARIANA [*Interrumpiendo, dramáticamente*]:
                                      ¿Qué dices?
ANGUSTIAS: ...han hallado   480
                        en el armario viejo
                        y se han tendido en ella

---

466 A prisoner in love's care: a highly stylised conceit or play on words
by which Fernando argues that since he is already imprisoned by his love
for Mariana, the bitterest form of life-sentence, he has no cares about
Pedrosa's jail. In his most recent utterances the young Fernando seems at
pains to reach a sophisticated mode of expression by which to impress
Mariana with his dignity, his merit and his maturity. It is still debatable,
however, whether Lorca achieves a convincing characterisation, and in
some respects Fernando is a casualty of the play's Romantic, melodramatic
mood.

MARIANA [*agitated and stammering*]: Take care.
FERNANDO [*at the door, putting on his hat*]:
          My heart is already imprisoned,
          so I have no need of care.   465
          A prisoner in love's care am I,
          and ever will be while I live.
MARIANA: Farewell. [*She takes a candlestick.*]
FERNANDO: Don't come out, Mariana.
          Time's horse is also galloping,
          and I must cross the bridge before   470
          Don Pedro. Till tomorrow then.
          [*They leave.*]
[*The stage is briefly empty. But no sooner have Mariana and Fernando left through one door than, Doña Angustias appears through the opposite door holding a candlestick. The lovely autumn perfume of the quinces fills the whole atmosphere.*]
ANGUSTIAS: Girl, where are you? Come quick!
          My goodness, what is this?
          Where were you?
MARIANA [*entering with a candlestick*]:
                       I went out
          with Fernando...
ANGUSTIAS: What games   475
          your children do invent!
          You must scold them.
MARIANA [*putting the candlestick down*]:
                       What for?
ANGUSTIAS: Mariana, it's the flag,
          the one you sew in secret...
MARIANA [*interrupting forcefully*]:
          What? Go on!
ANGUSTIAS: They found it   480
          tucked in the old cupboard,
          and wrapped themselves in it

---

478 the flag: appropriately, the First Engraving ends as it had begun, with a reference to the liberal flag. The device of having children play innocently with an ominous prop is typical of Lorca and is found for instance in *Blood Wedding* when girls play with a fatalistic skein of wool (*Obras completas*, II, 604 *et. seq.*).
480-1 They found it tucked in the old cupboard: foreshadowing the discovery of the flag in a secret place by Pedrosa in the Second Engraving.

```
                    fingiéndose los muertos!
                    Tilín, talán; abuela,
                    dile al curita nuestro                    485
                    que traiga banderolas
                    y flores de romero;
                    que traigan encarnadas
                    clavelinas del huerto.
                    Ya vienen los obispos,                    490
                    decían uri memento,
                    y cerraban los ojos
                    poniéndose muy serios.
                    Serán cosas de niños;
                    está bien. Mas yo vengo               495
                    muy mal impresionada,
                    y me da mucho miedo
                    la dichosa bandera.
MARIANA [Aterrada]:
                    ¿Pero cómo la vieron?
                    ¡Estaba bien oculta!                      500
ANGUSTIAS: Mariana, ¡triste tiempo
                    para esta antigua casa,
                    que derrumbarse veo,
                    sin un hombre, sin nadie,
                    en medio del silencio!                    505
                    Y luego, tú...
MARIANA [Desorientada y con aire trágico]:
                              ¡Por Dios!
ANGUSTIAS: Mariana, ¿tú qué has hecho?
                    Cercar estas paredes
                    de guardianes secretos.
MARIANA:     Tengo el corazón loco                     510
                    y no sé lo que quiero.
ANGUSTIAS: ¡Olvídalo, Mariana!
MARIANA [Con pasión]:
                    ¡Olvidarlo no puedo!
                    [Se oyen risas de niños.]
ANGUSTIAS [Haciendo señas para que Mariana calle]:
                    Los niños.
MARIANA:                     Vamos pronto.
                    ¿Cómo alcanzaron eso?                  515
```

---

483 pretending to be dead: the symbolic implications of the flag are clear
from the children's using it as a shroud. Its death associations are further
developed in their song, recounted by Angustias, for the bells, drapes,
reddened skin, Latin chants and closed eyes all evoke a funeral rite.
491 uri memento: from the religious maxim, *memento mori*, 'remember that
you have to die', the equally telegrammatic uri memento warns 'remember

```
                    pretending to be dead!
                    Ding-dong, ding-dong, Grandma,
                    they said:  go tell our priest              485
                    to bring some funeral drapes
                    and rosemary if he can;
                    we want pinks from the garden
                    coloured red like our hands.
                    See, here come the bishops,                 490
                    uri memento they chant...
                    And then they closed their eyes
                    and went all stiff and still.
                    It's only children's games,
                    I know, but I'll tell you                   495
                    it gave me a real fright.
                    The truth is I'm terrified
                    of that bedevilled flag!
MARIANA [disturbed]:
                    But how did they find it?
                    I hid it so carefully!                      500
ANGUSTIAS:  Mariana, a sad time
                    has come on this old house,
                    crumbling now about us,
                    with no man, no one... just
                    this silence everywhere.                    505
                    And you...
MARIANA [at a loss and with a tragic air]:
                              For pity's sake!
ANGUSTIAS:  What have you done, Mariana,
                    but fill these walls with secrets
                    and bring suspicion here?
MARIANA:    My heart is all deranged                            510
                    and knows not what it wants.
ANGUSTIAS:  Oh, forget him, Mariana!
MARIANA [passionately]:
                    I cannot forget him!
                    [Children's laughter is heard.]
ANGUSTIAS [gesturing to Mariana to keep quiet]:
                    The children.
MARIANA:                        Let's see, quickly.
                    But how did they find it?                   515
```

---

that you will burn', the syntactical order of the Latin coming from the
need to maintain assonance in e-o in the Spanish verse.
508 <u>fill these walls with secrets</u>: repeating her opinion, stated at the
beginning of the act, that Mariana is not behaving responsibily towards
those in her care, Angustias's lines effectively evoke a sense of the house
being in a state of seige.

ANGUSTIAS: Así pasan las cosas.
              ¡Mariana, piensa en ellos!
              [*Coge un candelabro.*]
MARIANA: Sí, sí; tienes razón.
              Tienes razón. ¡No pienso!
              [*Salen.*]
                    [*Telón*]

Mariana, painted by Francisco Enríquez and reproduced in 'El Album Granadino in 1856 (by kind permission of Antonina Rodrigo).

---

519 I don't think at all: the act ends on the note of love's irrationality, a point not only fitting to the historical character of Mariana Pineda but one which also makes her seem the epitome of the Romantic, literary heroine.

ANGUSTIAS: You know what children are.
Mariana, think of them!
[*She takes a candlestick.*]
MARIANA: You're right; I should, I know.
But I don't think at all!
[*They leave.*]
Curtain

*The Plaza Nueva in Granada near which Mariana lived, 1832, by
Girault de Prangey   (by kind permission of Antonina Rodrigo).*

ESTAMPA SEGUNDA

*Sala principal en la casa de Mariana. Entonación en grises, blancos
y marfiles, como una antigua litografía. Estrado blanco, a estilo
Imperio. Al fondo, una puerta con una cortina gris, y puertas
laterales. Hay una consola con urna y grandes ramos de flores de
seda morada y verde. En el centro de la habitación, un pianoforte
y candelabros de cristal. Es de noche. Están en escena la
Clavela y los Niños de Mariana. Visten la deliciosa moda infantil de
la época. La Clavela está sentada, y a los lados, en taburetes, los
niños. La estancia es limpia y modesta, aunque conservando ciertos
muebles de lujo heredados por Mariana.*

CLAVELA: No cuento más.
             [Se levanta.]
NIÑO *[Tirándole del vestido]*: Cuéntanos otra cosa.
CLAVELA: ¡Me romperás el vestido!
NIÑA *[Tirando]*:   Es muy malo.
CLAVELA *[Echándoselo en cara]*:
             Tu madre lo compró.
NIÑO *[Riendo y tirando del vestido para que se siente]*:
             ¡Clavela!
CLAVELA *[Sentándose a la fuerza y riendo también]*:
             ¡Niños!
NIÑA: El cuento aquel del príncipe gitano.
CLAVELA: Los gitanos no fueron nunca príncipes.   5
NIÑA: ¿Y por qué?

A white drawing-room in the Empire style: the predominance of white
continues and, if anything, is accentuated in this more formal room, thus
creating a tonal unity and sense of progression within the play that will
culminate in the convent setting of the final act. Empire here refers to the
Napoleonic Empire which dates from 1804, when furniture was modelled on
Greek and Roman designs.
silk flowers in purple and green: 'morada y verde' (in purple and green)
is omitted in the *Obras completas* but is found in Rivadeneyra, Losada and
Harrap. The detail seems well worth keeping.
**Mariana's Son and Daughter...dressed in the delightful children's fashion
of the day:** the children are not named by Lorca but correspond to her
son, José María, who would have been ten years old at this time, and her
first daughter, Úrsula María, who would have been nine years old had she
lived. In historical fact the situation was more complicated, for Mariana
lost her first daughter and gave birth to a second, illegitimate daughter in
1829 (Antonina Rodrigo, *op.cit.*, 99, 176). The second daughter was of
course too young for the purpose of the play and Lorca has wisely chosen
to simplify the family situation. Their dress, no doubt, would incorporate

SECOND ENGRAVING

The main room in Mariana's house. Different shades of white, grey and ivory, like an old-fashioned lithograph. A white drawing-room, in the Empire style. Upstage a door with a grey curtain and side doors. There is a console table with an urn containing sprays of silk flowers in purple and green. In the centre of the room stands a pianoforte with glass candelabra. It is night. On stage are Clavela and Mariana's Son and Daughter. They are dressed in the delightful children's fashion of the day. Clavela is sitting and the children are to each side of her on stools. The room is neat and modest, though certain expensive items of furniture inherited by Mariana may be seen.

CLAVELA: Right, no more stories.
             [*She gets up.*]
SON [*pulling at her dress*]:   Oh, tell us one more!
CLAVELA: You'll tear my dress!
SON [*pulling*]:   It's dowdy anyway!
CLAVELA [*getting her own back*]:
             A present from your mum.
SON [*laughing and pulling her by the dress to make her sit down*]:
                                          Clavela!
CLAVELA [*also laughing when she is forced to sit down*]:
                                          Children!
DAUGHTER: Let's hear that one about the gypsy prince.
CLAVELA: A gypsy prince? That's impossible!   5
DAUGHTER: And why is that?

---

the charming cuffs, tight stockings and pantaloons in the case of the boy, a full dress with lace frills and close fitting waist for the girl. The appearance of the two children on stage links well with the close of the previous act and it brings a light-hearted tone comparable with the gay mood of Mariana's young visitors, Amparo and Lucía, early in the First Engraving.

expensive items of furniture inherited by Mariana: though her historical background is not specified in the play, this detail accords with the fact that Mariana came from good stock on the paternal side. Her father, Mariano de Pineda y Ramírez (1754-1806), was a naval captain, and her grandfather had been a High Court Judge in Guatemala City from 1744, and, ironically, Chief of Police at the Granada Chancery from 1756. That the expensive items stand out in an otherwise modest room is consistent with Mariana having received no material benefit from her marriage to Manuel de Peralta, who had died in 1822, and with the fact that she was unable, owing to her own illegitimacy, to realize through the courts certain properties once owned by her father (Antonina Rodrigo, *op.cit.*, 26-7. 57-9, 45-6).

NIÑO: No los quiero a mi lado.
                Sus madres son las brujas.
NIÑA [*Enérgica*]:   ¡Embustero!
CLAVELA [*Reprendiéndola*]:
                ¡Pero niña!
NIÑA: Si ayer vi yo rezando
        al Cristo de la Puerta Real dos de ellos.
        Tenían unas tijeras así... y cuatro   10
        borriquitos peludos que miraban...
        con unos ojos... y movían los rabos
        dale que le das. ¡Quién tuviera alguno!
NIÑO [*Doctoral*]:
        Seguramente los habían robado.
CLAVELA: Ni tanto ni tan poco. ¿Qué se sabe?   15
        [*Los Niños se hacen burla sacando la lengua.*]
        ¡Chitón!
NIÑO: ¿Y el romancillo del bordado?
NIÑA: ¡Ay duque de Lucena! ¿Cómo dice?
NIÑO: Olivarito, olivo..., está bordando.
        [*Como recordando.*]
CLAVELA: Os lo diré; pero cuando se acabe,
        en seguida a dormir.
NIÑO: Bueno.
NIÑA: ¡Enterados!   20
CLAVELA [*Se persigna lentamente, y los Niños la imitan, mirandola*]:
        Bendita sea por siempre
        la Santísima Trinidad,

---

6 **I can't stand them near me:** a common enough prejudice, though not one
Lorca shares. Gypsies were ostracised by good Christian society, confined
to ghettos such as Granada's *Albaicín*, and generally regarded as idlers
and thieves, especially horse-thieves, as line 14 suggests. No doubt it was
their social deprivation, coupled with a certain folkloric mystique, which
encouraged Lorca to make them the protagonists of his celebrated volume
of poems, *Gypsy Ballads* (1927), just as he later gave the negro
prominence in *Poet in New York* (1930). For Lorca, the gypsy, like the
negro, represented an earthy life-force, that is, values which civilised
society had come to neglect.
8 **two of them in prayer:** the daughter suggests that gypsies, contrary to
popular belief, are good Christians.

Puerta Real: literally the 'Royal Gate', a bustling commercial centre
situated in the heart of Granada, only a stone's throw from Bibarrambla
Square. Three of Granada's principal streets meet at the Puerta Real,
namely, the Avenida de Genil, the street named after the poet Zorrilla
(called Calle de Mesones in Mariana's day) and the Calle de los Reyes
Católicos.

SON: I can't stand them near me.
      Their mothers are witches!
DAUGHTER [*forcefully*]:   You're a liar!
CLAVELA [*reproving her*]:
      Watch that tongue!
DAUGHTER: But yesterday I saw two
      praying to Christ at the Puerta Real.
      Great big scissors they had... and nearby, four   10
      small donkeys all covered in hair with eyes
      that stared and stared... and tails that kept
                                          swishing
      to and fro. Oh, if only I had one!
SON [*knowledgeably*]:
      I bet you anything they were stolen.
CLAVELA: Go on with you! You're a proper know-all!   15
      [*The children make fun of her, poking their
        tongues out.*]
      Oh, shush!
SON: Let's sing the one about the seamstress.
DAUGHTER: The Duke of Lucena! How does it go?
SON [*trying to remember*]:
      Olive, little olive... the girl's a-sewing...
CLAVELA: I'll sing it for you, but then, straightaway
      to bed, you promise?
SON: Promise!
DAUGHTER: Cross my heart!   20
CLAVELA [*slowly makes the sign of the cross, and the children,
        watching, copy her*]:
      Blessed be forever
      the Holy Trinity,

---

17 the Duke of Lucena: there follows a delightful *romancillo*, or short
ballad with a line of fewer than the customary eight syllables, on the Duke
of Lucena. Lucena, in the sub-province of Cordova and some seventy miles
west of Granada, is a small but historic town which was known as a centre
for Jews in the time of the Moors, from whom it was recaptured in 1240.
To my knowledge the title Count Lucena was only authorised in 1847,
which suggests that Lorca's ballad may well be entirely his own invention.
It is probably no more than coincidental that Mariana Pineda's mother was
a native of Lucena (Antonina Rodrigo, *op.cit.*, 25).
    The ballad's primary theme, that of a young girl sewing or
embroidering a flag for a nobleman whom she appears to love, is
conspicuously relevant to the play. It is a further example of children's
games, in this case a song, taking on more sinister meaning through
thematic connexion, in which sense it could be compared to the lullaby in
the second scene of *Blood Wedding*. Also noteworthy is the very natural
way in which Lorca introduces this set piece of poetry, having the
children struggle to remember snatches of it before finally rejoicing in
proper recollection.

y guarde al hombre en la sierra
y al marinero en el mar.
A la verde, verde orilla   25
del olivarito está...
NIÑA [*Tapando con una mano la boca a Clavela y continuando ella*]:
...una niña bordando.
¡Madre! ¿Qué bordará?
CLAVELA [*Encantada de que la Niña lo sepa*]:
Las agujas de plata,
bastidor de cristal,   30
bordaba una bandera,
cantar que te cantar.
Por el olivo, olivo,
¡madre, quién lo dirá!
NIÑO [*Continuando*]:
Venía un andaluz,   35
bien plantado y galán.
[*Aparece por la parte del fondo Mariana, vestida de amarillo
claro, un amarillo de libro viejo, y oye el romance, glosando
con gestos lo que en ella evoca la idea de bandera y muerte.*]
CLAVELA: "Niña, la bordadora,

23-4 <u>guard the men in the hills and sailors on the sea</u>: a double request,
so typical of Andalusian sentiment in that the province has these two
dimensions of mountains and sea. It is typical too of Lorca's patterning, as
in the repeated lines of his '*Romance sonámbulo*' (Sleep-walking Ballad):
'the horse on the mountain, and the ship on the sea'. The duality has
added application in the play in that Pedro is currently a fugitive in the
Alpujarra mountains while the hoped-for liberal uprising centres on
Torrijos's daring invasion by sea.

25 <u>By the green olive grove</u>: the olive grove - to which, for instance,
Paca la Roseta is taken in *The House of Bernarda Alba* - is a favourite
location for love in Spanish lyric poetry of the oral tradition, a tradition
Lorca knew intimately and whose symbolism and musicality he so effectively
recreates. Here is one delightful ancient example which suggests some
notoriety attaches to the olive grove:

Que no hay tal andar	What a lot of goings on
por el verde olivico,	up the green olive grove,
que no hay tal andar	what a lot of goings on
por el verde olivar.	up the olive grove so green.
	(Alonso and Blecua, *op.cit.*, 113)

The colour green is richly allusive in Lorca as in oral poetry. On the one
hand it conjures up notions of springtime and fertility, which of course
relate to the girl's youth in the Lucena ballad, while on the other, green
suggests the bitter taste of unripe fruit, or indeed the sour taste of olive,
a negative omen for love. This polarization is discussed in my article, 'The
Symbolic Ambivalence of "Green" in Garcia Lorca and Dylan Thomas', *The
Modern Language Review*, 67 (1972), 810-19. This article refers

guard the men in the hills
and sailors on the sea.
By the green olive grove   25
a young girl can be seen...
DAUGHTER [*putting her hand over Clavela's mouth and taking
          up the song*]:
          A young girl is sewing.
          Mother, what can it be?
CLAVELA [*delighted the child knows the song*]:
          With needles of silver
          and glass her sewing screen,   30
          she was sewing a flag
          and singing like a queen.
          By the green olive tree;
          mother, what can it mean?
SON [*continuing*]:
          There came an Andalusian,   35
          handsome and young was he.
[*Mariana appears at the door upstage, dressed in light yellow,
like the colour of an old book. Listening to the song, she
expresses in mime what the idea of the flag and death evoke
in her.*]
CLAVELA: 'Seamstress, my young lady,

---

particularly to '*Romance sonámbulo*' (Sleep-walking Ballad), which begins
with the famous line 'Verde que te quiero verde' (Green how I want you
green).
28 Mother, what can it be?: following the traditional format, since a great
many oral lyrics were addressed by young girls to their mother, often
asking for her advice.
29 With needles of silver: an almost magical heightening of reality comes
with such luxurious items, as in the case of the famous ballad of Count
Arnaldos who saw a ship decked out with 'silken sails and rigging of
gauze' (C.C. Smith, *op.cit.*, 208). In Lorca's ballad the finery also leads
us to suppose the items were gifts from the Duke of Lucena, that is,
tokens of his love.
35 There came an Andalusian: again much in traditional spirit, Lorca sets
the narrative in motion by introducing a male who will dialogue with the
young seamstress. This corresponds to the oral poem's 'gloss', an
expansion in narrative terms of the symbolic values implicit in the opening
picture. The line recalls the gloss of a well known traditional piece:

Venía el caballero,	There came a young gallant,
venía de Sevilla...	he came from Seville...
	(Alonso and Blecua, *op.cit.*, 44).

36+ dressed in light yellow: to match the scenic decor Mariana's dress
progressively lightens from mauve in the First Engraving, yellow in the
Second, to a brilliant white in the Third.
she expresses in mime: as a kind of micro-drama of the whole play's mood
and tension, Mariana's mime is an ingenious device which takes us back
momentarily to a pure, symbolic level of theatre.

	mi vida, ¡no bordar!,	
	que el duque de Lucena	
	duerme y dormirá."	40
NIÑA:	La niña le responde:	
	"No dices la verdad:	
	el duque de Lucena	
	me ha mandado bordar	
	esta roja bandera	45
	porque a la guerra va."	
NIÑO:	Por las calles de Córdoba	
	lo llevan a enterrar,	
	muy vestido de fraile	
	en caja de coral.	50

NIÑA [*Como soñando*]:

La albahaca y los claveles
sobre la caja van,
y un verderol antiguo
cantando el pío pa.

CLAVELA [*Con sentimiento*]:

"¡Ay duque de Lucena,   55
ya no te veré más!
La bandera que bordo
de nada servirá.
En el olivarito
me quedaré a mirar   60
cómo el aire menea
las hojas al pasar."

---

38 Don't sew upon that screen: in addition to paralleling the warnings given to Mariana about her flag, the situation recalls Penelope who, being importuned by many suitors in the absence of her husband Odysseus, forestalled them by insisting on finishing her tapestry.

40 lies sleeping at his ease: this euphemism for death is later echoed in the play when Pedrosa tells Mariana he has the power to make her 'sleep the deepest sleep of all' (line 215, Third Engraving). There is also a practical point to the motif since the ballad is intended to prepare the two children for bed. Lorca was very well informed on the topic of lullabies and related songs; in his essay on the subject he notes that: 'while the European lullaby has no other motive than to put the child to sleep, the Spanish tends to wound the child's sensibility', notably by introducing the idea of death. This 'technique of fear' is a 'procedure which instills silence' (*Obras completas*, I, 1045, 1050). Naturally, the unanswered mysteries which the lullaby or child's ballad implants in the mind are designed to make the child speculate as he moves from the realm of consciousness to imagination and dream.

46 to fly in the breeze: while the Duke of Lucena no doubt intended to do his Christian duty by slaying Moors, the colour red clearly has links with modern political ideas.

```
                don't sew upon that screen,
                the Duke of Lucena
                lies sleeping at his ease!              40
AUGHTER:        To him the girl replies:
                'You are lying, my liege:
                the Duke of Lucena
                bade me sew on this screen;
                he takes this flag to war              45
                to fly red in the breeze!
ON:             Through the streets of Cordova
                they bear him to his peace,
                dressed in a monk's habit
                his coffin a coral tree.               50
AUGHTER [as if dreaming]:
                Sweet basil and carnations
                to decorate the scene,
                while an old greenfinch sings
                on his coffin serene.
LAVELA [with feeling]:
                'Oh, Duke of Lucena,                   55
                forever gone from me!
                No longer have you use
                for the flag on my screen.
                But I'll stay here awhile
                with the green olive trees             60
                watching their leaves ripple
                as they blow in the breeze!
```

---

through the streets of Cordova: placenaming is an indispensable ature of the ballad and has a powerful focalising effect.

in a monk's habit: this was no doubt in honour of the Duke's Christian al, but the habit also reminds us of how Mariana's lover escaped from rison.

-3 coral tree...basil...carnations...greenfinch: this accumulation of lours again beautifies death; in addition, the greens and reds suggest spectively that the Duke was young and that he met his death violently.

-2 watching their leaves ripple/as they blow in the breeze: much in the irit of oral poetry, with its superlative feeling for nature, this image calls the traditional song:

De los álamos vengo, madre,	From the poplars I come, mother,
de ver cómo los menea el aire.	from seeing how the wind ripples them.
De los álamos de Sevilla	From the poplars of Seville
de ver a mi linda amiga,	from seeing my lovely girl,
de ver cómo los menea el aire...	from seeing how the wind ripples them...

(Dámaso Alonso and J.M. Blecua, op.cit., 47).

```
NIÑO:           "Adiós, niña bonita,
                espigada y juncal,
                me voy para Sevilla,                        65
                donde soy capitán."
CLAVELA:        Y a la verde, verde orilla
                del olivarito está
                una niña morena
                llorar que te llorar.                        70
```

[*Los Niños hacen un gesto de satisfacción. Han seguido el romance con alto interés.*]

MARIANA [*Avanzando*]:
```
                Es hora de acostarse.
```
CLAVELA [*Levantándose y a los niños*]:
```
                                ¿Habéis oído?
```
NIÑA [*Besando a Mariana*]:
```
                Mamá, acuéstanos tú.
```
MARIANA:
```
                                Hija, no puedo,
                yo tengo que coserte una capita.
```
NIÑO: ¿Y para mí?
CLAVELA [*Riendo*]:   ¡Pues claro está!
MARIANA: Un sombrero
```
                con una cinta verde y dos naranja.          75
                [Lo besa.]
```
CLAVELA: ¡A la costa, mis niños!
NIÑO [*Volviendo*]:   Yo lo quiero
```
                como los hombres, alto y grande, ¿sabes?
```
MARIANA: ¡Lo tendrás, primor mío!
NIÑA: Y entra luego;
```
                me gustará sentirte, que esta noche
                no se ve nada y hace mucho viento.          80
```

---

64 your waist like a reed: a narrow waist is essential to the Spanish conception of physical beauty for the male and female alike, as can be seen from the dress of flamenco dancers and bull-fighters' suits which are both designed to accentuate the slenderness of waist. Lorca develops many images to this effect, as in *The House of Bernarda Alba* where he describes a young male, 'tightly squeezed like a sheaf of wheat', *Obras completas*, II, 835.

65-6 bound for Seville to do my soldier's deed: one assumes that, his advance having been tacitly rejected, the speaker now wishes to impress his merit upon the young girl by doing heroic deeds. Thus the ballad offers the typical triangle of love in which the girl corresponds to Mariana, the Duke of Lucena to Don Pedro and the rejected young Andalusian to Fernando.

69 a girl with skin so dark: the theme of the *morena* or dark-skinned beauty has two primary implications here: first, it identifies the lower class of the girl *vis-à-vis* the Duke, for such skin is associated with the open-air, peasant life; second, as previously mentioned, it suggests her passionate nature and, by extension, the probability of her love for the Duke having been consummated. So strongly established is this second

```
SON:          'Fare thee well, handsome girl,
              with your waist like a reed,
              I am bound for Seville                        65
              to do my soldier's deed!
CLAVELA:      By the olive, olive grove
              she is still to be seen,
              a girl with skin so dark,
              and tears in eyes of green.                   70
```
[*The children are delighted, having followed the song with great interest.*]
MARIANA [*coming forward*]:
              It's time for bed now, children.
CLAVELA [*standing up with the children*]:   Did you hear?
DAUGHTER [*kissing Mariana*]:
              Oh mama, you put us to bed.
MARIANA: But child,
              I can't; I have to make you a bonnet.
SON: And something for me?
CLAVELA [*laughing*]:   Of course!
MARIANA: A big hat
              with one green band and two orange ribbons.   75
              [*She kisses him.*]
CLAVELA: To bed, now, children!
SON [*turning round*]:   Just like the men wear,
              mother, big and tall, you know what I mean?
MARIANA: Just so, my precious!
DAUGHTER: Will you tuck us in?
              I like to feel you near me when the night
              is black as pitch and there's a howling wind. 80

---

implication that in the following traditional piece the young speaker is at pains to deny that her dark skin means she has sinned:

Yo me soy la morenica,	I am the little dark girl,
Yo me soy la morená.	I am the girl so dark.
Lo moreno, bien mirado,	But darkness, well considered,
fue la culpa del pecado	was the fault of a sin
que en mi nunca fue hallado,	that never was found in me,
ni jamás se hallará.	nor will it ever be.

                    (Alonso and Blecua, *op.cit.*, 64).

The theme continued through into cultured Spanish poetry and is found, for instance, in the later Romantic poets, Gustavo Adolfo Bécquer (see his *Rimas*, number XI), and especially Rosalía de Castro who identified herself with the sinful tag in the poem beginning:

| A las rubias envidias | You envy blond girls |
| porque naciste con color moreno | because you were born with dark skin |

Rosalía de Castro, *En las orillas del Sar* (*On the Banks of the Sar*), *Obras completas* (Madrid: Aguilar, 1968), 645.
73 I can't: Mariana's inability to find time for her children is a poignant detail which, like her treatment of Fernando, is indicative of the cruel side-effects of single-minded passion.

MARIANA [*Bajo a Clavela*]:
                Cuando acabes, te bajas a la puerta.
CLAVELA: Pronto será; los niños tienen sueño.
MARIANA: ¡Que recéis sin reíros!
CLAVELA: ¡Sí, señora!
MARIANA [*En la puerta*]:
                Una salve a la Virgen y dos credos
                al Santo Cristo del Mayor Dolor,   85
                para que nos protejan.
NIÑA: Rezaremos
                la oración de San Juan y la que ruega
                por caminantes y por marineros.
                [*Salen Clavela y los niños. Pausa.*]
MARIANA [*En la puerta*]:
                Dormir tranquilamente, niños míos,
                mientras que yo, perdida y loca, siento   90
[*Lentamente*] quemarse con su propia lumbre viva
                esta rosa de sangre de mi pecho.
                Soñar en la verbena y el jardín
                de Cartagena, luminoso y fresco,
                y en la pájara pinta que se mece   95
                en las ramas del verde limonero.
                Que yo también estoy dormida, niños,
                y voy volando por mi propio sueño,
                como van, sin saber adónde van,
                los tenues vilanicos por el viento.   100
                [*Aparece Doña Angustias en la puerta y en
                un aparte.*]

---

88 protection for travellers and sailors: the same two aspects mentioned in the note to lines 23-4 are foregrounded again.
89 Sleep peacefully: there follows a fine soliloquy which facilitates transition from the children's gaiety to the play's more serious levels which come with Don Pedro's arrival, much in the same way as Mariana's first soliloquy punctuated the departure of her gay visitors and Fernando's entry (First Engraving, 168-187). The motif of sleeping dominates the soliloquy, thus following on naturally from the Duke of Lucena ballad; at the same time, it relates to two features in Mariana herself: firstly to the faith she puts in dreams or illusions, and secondly, to the ever present sense of her own fate.
93-4 verbena...Cartagena: this internal rhyme, which occurs also in the Spanish, gives the sprightly sense of children's song, from which the two motifs came. The verbena, a herbaceous plant known for its pleasant scent, has been attributed with magical powers since at least the time of the Romans, notably the power to protect the person who holds it. In folklore it became associated with certain festivals and especially Midsummer's morning, June 24th, known as the morning of St John, an occasion when the plant was deemed to have the power to reveal one's future love. In the following traditional-type lyric by Lope de Vega the

MARIANA [*whispering to Clavela*]:
        When they've gone to sleep go down to the door.
CLAVELA: I won't be long with these two sleepy-heads.
MARIANA: No laughing over prayers!
CLAVELA: Quite so, Señora.
MARIANA [*at the door*]:
        Say one Hail Mary and a special credo
        for Christ our Lord of the Deepest Sorrow,   85
        to ask Him to protect us.
DAUGHTER: And we'll say
        the prayer of Saint John, and the one that begs
        protection for travellers and sailors.
        [*Clavela and the children leave. Pause.*]
MARIANA [*at the door*]:
        Sleep peacefully, my children, sleep in peace;
        forget your mother whose tormented mind   90
[*slowly*]   burns with the fire of a blood red flower
        which sprouts its living flame within her heart.
        Dream of the verbena and of the garden
        of Cartagena with its sunlit air,
        dream of the speckled bird who perches high   95
        among the branches of the lemon tree.
        For I too am sleeping now, my children,
        and am borne away on the wings of dreams
        just as the down of thistle flies without
        destination on the wings of the wind.   100
        [*Doña Angustias appears at the door.*]

---

young female speaker is in too bad a mood to have anything to do with it:

Ya no cogeré verbena	No more will I pick verbena
la mañana de San Juan,	on the morning of St John,
pues mis amores se van.	for my true love has gone.
	(Alonso and Blecua, *op.cit.*, 194).

Cartagena is a city in the province of Murcia, adjoining Andalusia, on Spain's south-eastern Mediterranean coast. In 1905 it had a population of no more than 20,000, but around 220 B.C. it was the great port for the Carthaginians who then controlled most of the peninsula. It is perhaps coincidental that the city's main park is Bolivar Park, which has a statue to the great Liberator of South America who was Mariana's contemporary.

96 the lemon tree: abruptly bringing to an end the hopeful images associated with her children, this inauspicious emblem of bitterness returns us once more to Mariana's sombre mood. For a penetrating discussion of citrus symbolism see Stephen Reckert, *Lyra Minima: Structure and Symbol in Iberian Traditional Verse* (Portsmouth: Eyre and Spottiswoode, 1970), especially the second essay.

99 the down of thistle: though a fairly standard image, as a metaphor of Mariana's psychological state it recalls Lorca's disturbing surrealist drawing entitled 'Eye and Thistles', *Obras completas*, I, 1244.

ANGUSTIAS: Vieja y honrada casa, ¡qué locura!
[*A Mariana.*]
Tienes una visita.
MARIANA: ¿Quién?
ANGUSTIAS: ¡Don Pedro!
[*Mariana sale corriendo hacia la puerta.*]
¡Serénate, hija mía! ¡No es tu esposo!
MARIANA: Siempre tienes razón. ¡Pero no puedo!
[*Mariana llega corriendo a la puerta en el momento en que Don
Pedro entra por ella. Don Pedro tiene treinta y seis años. Es
un hombre simpático, sereno y fuerte. Viste correctamente y
habla de una manera dulce. Mariana le tiende los brazos y le
estrecha las manos. Doña Angustias adopta una triste y
reservada actitud.*]
PEDRO [*Efusivo*]:
Gracias, Mariana, gracias.   105
MARIANA [*Casi sin hablar*]:
Cumplí con mi deber.
[*Durante esta escena dará Mariana muestras de una vehemen-
tísima y profunda pasión.*]
PEDRO [*Dirigiéndose a Doña Angustias*]:
Muchas gracias, señora.
ANGUSTIAS [*Triste*]:
¿Y por qué? Buenas noches.
[*A Mariana.*]
Yo me voy con los niños.
[*Aparte.*]
¡Ay, pobre Marianita!   110
[*Sale. Al salir Angustias, Pedro, efusivo, enlaza a Mariana
por el talle.*]
PEDRO [*Apasionado*]:
¡Quién pudiera pagarte lo que has hecho por mí!
Toda mi sangre es nueva, porque tú me la has dado

---

104 <u>You're right, as always</u>: The *Obras completas* omits 'siempre' (as
always), but the line requires it to scan as a hendecasyllable and 'siempre'
is found in Rivadeneyra, Losada and Harrap.
104+ <u>Mariana takes him by the hands</u>: Angustias's presence on stage
ensures that, out of modesty, Mariana's first contact with Don Pedro is
more formal than effusive. This sets the tone for the ensuing dialogue
which, though amorous, is characterised by Mariana's repressing or
subduing her deepest feelings in deference to Don Pedro's correctness
and, ultimately, to his wish to put political issues first.
111 <u>Oh Mariana</u>: significantly at this point, with Don Pedro and Mariana
alone on stage, the line of verse lengthens. While no doubt appropriate to
the tense mood, the longer line also encourages a more mannered and even
bombastic type of utterance, especially since the speeches themselves are
quite long. Far from faulting Lorca, however, I suggest that here we have

ANGUSTIAS [*aside*]:
  What a commotion in this respected house!
  [*To Mariana.*]
  You have a visitor.
MARIANA: Who?
ANGUSTIAS: Don Pedro!
  [*Mariana runs towards the door.*]
  Keep calm, my child; he's not your husband yet!
MARIANA [*fully acknowledging the point*]:
  You're right, as always. But I can't help myself!
[*Mariana reaches the door in a rush just as Don Pedro enters. Don
Pedro is thirty-six years old. He is an attractive man, calm and
strong. He is correct in his dress and he speaks in a soft voice.
Mariana holds her arms out to him and takes him by the hands.
Doña Angustias adopts a discreet but somewhat melancholy attitude.*]
PEDRO [*effusively*]:
  My deepest thanks, Mariana.   105
MARIANA [*almost unable to speak*]:
  I did what duty required.
[*Throughout this scene Mariana displays a deep and vehement
passion.*]
PEDRO [*to Doña Angustias*]:
  My thanks to you too, Señora.
ANGUSTIAS [*sadly*]:
  There is no need. Good night, then.
  [*To Mariana.*]
  I'll go to see the children.
  [*Aside.*]
  Oh my poor and dear Mariana!   110
[*She leaves, whereupon Don Pedro excitedly takes Mariana by
the waist.*]
PEDRO [*passionately*]:
  Oh Mariana, if only I could repay you!
  Thanks to you I am entirely invigorated

---

an example of subtle characterization through language. In particular, Don
Pedro is presented as a typically ardent liberal, well practised in the art
of rhetoric and debate. This, as Raymond Carr notes, was very much a
part of Liberalism, since, having been deprived of a proper democratic
forum, '(T)he only bases for such an organization were journalistic cliques
and the *tertulia*, evening gatherings of familiar acquaintance. This reliance
on the compulsive power of oratory started a rhetorical tradition which in
the long run weakened liberalism' (*op.cit.*, 95). In marked contrast to Don
Pedro, Mariana is less adept at speech making, as line 118 suggests: <u>When
I am at your side the words escape me.</u> In short, the longer line is <u>more</u>
suited to the logic of argument than to the instinctual level of passion,
and it thereby simultaneously points up Mariana's frustration and the
perhaps less than convincing utopianism of Don Pedro.

95

exponiendo tu débil corazón al peligro.
¡Ay, qué miedo tan grande tuve por él, Mariana!
MARIANA [*Cerca y abandonada*]:
        ¿De qué sirve mi sangre, Pedro, si tú murieras?   115
        Un pájaro sin aire, ¿puede volar? ¡Entonces!...
        [*Bajo.*]
        Yo no podré decirte cómo te quiero nunca;
        a tu lado me olvido de todas las palabras.
PEDRO [*Con voz suave*]:
        ¡Cuántos peligros corres sin el menor desmayo!
        ¡Qué sola estás, cercada de maliciosa gente!   120
        ¡Quién pudiera librarte de aquellos que te acechan
        con mi propio dolor y mi vida, Mariana!
        ¡Día y noche, qué largos sin ti por esa sierra!
MARIANA [*Echando la cabeza en el hombro y como soñando*]:
        ¡Así! Deja tu aliento sobre mi frente. Limpia
        esta angustia que tengo y este sabor amargo;   125
        esta angustia de andar sin saber dónde voy,
        y este sabor de amor que me quema la boca.
[*Pausa. Se separa rápidamente del caballero y le coge los codos.*]
        ¡Pedro! ¿No te persiguen? ¿Te vieron entrar?
PEDRO: Nadie.
        [*Se sienta.*]
        Vives en una calle silenciosa, y la noche
        se presenta endiablada.
MARIANA: Yo tengo mucho miedo.   130
PEDRO [*Cogiéndole una mano*]:
        ¡Ven aquí!
MARIANA [*Se sienta*]:   Mucho miedo de que esto se adivine,
        de que pueda matarte la canalla realista.
        Y si tú... [*Con pasión*]
             yo me muero, lo sabes, yo me muero.
PEDRO [*Con pasion*]:
        ¡Marianita, no temas! ¡Mujer mía! ¡Vida mía!
        En el mayor sigilo conspiramos. ¡No temas!   135
        La bandera que bordas temblará por las calles
        entre el calor entero del pueblo de Granada.
        Por ti la Libertad suspirada por todos
        pisará tierra dura con anchos pies de plata.
        Pero si así no fuese; si Pedrosa...
MARIANA [*Aterrada*]:   ¡No sigas!   140
PEDRO: ... sorprende nuestro grupo y hemos de morir...
MARIANA: ¡Calla!
PEDRO: Mariana, ¿qué es el hombre sin libertad? ¿Sin esa
        luz armoniosa y fija que se siente por dentro?
        ¿Cómo podría quererte no siendo libre, dime?

and reborn, for you risked your tender heart for me.
How much I have feared for your safety, Mariana!
ARIANA [*near him, with abandon*]:
What use would my life be, Pedro, if you should die?
A bird deprived of air can hardly fly. And so...
[*Quietly*]
But I can never say how much you mean to me;
when I am at your side the words escape me.
EDRO [*gently*]:
What dangers you endure with no sign of weakness!
Alone and undefended, beseiged by enemies!   120
If only I could bear your suffering, Mariana,
and with my own blood free you from your enemies!
Days and nights in the hills were endless without you!
ARIANA [*putting her head on his shoulders and as if dreaming*]:
There, now! Let your breath blow soft upon my forehead.
Blow away my anguish and all my bitter thoughts; 125
this anguish that comes from uncertainty and fear,
this bitter taste of love that burns inside my mouth.
ause. She breaks out of his embrace and holds him by the elbows.]
Did anyone follow you to my house, Pedro?
EDRO: No one!
[*He sits down.*]
Mariana, this house is in a secluded street,
and it's as dark as hell tonight.
ARIANA: I'm so afraid.   130
EDRO [*taking her by the hand*]:
Come here!
ARIANA [*sitting down*]:
I fear their eyes are watching everywhere,
that you will fall into their cursed Royalist hands;
for if they kill you... [*passionately*]
then I'd be quick to follow.
EDRO [*passionately*]:
Marianita, don't distress yourself, my dear love!
Our conspiracy is a well guarded secret.   135
The flag that you embroider will proudly flutter
through Granada and warm the hearts of all its people.
Because of you, Liberty, so loved by us all,
will dance in silver shoes upon this land of ours.
But if by chance we fail; if Pedrosa...
ARIANA [*unnerved*]:   Stop there!   140
DRO   ... discovers our plot and we have to die...
ARIANA: Please, stop!
DRO: But Mariana, what is a man without liberty?
Without that bright and faithful flame he feels inside?
Could I aspire to love you if I were not free?

97

<pre>
                ¿Cómo darte este firme corazón si no es mío?   145
                No temas; ya he burlado a Pedrosa en el campo,
                y así pienso seguir hasta vencer contigo,
                que me ofreces tu amor y tu casa y tus dedos.
MARIANA: ¡Y algo que yo no sé decir, pero que existe!
                ¡Qué bien estoy contigo! Pero aunque alegre noto 150
                un gran desasosiego que me turba y enoja;
                me parece que hay hombres detrás de las cortinas,
                que mis palabras suenan claramente en la calle.
PEDRO [Amargo]:
                ¡Eso sí! ¡Qué mortal inquietud, qué amargura!
                ¡Qué constante pregunta al minuto lejano!   155
                ¡Qué otoño interminable sufrí por esa sierra!
                ¡Tú no lo sabes!
MARIANA: Dime: ¿corriste gran peligro?
PEDRO: Estuve casi en manos de la justicia,
                [Mariana hace un gesto de horror.]
                                                    pero
                me salvó el pasaporte y el caballo que enviaste
                con un extraño joven, que no me dijo nada.   160
MARIANA [Inquieta y sin querer recordar]:
                Y dime.
PEDRO: ¿Por qué tiemblas?
MARIANA [Nerviosa]:   Sigue... ¿Después?
PEDRO: Después
                vagué por la Alpujarra. Supe que en Gibraltar
                había fiebre amarilla; la entrada era imposible,
                y esperé bien oculto la ocasión. ¡Ya ha llegado!
                Venceré con tu ayuda. ¡Mariana de mi vida!   165
                ¡Libertad, aunque con sangre llame a todas las puerta
MARIANA [Radiante]:
                ¡Mi victoria consiste en tenerte a mi vera!
</pre>

145-6 Could I give this heart if it were not mine/to give?: a conceit which
neatly integrates the themes of freedom and love, but one in which the
lack of originality smacks of rehearsed rather than spontaneous thought.
This is Pedro's fourth rhetorical question in as many lines, and his use of
such a well known oratorical device is again a little mannered.
154 I too have felt...: rather than trying to appease Mariana, Pedro turns
the conversation to his own trials and tribulations. The exclamations which
pepper his speech here, as in lines 119-123, are another feature of his
oratory.
160 that strange young man who spoke not a word: Fernando's silence
puzzled Don Pedro, but its cause is touchingly clear to us.
Gibraltar...yellow fever: 'For a long time now the Spanish liberals have
had their headquarters in Gibraltar', wrote the Marquis de Custine, who
arrived in Granada shortly after Mariana's execution (see Antonina
Rodrigo, op.cit., 166). Gibraltar, of course, is the famous Rock which
juts out into the Mediterranean at Spain's southern extreme. Known in

Could I give you this heart if it were not mine   145
to give? Don't fret. I fooled Pedrosa in the hills
and will again, with your help, until we triumph,
until the day we live in peace as man and wife.
[*He kisses her hands.*]

MARIANA: I long for that day, when dream becomes reality!
How happy I am with you! But at the same time   150
I feel a great unease that gnaws away at me
and I imagine men hiding behind curtains
and that my words ring loud and clear down in the street.

PEDRO [*bitterly*]:
I too have felt the bitterest taste of anguish,
agonising over an uncertain future!   155
What an endless Autumn I suffered in those hills!
You've no idea...!

MARIANA: And was your life in peril?

PEDRO: I almost fell into the hands of the police,
[*Mariana looks horrified.*]
but got away thanks to the passport and the horse
you sent with that strange young man who spoke not a word.

MARIANA [*disturbed and not wanting to remember*]:
And what then?
[*Pause.*]

PEDRO: Why do you tremble?

MARIANA [*nervously*]:   Go on, what then?

PEDRO: I wandered the Alpujarra. Unable to make
for Gibraltar, where I knew there was yellow fever,
I bided my time and kept low. And now the time
has come! At last, together, my love, we'll triumph!
Freedom, though with bloody hands, knock on all our doors!

MARIANA [*radiantly*]:
My triumph consists in having you at my side!

Classical times as one of the two Pillars of Hercules, it was conquered by
the Moors in 711 (from whom comes its name, *Gebel al Tarik*, meaning
Tarik's castle). Reconquered by Christians in 1462, it was lost by Spain to
Britain in 1704 during the War of Succession.

    The infectious and often fatal disease of yellow fever came from the
tropics, especially the Caribbean, and is a virus transmitted by mosquito.
In Europe it was largely confined to the seaports of Spain and Portugal,
where there were sporadic epidemics in the eighteenth and early nineteenth
centuries, notably in Barcelona in 1821.

166 Freedom, though with bloody hands...: another rousing image which,
like many that link freedom with a violent struggle, has a hollow ring in
the context of Pedro's subsequent actions.

167 My triumph consists...: Mariana's emphasis consistently falls on the
immediate personal relationship. In this speech the healing power of love
so transcends politics that we are left in little doubt that Mariana is a
reluctant conspirator.

En mirarte los ojos mientras tú no me miras.
Cuando estás a mi lado olvido lo que siento
y quiero a todo el mundo: 170
hasta al rey y a Pedrosa.
Al bueno como al malo.   ¡Pedro!, cuando se quiere
se está fuera del tiempo,
y ya no hay día ni noche, ¡sino tú y yo!
PEDRO [*Abrazándola*]:   ¡Mariana!
Como dos blancos ríos de rubor y silencio,   175
así enlazan tus brazos mi cuerpo combatido.
MARIANA [*Cogiéndole la cabeza*]:
Ahora puedo perderte, puedo perder tu vida.
Como la enamorada de un marinero loco
que navegara eterno sobre una barca vieja,
acecho un mar oscuro, sin fondo ni oleaje,   180
en espera de gentes que te traigan ahogado.
PEDRO: No es hora de pensar en quimeras, que es hora
de abrir el pecho a bellas realidades cercanas
de una España cubierta de espigas y rebaños,
donde la gente coma su pan con alegría,   185
en medio de estas anchas eternidades nuestras
y esta aguda pasión de horizonte y silencio.
España entierra y pisa su corazón antiguo,
su herido corazón de Península andante,
y hay que salvarla pronto con manos y con dientes. 190
MARIANA [*Pasional*]:
Y yo soy la primera que lo pide con ansia.
Quiero tener abiertos mis balcones al sol
para que llene el suelo de flores amarillas

---

178 the lovesick woman of a crazy sailor: Mariana returns to a traditional
topic more appropriate to her sensitivity. The woman who pines at the sea
shore was especially prominent in the oral lyric of Galicia and Portugal;
for instance,

Ondas do mar de Vigo	Waves of the sea of Vigo,
se vistes meu amigo!	if you should see my lover!
E ai, Deus, se verrá cedo!	Oh, God, may he come back soon!
Ondas do mar levado,	Waves of the stormy sea,
se vistes meu amado!	if you should see my man!
E ai, Deus, se verrá cedo!	Oh God, may he come back soon!

See *Poesia medieval. I. Cantigas de amigo*, ed. Hernani Cidade (Lisbon:
Textos Literarios, 1959), 4.
The topic is also treated in Castilian, as in the haunting poem which
begins:

Miraba la mar	She stood looking at the sea,
la mal casada,	the unhappy wife,
que miraba la mar	looking at the sea:
cómo es ancha y larga...	how big and wide it is...
	(Alonso and Blecua, *op.cit.*, 86).

182 This is no time for daydreams: it is increasingly evident that the two

100

Looking into your eyes while you're not watching mine.
When you are here with me I forget all my fears
and I love everybody,   170
the King, Pedrosa even,
the good and the bad alike. Pedro, when one loves
one feels somehow beyond time,
no longer is there day and night, just you and me!

PEDRO [*embracing her*]:
Mariana, your arms embrace my worn out body   175
like two white rivers of modesty and silence.

MARIANA [*her hands holding his head*]:
Now I can lose you, now I can let your life go.
Like the lovesick woman of a crazy sailor
who always took to sea in a ricketty boat,
I will look out upon the dark and bottomless   180
waves and watch for your body to be brought home
                                                      drowned.

PEDRO:
This is no time for daydreams, Mariana, but time
to open up our hearts to new realities,
to a new Spain that is covered in wheat and flocks,
where the common people eat their bread peacefully
amid these broad and everlasting plains of ours
where the stark horizon emits a silent pang.
Now Spain batters and tramples upon its old heart,
its ravaged heart of peninsular chivalry,
which we must resurrect with our hands and our nails.

MARIANA [*passionately*]:
And I am the first who would rush to its rescue.
I wish to see my windows open to the sun,
my balcony floor all strewn with golden flowers,

---

lovers are speaking at cross purposes. Mariana's real fears, indeed her
nightmares, are dismissed by Pedro as daydreams, while his own
fancifully-formed wishes for Spain's future are to him realities. His
subsequent images, however, in their epic dimension, beautifully evoke the
ideal of democracy and brotherhood.
186-7 everlasting plains...silent pang: the image is rare inasmuch as it
goes beyond the play's Andalusian confines and instead evokes the grand
vistas of the Castilian *meseta* or tableland.
188 peninsular chivalry: Pedro patriotically laments the loss of traditional
Spanish values; but this allusion to the glories of the past – implicitly to
the Reconquest and the Empire – is somewhat reactionary in spirit and at
odds with the progressive and even socio-economic imagery of lines 184-5.
Thus the speech as a whole, while poetically impressive, is something of a
political muddle; though that in itself is not uncharacteristic of Spanish
Liberalism which could not evolve a liberal policy towards the colonies (see
R. Carr, *op.cit.*, 143), and certainly never came to terms with the two
horns of progress and tradition, a dilemma which was to dominate Spanish
thinking for the next hundred years. The further echo in Lorca's image of
peninsular chivalry is that of Don Quixote, the supreme idealist, heroic
and deluded, whose spirit is present in both Pedro and Mariana.

y quererte, segura de tu amor sin que nadie
me aceche, como en este decisivo momento.   195
[*En un arranque.*]
¡Pero ya estoy dispuesta!
PEDRO [*Entusiasmado, se levanta*]:   ¡Así me gusta verte,
hermosa Marianita!   Ya no tardarán mucho
los amigos, y alienta
ese rostro bravío y esos ojos ardientes
[*Amoroso*]
sobre tu cuello blanco, que tiene luz de luna.   200
[*Fuera comienza a llover y se levanta el viento.   Mariana hace
señas a Pedro de que calle.*]
CLAVELA [*Entrando*]:
Señora... Me parece que han llamado.
[*Pedro y Mariana adoptan actitudes indiferentes.*]
CLAVELA [*Dirigiéndose a Don Pedro*]
¡Don Pedro!
PEDRO [*Sereno*]:   ¡Dios te guarde!
MARIANA: ¿Tú sabes quién vendrá?
CLAVELA: Sí, señora; lo sé.
MARIANA: ¿La seña?
CLAVELA: No la olvido.   205
MARIANA: Antes de abrir. que mires por la mirilla grande.
CLAVELA: Así lo haré, señora.
MARIANA: No enciendas luz ninguna,
pero ten en el patio
un velón prevenido,   210
y cierra la ventana del jardín.
CLAVELA [*Marchándose*]:   En seguida.
MARIANA: ¿Cuántos vendrán?
PEDRO: Muy pocos.
Pero los que interesan.
MARIANA: ¿Noticias?
PEDRO: Las habrá
dentro de unos instantes.   215
Si, al fin, hemos de alzarnos,
decidiremos.
MARIANA: ¡Calla!
[*Hace ademán a Don Pedro de que se calle, y queda escuchando.
Fuera se oye la lluvia y el viento.*]
¡Ya están aquí!
PEDRO [*Mirando el reloj*]:   Puntuales,

---

196 But I am ready: Mariana's resolution seems to owe most to her
awareness that this is the only way to Pedro's heart.
200 your lovely moonlight neck aglow: the combination of two fatalistic
motifs, moon and neck, follows hard upon Mariana's decision to go through

and I wish to love you, confident of your love,
with no fears that anyone is spying on us.　　　195
[*In a burst of feeling.*]
But I am ready to meet the moment's challenge!
PEDRO [*standing up, enthused*]:
Bravo, Mariana, my precious. It won't be long
before our friends come to ease
your worried brow. Then we shall see your eyes burning
with passion, [*lovingly*] and your lovely moonlight neck
aglow.
[*Outside it starts to rain and the wind rises up. Mariana gestures to
Pedro to be silent.*]
CLAVELA [*entering*]:
Señora... I think they have come.
[*Pedro and Mariana adopt more formal postures.*]
CLAVELA [*moving towards Don Pedro*]
Don Pedro!
PEDRO [*serene*]:　　　God bless you!
MARIANA:　　You know who's coming now?
CLAVELA:　　Yes, señora, I know.
MARIANA:　　The password?
CLAVELA:　　　　　　I'll remember.　　　205
MARIANA:　　Before you open the door, look through the peephole.
CLAVELA:　　I will, of course, Señora.
MARIANA:　　Use no candle at all,
but keep a brass lamp lit
dimly in the patio,　　　210
and close the window to the garden.
CLAVELA [*leaving*]:　　　　　　Straightaway.
MARIANA:　　How many are coming?
PEDRO:　　Few, but all committed.
MARIANA:　　Is there news?
PEDRO:　　　　　　There will be,
within a few minutes.　　　215
We'll decide if it's time
at last to rise.
MARIANA:　　　　　　Quiet!
[*She motions to Don Pedro to be silent and listens attentively. Wind
and rain are heard outside.*]
They are here!
PEDRO [*looking at his watch*]:
Right on time,

---

with the conspiracy, and it therefore brings the lovers' dialogue to a
suitably prophetic close.
06 Before you open the door: Mariana's precautions here contrast with
Pedro's imprudent confidence in their safety, as expressed for instance in
lines 128 and 236.

103

	como buenos patriotas.	
	¡Son gente decidida!	220
MARIANA:	¡Dios nos ayude a todos!	
PEDRO:	¡Ayudará!	
MARIANA:	¡Debiera,	
	si mirase a este mundo!	

[*Mariana, corriendo, avanza hasta la puerta y levanta la gran cortina del fondo.*]

¡Adelante, señores!

[*Entran tres caballeros con amplias capas grises; uno de ellos lleva patillas. Mariana y Don Pedro los reciben amablemente. Los caballeros dan la mano a Mariana y a Don Pedro.*]

MARIANA [*Dando la mano al Conspirador 1.°*]:
    ¡Ay, qué manos tan frías!

CONSPIRADOR 1.° [*Franco*]:   ¡Hace un frío   225
que corta! Y me he olvidado de los guantes;
pero aquí se está bien.

MARIANA: ¡Llueve de veras!

CONSPIRADOR 3.° [*Decidido*]:
El Zacatín estaba intransitable.

[*Se quitan las capas, que sacuden de lluvia.*]

CONSPIRADOR 2.° [*Melancólico*]:
La lluvia, cómo un sauce de cristal,
sobre las casas de Granada cae.   230

CONSPIRADOR 3.°:
Y el Darro viene lleno de agua turbia.

MARIANA: ¿Les vieron?

CONSPIRADOR 2.° [*Melancólico. Habla poco y pausadamente*]:
¡No! Vinimos separados
hasta la entrada de esta oscura calle.

224+ <u>Three men enter dressed in long grey cloaks</u>: an impressive entry which makes the stage a striking picture evocative of the Romantic period and of the mood of intrigue. As we have already seen (note to line 205, First Engraving), Richard Ford was most impressed with Spanish cloaks: 'The ample folds and graceful draping give breadth and throw an air of stately decency – nay, dignity – over the wearer'. He also offers the following advice about how to wear a cloak: 'either the *capa* is allowed to hang simply down from the shoulders, or it is folded in the *embozo*, or *a lo majo*: the *embozar* consists in taking up the right front fold and throwing it over the left shoulder, thus muffling up the mouth, while the end of the fold hangs halfway down the back behind... it is extremely difficult to do this neatly, although all Spaniards can... There is no end of proverbs on the cloak', he says, and he gives three:

"Una buena capa, todo tapa"   A good cloak conceals all.

"Por sol que haga, no dejes tu capa en casa"   However sunny it is, don't leave your cloak at home.

"Debajo mi manto, veo y canto"   Beneath my cloak, I see all and sing.

	just like good patriots;	
	all men of resolution!	220
MARIANA:	May God help our just cause!	
PEDRO:	He will!	
MARIANA:	Indeed, he should,	
	if he could see Spain's plight!	

[*She crosses towards the door and lifts the large curtain upstage.*]
                    Gentlemen, come in, please!
[*Three men enter dressed in long grey cloaks; one of them has whiskers. Mariana and Don Pedro give them a warm welcome. Each shakes the hand of Mariana and Don Pedro.*]
MARIANA [*giving her hand to the First Conspirator*]:
                    How cold your hands are!
FIRST CONSPIRATOR [*forthrightly*]:   There's an icy chill   225
                    outside and I had forgotten my gloves.
                    But we'll warm up in here.
MARIANA: It's raining hard!
THIRD CONSPIRATOR [*firmly*]:
                    Pouring! The Zacatín was impassable.
                    [*They take off their cloaks, shaking the rain
                        from them.*]
SECOND CONSPIRATOR [*sadly*]:
                    Tonight the rain falls like a great weeping
                    willow on all the rooftops of Granada.   230
THIRD CONSPIRATOR:
                    The Darro is awash with muddy water.
MARIANA: Did anyone see you?
SECOND CONSPIRATOR [*who says little and speaks slowly*]:
                                No. We each came
                    separately to meet in this dark street.

(A proverb which is a near equivalent to the English idiom of laughing up one's sleeve)
Richard Ford, *op.cit.*, 303-7.
228 <u>The Zacatín was impassible</u>: the Zacatín often flooded with water from the Darro river, as Richard Ford delightfully recounts: 'The Darro, after washing the base of the Alhambra, flows under the Plaza Nueva, being arched over; and when swelled by rains, there is always much risk of its blowing up this covering. Such says the *Seguidilla* (song), is the portion which Darro will bear to his bride the Xenil:

"Darro tiene prometido,	The Darro has promised
El casarse con Xenil,	to marry the Genil,
y le ha de llevar en dote,	and as a dowry will bring
Plaza Nueva y Zacatín."	the Plaza Nueva and Zacatín.
	(*op.cit.*, 575-6).

229-31 <u>Tonight the rain...muddy water</u>: besides its pictorial appeal, Lorca's imagery of the foul weather prepares us for news unfavourable to the conspirators, a point which is later made plain (line 308).

CONSPIRADOR 1.°:
          ¿Habrá noticias para decidir?
PEDRO: Llegarán esta noche, Dios mediante.   235
MARIANA: Hablen bajo.
CONSPIRADOR 1.° [*Sonriendo*]:
          ¿Por qué, doña Mariana?
          Toda la gente duerme en este instante.
PEDRO: Creo que estamos seguros.
CONSPIRADOR 3.°:   No lo afirmes;
          Pedrosa no ha cesado de espiarme,
          y aunque yo lo despisto sagazmente,   240
          continúa en acecho, y algo sabe.
[*Unos se sientan y otros quedan de pie, componiendo una bella estampa.*]
MARIANA: Ayer estuvo aqui.
          [*Los caballeros hacen un gesto de extrañeza.*]
          ¡Como es mi amigo
          no quise, porque no debía, negarme!
          Hizo un elogio de nuestra ciudad;
          pero mientras hablaba, tan amable,   245
          me miraba... no sé... ¡como sabiendo!,
          [*Subrayando*] de una manera penetrante.
          En una sorda lucha con mis ojos
          estuvo aquí toda la tarde,
          y Pedrosa es capaz... ¡de lo que sea!   250
PEDRO: No es posible que pueda figurarse...
MARIANA: Yo no estoy muy tranquila, y os lo digo
          para que andemos con cautela grande.
          De noche, cuando cierro las ventanas,
          imagino que empuja los cristales.   255
PEDRO [*Mirando el reloj*]:
          Ya son las once y diez. El emisario
          debe estar ya muy cerca de esta calle.
CONSPIRADOR 3.° [*Mirando el reloj*]:
          Poco debe tardar.
CONSPIRADOR 1.°:   ¡Dios lo permita!
          ¡Que me parece un siglo cada instante!
[*Entra Clavela con una bandeja de altas copas de cristal tallado y un frasco lleno de vino rojo, que deja sobre el velador. Mariana habla con ella.*]
PEDRO: Estarán sobre aviso los amigos.   260

---

244 Granada's beauty: Pedrosa, a Castilian, was evidently trying to ingratiate himself by appealing to Mariana's provincial pride, a typical Andalusian feature illustrated in the rhyme,

    'Quien no ha visto Granada   Who hasn't seen Granada
    no ha visto nada'   hasn't seen anything

FIRST CONSPIRATOR:
              Will there be information to act on?
PEDRO: Vital news will come tonight, God willing.   235
MARIANA: Speak quietly please.
FIRST CONSPIRATOR [*smiling*]:   But why, Doña Mariana?
              At this hour all Granada is asleep.
PEDRO: I think we are quite safe.
THIRD CONSPIRATOR: Don't be so sure;
              Pedrosa has kept a close watch on me,
              and though I shook his bloodhounds off, thank God,
              he knows a thing or two and won't give up.
[*Some sit down while others remain standing, forming an
attractive engraving.*]
MARIANA: He came here yesterday.
              [*The men show their surprise.*]
                              Since he's a friend...
              I was in no position to stop him.
              He spoke at length about Granada's beauty,
              but as his words fell sweetly from his tongue   245
              he looked at me... as if... as if he knew...
              [*emphatically*] for he has eyes that look right into me.
              He spent a good few hours in this house;
              his eyes were always so intent on mine.
              I think he might well know... well, anything!   250
PEDRO: You mean you think that he could be aware...?
MARIANA: I'm very uneasy at the moment,
              and all I say is that we must proceed
              with caution. At night, closing my windows,
              I sometimes think he's there in every pane.   255
PEDRO [*looking at the clock*]:
              Look, it's ten past eleven already.
              The messenger must be well on his way.
THIRD CONSPIRATOR [*looking at the clock*]:
              He should be here within minutes.
FIRST CONSPIRATOR: God willing!
              To me each second's an eternity!
[*Clavela enters carrying a tray with long stemmed cut glasses and
a bottle of red wine which she puts down on the pedestal table.
Mariana speaks to her*]:
PEDRO: Our friends will now have been put on alert.   260

---

which is, in turn, a response to the better known:
    'Quien no ha visto Sevilla   Who hasn't seen Seville
    no ha visto una maravilla'   hasn't seen a marvel.
247 he has eyes that look right into me: introducing one of the main
points in Pedrosa's characterization, his penetrating, sleuth eyes.

CONSPIRADOR 1.º:
Enterados están. No falta nadie.
Todo depende de lo que nos digan
esta noche.
PEDRO: La situación es grave,
pero excelente si la aprovechamos.
[Sale Clavela, y Mariana corre la cortina.]
Hay que estudiar hasta el menor detalle,   265
porque el pueblo responde, sin dudar.
Andalucía tiene todo el aire
lleno de Libertad. Esta palabra
perfuma el corazón de sus ciudades,
desde las viejas torres amarillas   270
hasta los troncos de los olivares.
Esa costa de Málaga está llena
de gente decidida a levantarse:
pescadores del Palo, marineros
y caballeros principales.   275
Nos siguen pueblos como Nerja, Vélez,
que aguardan las noticias, anhelantes.
Hombres de acantilado y mar abierto,
y, por lo tanto, libres como nadie.
Algeciras acecha la ocasión,   280
y en Granada, señores de linaje
como vosotros exponen su vida
de una manera emocionante.
¡Ay, qué impaciencia tengo!
CONSPIRADOR 3.º: Como todos
los verdaderamente liberales.   285
MARIANA [*Tímida*]:
Pero ¿habrá quién os siga?
PEDRO [*Convencido*]:   Todo el mundo.
MARIANA: ¿A pesar de este miedo?
PEDRO [*Seco*]:   Sí.

274-6 Palo...Nerja and Vélez: all are small towns on the Andalusian coast
near Málaga; the first two, properly speaking, being fishing villages,
while even the more renowned Vélez Málaga, to give the town its full
name, had a population of only 24,000 in the 1905 census. Thus, in failing
to mention the more significant towns, Pedro's references have a somewhat
idealistic democratic ring and do not inspire absolute confidence in the
practical chances of the uprising. Well might we wonder how the fishermen
were to be mobilised; indeed Pedro seems to be indulging in what Richard
Carr calls 'the myth of the free man's superiority over the trained slave
army' (*op.cit.*, 140). We might also bear in mind Carr's severe comment:

FIRST CONSPIRATOR:
        Each one will be informed, every last man.
        So much depends on what we hear tonight.
PEDRO: The situation is most critical,
        but also propitious to our purpose.
        [*Clavela leaves and Mariana draws the curtain.*]
        We must consider all aspects in detail,   265
        since those who follow us give all their trust.
        This Andalusian air of ours is radiant
        with Liberty's light, and the word Liberty
        is a fragrance in our southern cities;
        it blows from our historic sunlit towers   270
        and cools the trunks of our green olive groves.
        Down south the coast of Malaga is full
        of men who have made up their minds to rise:
        the humble fishermen around Palo,
        for instance, but also sailors and men   275
        of standing. Towns such as Nerja and Vélez
        are waiting anxiously for our signal.
        Men who live by those rugged cliffs, their faces
        open to the sea, are free like the waves.
        In Algeciras they wait impatiently,   280
        and in Granada men of highest stock
        like you are risking all without a thought
        for safety. It moves my heart to see you.
        I'm burning with impatience!
THIRD CONSPIRATOR: So are we,
        and all who are of Liberal thinking.   285
MARIANA [*nervously*]:
        Are so many ready to rise?
PEDRO [*convinced*]:   They are!
MARIANA: In spite of the danger?
PEDRO [*sharply*]:   Yes.

'The total lack of response to Torrijos's desperate invasion proves that even there [Andalusia] the countryside was firmly loyal to Ferdinand VII' (*ibid.*, 152n).
280 Algeciras: a port near Gibraltar in the sub-province of Cadiz with some 13,000 inhabitants; it takes its name from the Arabic *Al-Djezirah al Hadra*, meaning the green island, and was recaptured from the Moors in 1309.
286 Are so many ready to rise?: this and her next question hint at Mariana's scepticism, while Pedro's curt replies may suggest his impatience with her interfering in the business of men.

MARIANA: No hay nadie
           que vaya a la Alameda del Salón
           tranquilamente a pasearse,
           y el café de la Estrella está desierto.   290
PEDRO [*Entusiasta*]:
           ¡Mariana, la bandera que bordaste
           será acatada por el rey Fernando,
           mal que le pese a Calomarde!
CONSPIRADOR 3.°:
           Cuando ya no le quede otro recurso
           se rendirá a las huestes liberales,   295
           que aunque se finja desvalido y solo,
           no cabe duda que él hace y deshace.
MARIANA: ¿No es Fernando un juguete de los suyos?
CONSPIRADOR 3.°:
           ¿No tarda mucho?
PEDRO [*Inquieto*]:   Yo no sé decirte.
CONSPIRADOR 3.°:
           ¿Si lo habrán detenido?
CONSPIRADOR 1.°:   No es probable.   300
           Oscuridad y lluvia le protegen,
           y él está siempre vigilante.
MARIANA: Ahora llega.
PEDRO;   Y al fin sabremos algo.
           [*Se levantan y se dirigen a la puerta.*]
CONSPIRADOR 3.°:
           Bien venido, si buenas cartas trae.
MARIANA [*Apasionada, a Pedro*]:
           Pedro, mira por mí. Sé muy prudente,   305
           que me falta muy poco para ahogarme.
[*Aparece por la puerta el Conspirador 4.°. Es un hombre fuerte;
campesino rico. Viste el traje popular de la época: sombrero
puntiagudo de alas de terciopelo, adornado con borlas de seda:
chaqueta con bordados y aplicaduras de paño de todos los colores*]

287-8 But scarcely/a soul is to be seen these days...: in contrast to Don
Pedro's epic evocation of Andalusia in lines 267-283, Mariana's pessimism
about the conspiracy's chances is based on what she has seen with her
own eyes. Salón Avenue is a promenade which runs alongside the River
Genil where liberals would have gathered to debate, as no doubt they did
in such cafes as the presumably fictitious Café Estrella, literally 'Star'
cafe.
293 Calomarde: Francisco Tadeo Calomarde, who was humbly born in
Teruel in 1773 and died in exile in Toulouse in 1842, was Ferdinand VII's
right-hand man in the last ten years of his reign. Initially associated with
the Cadiz liberals, Calomarde became an arch-royalist responsible for the
execution of numerous constitutionalists and liberal agitators. Though
instrumental in repealing the Salic Law, so that Ferdinand's daughter
might succeed to the throne, at the end of Ferdinand's reign Calomarde

MARIANA: But scarcely
          a soul is to be seen these days taking
          a quiet stroll down Salón Avenue,
          while Café Estrella is quite deserted.   290
PEDRO [*eagerly*]:
          Mariana, the flag that you sewed for us
          will be accepted by King Fernando,
          whether Calomarde likes it or not!
THIRD CONSPIRATOR:
          When he can find no other card to play
          he'll concede to the Liberal masses,   295
          for though he acts as if he had no power
          there's no doubt he's the one who calls the tune.
MARIANA: But isn't Fernando merely a puppet?
THIRD CONSPIRATOR:
          Our friend is very late.
PEDRO [*anxiously*]:   It worries me.
THIRD CONSPIRATOR:
          Perhaps they caught him.
FIRST CONSPIRATOR: That's most unlikely.   300
          The darkness and the rain give him good cover,
          and he's a man who takes the utmost care.
MARIANA: He's coming now.
PEDRO: At last we'll know for sure.
          [*They get up and go towards the door.*]
THIRD CONSPIRATOR:
          He's very welcome, if he brings good news.
MARIANA [*passionately, to Pedro*]:
          Be cautious, Pedro, and watch out for me,   305
          I feel the waters swirl above my head.
[*The Fourth Conspirator appears at the door. He is a robust man,
a rich, country type. He wears the provincial dress of the period:
a sharp-pointed hat with velvet brim and silk tassels; a jacket with
embroidered motifs and highly coloured trimmings at the elbows,*

---

turned Carlist – a supporter of the rival pretender, Carlos – for which
mistake he spent his last years in exile. For his vindictive persecution of
the liberals, and for such reactionary measures as the closure of the
universities, the years of his ministry are often called "the ominous decade
of Calomarde", while the phrase "not even in Calomarde's time" is
proverbial.
298 **But isn't Fernando merely a puppet?:** Mariana voices a popular
misconception in thinking Calomarde is more in command than the King.
Notable, however, is that none of the men bothers to answer her question.
306+ **The Fourth Conspirator:** there follows a remarkably detailed
description of the fine dress of this country gentleman who is evidently
one of the 'men of highest stock' whom Pedro had earlier referred to (line
281). The finery reminds us that Spanish Liberalism drew its support from
the gentry not the working class.

en los codos, en la bocamanga y en el cuello. El pantalón, de
vueltas, sujeto por botones de filigrana, y las polainas, de cuero,
abiertas por un costado, dejando ver la pierna. Trae una dulce
tristeza varonil. Todos los personajes están de pie cerca de la
puerta de entrada. Mariana no oculta su angustia, y mira, ya
al recién llegado, ya a Don Pedro, con un aire doliente y escrutador.
CONSPIRADOR 4.°:
        ¡Caballeros! ¡Doña Mariana!
        [*Estrecha la mano de Mariana.*]
PEDRO [*Impaciente*]:   ¿Hay noticias?
CONSPIRADOR 4.°:
        ¡Tan malas como el tiempo!
PEDRO: ¿Qué ha pasado?
CONSPIRADOR 1.° [*Irritado*]:
        Casi lo adivinaba.
MARIANA [*A Pedro*]:   ¿Te entristeces?
PEDRO: ¿Y las gentes de Cádiz?
CONSPIRADOR 4.°:   Todo en vano.   310
        Hay que estar prevenidos. El Gobierno
        por todas partes nos está acechando.
        Tendremos que aplazar el alzamiento,
        o luchar o morir, de lo contrario.
PEDRO [*Desesperado*]:
        Yo no sé qué pensar; que tengo abierta   315
        una herida que sangra en mi costado,
        y no puedo esperar, señores míos.
CONSPIRADOR 3.° [*Fuerte*]:
        Don Pedro, triunfaremos esperando.
        La situación no puede durar mucho.
CONSPIRADOR 4.° [*Fuerte*]:
        Ahora mismo tenemos que callarnos.   320
        Nadie quiere una muerte sin provecho.
PEDRO [*Fuerte también*]:
        Mucho dolor me cuesta.
MARIANA [*Angustiada*]:   ¡Hablen más bajo!
        [*Se pasea.*]
CONSPIRADOR 4.°:
        España entera calla, ¡pero vive!
        Guarde bien la bandera.
MARIANA: La he mandado
        a casa de una vieja amiga mía,   325
        allá en el Albaicín, y estoy temblando.

---

309 <u>Cadiz:</u> a large city and naval port in western Andalusia, historically
the <u>focal</u> centre of liberals since it was here that they proclaimed the
Constitution of 1812 and here too, in 1820, General Riego pronounced his
coup (see Introduction).
326 <u>Albaicín:</u> a colourful district in Granada, facing the Alhambra palace.
Opulent in Moorish times, today only a few ruins remain of its former

wrists and neck. His trousers have decorative linings and are
secured with filigree buttons, and his leather gaiters are open on
one side where his legs are bare. His manliness is tempered by
his subdued mood. Everyone is standing near the door through
which he enters. Mariana does not disguise her anguish and she
looks rapidly in turn at Don Pedro and at the new arrival, her eyes
alert and sorrowful.]

FOURTH CONSPIRATOR:
        Gentlemen! Doña Mariana!
        [*He offers his hand to Mariana.*]
PEDRO [*impatiently*]:   What news?
FOURTH CONSPIRATOR:
        As foul as the weather outside!
PEDRO: What's happened?
FIRST CONSPIRATOR [*exasperated*]:
        I might have guessed.
MARIANA [*to Pedro*]:   Don't be disappointed.
PEDRO: And those in Cadiz?
FOURTH CONSPIRATOR: It was all in vain.   310
        We have to face it square. The Government
        has placed its troops in every corner.
        Our rising must be postponed for a while,
        or else it's a question of fight and die.
PEDRO [*desperately*]:
        I don't know what to think; I feel as if   315
        my side were open with a running wound.
        I say there is no time to wait, my friends.
THIRD CONSPIRATOR [*forcefully*]:
        Don Pedro, if we wait we're sure to triumph;
        things cannot go on like this much longer.
FOURTH CONSPIRATOR [*forcefully*]:
        Discretion is the better part of valour;   320
        to die in vain would just betray our cause.
PEDRO: But I've run out of patience.
MARIANA [*anxiously*]:   Please, speak softly!
        [*She walks about the room.*]
FOURTH CONSPIRATOR:
        All Spain awaits with quiet patience,
        and it lives on! Put the flag in safe keeping.
MARIANA: I've sent it off to someone I can trust,   325
        living in the Albaicín. Though I think

---

splendour, and the district, with its large gypsy population, has long
been among Granada's poorest. Lorca is faithful to history in this
reference, for Mariana Pineda sent the flag to two sisters in the Albaicín
who were asked to embroider it. The news got out; Pedrosa discovered the
flag and then claimed his men had found it at Mariana's house, a detail
Lorca does not use.

Quizá estuviera aquí mejor guardada.
PEDRO: ¿Y en Málaga?
CONSPIRADOR 4.°:   En Málaga, un espanto.
El canalla de González Moreno...
No se puede contar lo que ha pasado.   330
*[Expectación vivísima. Mariana, sentada en el sofá, junto a
Don Pedro, después de todo el juego escénico que ha realizado,
oye anhelante lo que cuenta el Conspirador 4.°.]*
Torrijos, el general
noble, de la frente limpia,
donde se estaban mirando
las gentes de Andalucía,
caballero entre los duques,   335
corazón de plata fina,
ha sido muerto en las playas
de Málaga la bravía.
Le atrajeron con engaños
que él creyó, por su desdicha,   340
y se acercó, satisfecho,

Lorca describes the Albaicín in a youthful work of poetic prose, 'Impressions' (1917): 'The Albaicín has vague and passionate sounds and is wrapped up in its smooth tinsels of dark light. The mist stirs its sad and dreamy houses, and it seems as if they want to tell us something about the grand things they once saw' (*Obras completas*, I, 929). Again: 'in the blurred palimpsest of the Albaicín echoes loom of lost cities' (*ibid.*, 989).
329 <u>González Moreno.</u> the villain of the ballad which is about to be narrated, Vicente Gonzalez Moreno (1778-1839) was Military Governor of Malaga at the time of Torrijos's abortive uprising in 1831. He was to be known by liberals as *el verdugo de Málaga* (the Malaga executioner) for the way he deceived Torrijos into landing his ships and then arresting him and having him shot. Fernando VII rewarded Moreno by making him Captain General of Granada. After Ferdinand's death Moreno became a Carlist general and, with some ironic justice, was bayonetted by fellow Carlists in Navarre in 1839 when attempting to flee to France after the Carlist cause had collapsed.
331 <u>Torrijos:</u> General José María de Torrijos (1791-1831), a liberal hero of noble birth whose daring anti-royalist uprising in 1831 is used by Lorca as the cornerstone of the play's conspiracy. Torrijos had fought as a youth in the War of Independence, was active in Riego's constitutional triennium, 1820-23, then fled from royalist persecution to France and England. In 1830 he went to Gibraltar to await a propitious moment to return to Spain. In January 1831 he disembarked with two hundred men near Algeciras, but was forced by royalists to sail back to Gibraltar. He was then encouraged by González Moreno to attempt another landing near Malaga. Moreno corresponded at length with Torrijos, assuring him that as soon as he set foot on Spanish soil all would be ready to assist his triumphant coup. Convinced of this, Torrijos set sail with just fifty-two men in two small boats on the night of December 1st, 1831. He was intercepted by

it might have been safer to keep it here.
PEDRO: What happened in Malaga?
FOURTH CONSPIRATOR: Terrible news
          from Malaga, where González Moreno,
          the dog... I wish I didn't bring this news.   330
*[There is a terrible feeling of suspense. Mariana, after all her
previous movement about the stage, is now seated next to Don
Pedro on the sofa, and she listens keenly to what the Fourth
Conspirator relates.]*
          Torrijos, that brave general
          of noble face and lineage,
          Torrijos, that emblem of pride,
          of honour and of tutelage,
          there where all good Andalusians   335
          prayed for his ships' safe anchorage,
          there on Malaga's bloody sands
          he met his death in cold outrage.
          Innocent to their wily ploys,
          his heart as ever unafraid,   340
          he was lured there to disembark

---

coastguards and diverted from the proposed point of disembarkation to land in fact at Fuengirola, then a small fishing village, where, not surprisingly, his unfurling of the tricolour and rousing call to 'Liberty!' did not meet with the promised support. Believing that the hostile villagers were simply not party to the conspiracy, Torrijos led his men on without returning fire until they came within a short distance of Malaga on December 4. Promptly surrounded by royalist troops, the puzzled Torrijos surrendered next day. He and his fifty-two men were executed in Malaga on December 11, his request to face the firing squad without a blindfold being refused. Some years later a monument was erected in his honour in Riego Square, Malaga, while his disastrous venture was also commemorated in a sonnet by the major Romantic poet José de Espronceda, *Poesías líricas* (Madrid: Espasa-Calpe, 1968), 43.

Lorca's treatment of the episode in the ensuing ballad is largely faithful to history though he does contract events for greater dramatic effect, notably by suggesting that Torrijos and his men were slain immediately upon landing. Most significant, however, as pointed out in the Introduction, is that Torrijos's fateful venture came some months after Mariana Pineda's execution on May 26, 1831. Presumably Lorca chose to include this, rather than one of the several liberal uprisings which occurred before Mariana's death, because the episode has such a strong sense of pathos and it illustrates both the naïveté of liberal idealism and the cynical cunning of the royalists.

In treating an historical event of great moment, Lorca's ballad adheres to the original principle of the ballad genre which served in ancient times as a kind of news bulletin, informing people of developments in the wars between the Christian kingdoms and especially of progress in the Reconquest. Once again, as in the ballad on the bullfight at Ronda, Lorca does not fail to exploit to the full those poetic devices traditionally found in the genre.

con sus buques, a la orilla.
¡Malhaya el corazón noble
que de los malos se fía!,
que al poner el pie en la arena   345
lo prendieron los realistas.
El vizconde de La Barthe,
que mandaba las milicias,
debió cortarse la mano
antes de tal villanía,   350
como es quitar a Torrijos
bella espada que ceñía,
con el puño de cristal,
adornado con dos cintas.
Muy de noche lo mataron   355
con toda su compañía.
Caballero entre los duques,
corazón de plata fina.
Grandes nubes se levantan
sobre la tierra de Mijas.   360
El viento mueve la mar
y los barcos se retiran
con los remos presurosos
y las velas extendidas.
Entre el ruido de las olas   365
sonó la fusilería,

---

347 the Viscount of La Barthe: though of dubious historical veracity, the introduction of a French figure helps to offset Spanish culpability in the affair and is consistent with the ballad's patriotic spirit. It also reminds us of Ferdinand VII's reliance upon French soldiers to restore him as absolute monarch in 1823 and it insinuates that the King rules by force, without popular support.

352 stripped Torrijos of his blade: in keeping with the traditional ballad's reliance upon clear external signs, this action emphasises the great injury done to Torrijos whose honour as a gentleman is totally identified with his sword. Swords were often the focus of attention in ballads, notably in the great epic *Poem of the Cid* where the Cid is given the formulaic appelation 'he who girded his sword in a lucky hour', and indeed the Cid's two most prized swords have their own names, *Colada* and *Tizona*. (A new translation of the *Poem of the Cid* by P. Such and J. Hodgkinson is shortly to be published in the present series.) It is further typical of the ballad to dwell upon a detail - such as the description of Torrijos's sword in lines 353-4 - in the midst of a rapid narrative account of a complex historical event, for this sudden close-up arrests the attention and gives a remarkable sense of authenticity.

355 In the depth of night they killed him: the line recalls the popular ballad which Lope de Vega, a major seventeenth-century playwright, gave dramatic form to in *The Knight from Olmedo*.

and fell into an ambuscade.
Unlucky is that noble soul
who is by feigning friends betrayed,
no sooner did his foot touch sand   345
than came the Royalist fusillade.
It was the Viscount of La Barthe
whom the militia scum obeyed,
but history will dishonour him
for the villainous part he played.   350
His were the felonious hands
that stripped Torrijos of his blade,
that famous steel of glinting cup
with double straps in finest suede.
In the depth of night they killed him   355
and all felt it a privilege
to die for their emblem of pride,
of honour and of tutelage.
Above the scarp where Mijas stands
black clouds were rising in a gale,   360
the sea, lashed by fearsome winds,
was swelling higher than their sails;
and so it was that some with oars
and others, blown adrift, turned tail,
when in the din of crashing surf   365
they heard the crack of bullet hail,

357-8 emblem of pride,/of honour and of tutelage: echoing lines 333-4,
after the fashion of the ancient ballad.
359 Mijas: situated some twenty miles west of Malaga, Mijas is a small,
white-washed, ancient town which is perched in an enclave on the rocky
slopes of Mijas Mountain, from where it overlooks Fuengirola and the
Mediterranean. A sundial and a primitive bull-ring are two remaining
attractions of a town which, due to its peculiar location, has not suffered
the recent gargantuan tourist development of the coastal villages below.
359-62 scarp...clouds...sails: an effective use of three indices of height
to give a sense of the sea's turbulence. The bad weather partly explains
and at the same time augurs Torrijos's disaster, as in the case of the
ancient ballad which begins:

Los vientos eran contrarios,	The winds were contrary,
la luna estaba crecida,	the moon was full,
los peces daban gemidos	the fish were moaning
por el mal tiempo que hacía	at the foulness of the weather
cuando el rey don Rodrigo...	when King Don Rodrigo...
	(C.C. Smith, *Spanish Ballads*, 54).

(A new translation of some ballads by Roger Wright is shortly to appear in
the present series.)
363-4 some with oars/and others, blown adrift, turned tail: a parallelism
of action which is typical of the oral tradition. A further example comes in
lines 373-7 when both the sailors at sea and the women on shore cry with
profuse tears, bringing the ballad to an appropriately pathetic end.

y muerto quedó en la arena,
sangrando por tres heridas,
el valiente caballero,
con toda su compañía.   370
La muerte, con ser la muerte,
no deshojó su sonrisa.
Sobre los barcos lloraba
toda la marinería,
y las más bellas mujeres,   375
enlutadas y afligidas,
lo van llorando también
por el limonar arriba.
PEDRO [*Levantándose, después de oír el romance*]:
Cada dificultad me da más bríos.
Señores, a seguir nuestro trabajo.   380
La muerte de Torrijos me enardece
para seguir luchando.
CONSPIRADOR 1.º:
Yo pienso así.
CONSPIRADOR 4.º: Pero hay que estarse quietos;
otro tiempo vendrá.
CONSPIRADOR 2.º [*Conmovido*]:
¡Tiempo lejano!
PEDRO: Pero mis fuerzas no se agotarán.   385
MARIANA [*Bajo, a Pedro*]:
Pedro, mientras yo viva...
CONSPIRADOR 1.º: ¿Nos marchamos?
CONSPIRADOR 3.º:
No hay nada que tratar. Tienes razón.
CONSPIRADOR 4.º:
Esto es lo que tenía que contaros,
y nada más.
CONSPIRADOR 1.º: Hay que ser optimistas.
MARIANA: ¿Gustarán de una copa?
CONSPIRADOR 4.º: La aceptamos   390
porque nos hace falta.
CONSPIRATOR 1.º: ¡Buen acuerdo!
[*Se ponen de pie y cogen sus copas.*]
MARIANA [*Llenando los vasos*]:
¡Cómo llueve!
[*Fuera se oye la lluvia.*]
CONSPIRADOR 3.º: ¡Don Pedro está apenado!
CONSPIRADOR 4.º:
¡Como todos nosotros!
PEDRO: ¡Es verdad!

---

386 <u>But Pedro</u>: here Mariana is interrupted in mid sentence, and the men,
Pedro included, seem not at all mindful of her.

then saw, amazed, their leader fall
in dead weight to the salty shale,
and in his triple wounds they read
a sign it was to no avail.   370
Death, even as he lay dying,
could never strip his smile away.
But out at sea all sailors' cheeks
were wet with grief as well as spray,
and on the shore, in mourning black,   375
the loveliest women of the bay
let huge tears fall as they went off
to grieve in lemon groves that day.

PEDRO [*standing up after hearing the ballad*]:
    Each setback only makes me more determined.
    Gentlemen, shall we follow through our cause?   380
    Torrijos' death is just the spur I need
    to go on fighting!

FIRST CONSPIRATOR: I am of that mind.

FOURTH CONSPIRATOR:
    But we must wait and bide our time a while.
    Our turn will come.

SECOND CONSPIRATOR [*emotionally*]
              That day's a long way off!

PEDRO: No more procrastination can I bear.   385

MARIANA [*quietly to Pedro*]:
    But Pedro, as long as I live...

FIRST CONSPIRATOR: Shall we
    depart?

THIRD CONSPIRATOR:
        Why not? There's nothing else for us to do.

FOURTH CONSPIRATOR:
    I've told you all I had to tell;
    there's nothing more.

FIRST CONSPIRATOR: We must think positively.

MARIANA: Perhaps you'd like a drink before you go?   390

FOURTH CONSPIRATOR:
    We could do with one.

FIRST CONSPIRATOR: Yes, I quite agree.

[*They stand up and take their glasses.*]

MARIANA [*filling the glasses*]:
    And how it rains!
    [*Pouring rain can be heard offstage.*]

THIRD CONSPIRATOR:
        Don Pedro looks subdued.

FOURTH CONSPIRATOR:
    Like every one of us!

PEDRO: That's very true!

MARIANA: Y tenemos razones para estarlo.
Pero a pesar de esta opresión aguda 395
y de tener razones para estarlo...
[Levantando la copa.]
"Luna tendida, marinero en pie",
dicen allá, por el Mediterráneo,
las gentes de veleros y fragatas.
¡Como ellos, hay que estar siempre acechando! 400
[Como en sueños.]
"Luna tendida, marinero en pie."

PEDRO *[Con la copa]*:
Que sean nuestras casas como barcos.

[Beben. Pausa. Fuera se oyen aldabonazos lejanos. Todos quedan con las copas en la mano, en medio de un gran silencio.]

MARIANA: Es el viento que cierra una ventana.

[Otro aldabonazo.]

PEDRO: ¿Oyes, Mariana?

CONSPIRADOR 4.º: ¿Quién será?

MARIANA *[Llena de angustia]*: ¡Dios santo!

PEDRO *[Acariciador]*:
¡No temas! Ya verás cómo no es nada. 405

[Todos están con las capas puestas, llenos de inquietud.]

CLAVELA *[Entrando casi ahogada]*:
¡Ay señora! ¡Dos hombres embozados,
y Pedrosa con ellos!

MARIANA *[Gritando, llena de pasión]*:
¡Pedro, vete!
¡Y todos, Virgen santa! ¡Pronto!

PEDRO *[Confuso]*: ¡Vamos!

[Clavela quita las copas y apaga los candelabros.]

CONSPIRADOR 4.º:
Es indigno dejarla.

MARIANA *[A Pedro]*: ¡Date prisa!

PEDRO: ¿Por dónde?

MARIANA *[Loca]*:
¡Ay! ¿Por dónde?

CLAVELA: ¡Están llamando! 410

MARIANA *[Iluminada]*:
¡Por aquella ventana del pasillo
saltarás fácilmente! Ese tejado
está cerca del suelo.

CONSPIRADOR 2.º: ¡No debemos
dejarla abandonada!

---

408 Let's go: Pedro's reaction to leave Mariana is hardly that of a gallant, a point underlined immediately by the Fourth Conspirator's remark in line 409 and again by the Second Conspirator in lines 413-14.

<pre>
                And we have every reason to feel low.
MARIANA: In spite of all the trials we must suffer   395
                and worthy reasons for our melancholy...
                [She raises her glass.]
                "When the moon has set, sailors must keep watch".
                That's what they say on the Mediterranean,
                those men who sail the frigates and tall ships.
                Like them we need to keep our eyes wide open!   400
                [As though dreaming.]
                "When the moon has set, sailors must keep watch".
PEDRO [with his glass]:
                And may our houses be like their tall ships.
[They down their drinks. Pause. Offstage a distant knocking is
heard. They all stand holding their glasses in utter silence.]
MARIANA: It was the wind slamming a window shut.
                [Another knock.]
PEDRO: Did you hear that?
FOURTH CONSPIRATOR: Who can it be?
MARIANA [distraught]:   My God!
PEDRO [soothingly]:
                Keep calm, Mariana. Probably there's nothing   405
                to worry about.
[Now they all have their cloaks on and they stand waiting in
great anxiety.]
CLAVELA [entering breathlessly]:
                                Señora, two men
                in cloaks, Pedrosa with them!
MARIANA [crying out passionately]:   Go, Pedro!
                All of you, quick! Holy Virgin!
PEDRO [disorientated]:   Let's go!
[Clavela takes their glasses and extinguishes the candlestick.]
FOURTH CONSPIRATOR:
                To leave her is dishonourable.
MARIANA [to Pedro]:   Quickly!
PEDRO: Which way?
MARIANA [in a frenzy]: You're right! Which way?
CLAVELA: Another knock!
MARIANA [thinking quickly]:
                Your only chance is through the passage window.
                It leads onto a roof from where you'll jump
                to ground quite easily.
SECOND CONSPIRATOR: But it's unworthy
                to leave her all alone!
</pre>

---

397 <u>When the moon has set, sailors must keep watch</u>: Mariana's proverb is
as delightful as it is apt, reminding the conspirators of the continuing
need for vigilance.

121

PEDRO [*Enérgico*]: ¡Es necesario!
¿Cómo justificar nuestra presencia? 415
MARIANA: Sí, sí, vete en seguida. ¡Ponte a salvo!
PEDRO [*Apasionado*]:
¡Adiós, Mariana!
MARIANA: ¡Dios os guarde, amigos!
[*Van saliendo rápidamente por la puerta de la derecha. Clavela
está asomada a una rendija del balcón, que da a la calle. Mariana,
en la puerta, dice.*]
¡Pedro..., y todos, que tengáis cuidado!
[*Cierra la puertecilla de la izquierda, por donde han salido los
Conspiradores, y corre la cortina. Luego, dramática.*]
¡Abre, Clavela! Soy una mujer
que va atada a la cola de un caballo. 420
[*Sale Clavela. Se dirige rápidamente al
fortepiano.*]
¡Dios mío, acuérdate de tu pasión
y de las llagas de tus manos!
[*Se sienta y empieza a cantar la canción del "Contrabandista",
original de Manuel García: 1808.*]
Yo que soy contrabandista
y campo por mis respetos
a todos los desafío, 425
pues a nadie tengo miedo.
¡Ay! ¡Ay!
¡Ay muchachos! ¡Ay muchachas!
¿Quién me compra hilo negro?
Mi caballo está rendido 430
¡Y yo me muero de sueño!
¡Ay!
¡Ay! Que la ronda ya viene
y se empezó el tiroteo.
¡Ay! ¡Ay! Caballito mío, 435
caballo mío careto.

---

420 whom fate has leashed to a runaway horse: the horse is a frequent
symbol in Lorca, and one which interconnects the two themes of passion
and fate. When, in *Blood Wedding*, Leonardo tries to explain his illicit
attraction to the Bride, he says: 'I was riding a horse/and the horse
went to your door', *Obras completas*, II, 600.
422+ Manuel García: Manuel Vicente García (1775–1832) was a famous tenor
and composer from Seville. After rising to fame in Madrid he sang in
Paris, London, Naples and New York and was given principal roles by
Rossini in many operas, including *The Barber of Seville*. His own
compositions have not stood the test of time, but one opera, *El poeta
calculista*, was written in imitation of folk song and included 'The
Smuggler' which became immensely popular. Ironically, Manuel García was
himself attacked by bandits in Veracruz, Mexico, whereupon he returned a
much poorer man to Paris and there founded a school for singers. Lorca's

PEDRO [*forcefully*]:   Though necessary!
        How could we justify our presence here?   415
MARIANA: Of course, you're right. Go quickly! Save yourselves!
PEDRO [*passionately*]:
              Farewell, Mariana!
MARIANA: Friends, God save you all!
[*They leave in haste through the door on the right. Clavela peers
through a slit in the balcony window which overlooks the street.
Mariana is by the door.*]
              And Pedro... all of you, take utmost care!
[*She closes the little side-door through which the Conspirators
have left and draws the curtain. Her voice is now intensely
dramatic.*]
              Clavela, let them in! I feel like one
              whom fate has leashed to a runaway horse!   420
              [*Clavela leaves. Mariana goes quickly to the
                pianoforte.*]
              Oh Lord, think now on your bitter Passion,
              the wounds injustice hammered through your hands!
[*She sits down and begins to sing a song called 'The Smuggler',
written by Manuel García in 1808.*]
              I'm a bonny smuggler
              and smuggling keeps me free;
              I back down to no man   425
              and no man frightens me.
                   Hey! Hey! Hey!
              Hey laddies, hey lassies!
              Come buy my black thread.
              My horse is whipped and blown   430
              and like me is half dead.
                   Hey! Hey! Hey!
              Hey, see the soldiers coming,
              and everybody quakes.
              Hey, see my black beauty,   435
              come on for heaven's sake!

---

use of Manuel García's song is some measure of how well researched the
period aspect of *Mariana Pineda* is.
423 I'm a bonny smuggler: the theme of the fugitive who enjoys a freedom
outside the law is typically Romantic, the most famous example being
Espronceda's 'Canción del pirata' (Pirate's Song), with the refrain that
begins:

| Que es mi barco mi tesoro, | For my boat is my treasure, |
| que es mi Dios la libertad... | and my God is liberty... |

José de Espronceda, *Poesías líricas* (Madrid: Espasa Calpe, 1968), 28.
430-1 My horse...like me is half dead: Lorca wrote several poems on this
theme. In his well-known '*Canción de jinete*' (Rider's Song) the fugitive
knows that he will be killed before he reaches Cordova, while in '*Canción
del jinete (1860)*' (Rider's Song - 1860) the refrain is:

                    ¡Ay!
          ¡Ay! Caballo, ve ligero.
          ¡Ay! Caballo, que me muero.
                    ¡Ay!   440

[*Ha de cantar con un admirable y desesperado sentimiento,
escuchando los pasos de Pedrosa por la escalera.*]
[*Las cortinas del fondo se levantan y aparece Clavela, aterrada,
con el candelabro de tres bujías en una mano y la otra puesta
sobre el pecho. Pedrosa es un tipo seco, de una palidez
intensa y de una admirable serenidad. Dirá las frases con
ironía muy velada y mirará minuciosamente a todos lados, pero
con correción. Es antipático. Hay que huir de la caricatura.
Al entrar Pedrosa, Mariana deja de tocar y se levanta del
fortepiano. Silencio.*]
MARIANA: Adelante.
PEDROSA [*Adelantándose*]:
              Señora, no interrumpa
              por mí la cancioncilla que ahora mismo
              entonaba.
              [*Pausa.*]
MARIANA [*Queriendo sonreír*]:
                    La noche estaba triste
              y me puse a cantar.
              [*Pausa.*]
PEDROSA: He visto luz
              en su balcón y quise visitarla.   445
              Perdone si interrumpo sus quehaceres.
MARIANA: Se lo agradezco mucho.
PEDROSA: ¡Qué manera
              de llover!
[*Pausa. En esta escena habrá pausas imperceptibles y
rotundos silencios instantáneos, en los cuales luchan
desesperadamente las almas de los dos personajes. Escena
delicadísima de matizar, procurando no caer en exageraciones
que perjudiquen su emoción. En esta escena se ha de notar
mucho más lo que no se dice que lo que se está hablando. La
lluvia, discretamente imitada y sin ruido excesivo, llegará de
cuando en cuando a llenar silencios.*]
MARIANA [*Con intención*]:
                    ¿Es muy tarde?
              [*Pausa.*]

Caballito negro.	Little black horse.
¿Dónde llevas tu jinete muerto?	Where are you taking your dead rider
	(*Obras completas*, I, 313, 307)

In all these pieces the narrative level of smuggling and of being hounded
by the authorities is ultimately no more than a vehicle for expressing the
psychical notion of a fatalistic motivation; the horse, representing
instinctual drive, has taken over the rider's will and reason, and leads

Hey! Hey! Hey!
Hey beauty, gallop fast.
Hey beauty, this can't last.
Hey! Hey! Hey!   440
[*This must be sung with an acute sense of desperation as
Mariana listens to Pedrosa's steps on the stairway.*]
[*The curtains upstage rise and Clavela appears. She looks
terrified, with one hand on her breast and the other holding
a candelabrum of three candles. Pedrosa, cloaked and dressed
in black, enters behind her. Pedrosa is a cold fish, intensely
pale, but completely composed. He speaks with veiled irony,
correct in manner, studying everything closely with his eyes.
Though he is thoroughly dislikable, it is important to avoid
caricature. When Pedrosa enters Mariana stops playing and
gets up from the pianoforte. Silence.*]
MARIANA: Come in.
PEDROSA [*coming forward*]:
                  Señora, please, on my account
            don't interrupt that handsome little ditty
            you were singing.
            [*Pause.*]
MARIANA [*trying to smile*]:   The night had such a scowl
            I thought I'd cheer it up.
            [*Pause.*]
PEDROSA: I saw some light
            in your front balcony and took the chance   445
            to visit; but if it's inconvenient...
MARIANA: I'm very glad you did.
PEDROSA: Have you ever
            seen such rain!
[*Pause. In this scene there will be many imperceptible pauses
and sudden gaping silences as the two characters struggle
desperately with unspoken thoughts. It is a challenging and
subtle scene to carry off, and exaggeration should be avoided
at all costs. What is not said is of far greater importance than
the actual dialogue. The sound of rain, discreet rather than
loud; will fill the silences from time to time.*]
MARIANA [*hinting*]:   It must be getting late now.

---

him to an inevitable death. Both the narrative and psychical levels are
fully operational in the play's song.
440+ <u>Pedrosa:</u> the Spanish word for 'stone' is *piedra*, by which association
the name of Granada's Chief of Police suggests such adjectival concepts as
'stony' or 'stone-like'. His stiff, correct manner and, ultimately, his
complete lack of compassion for Mariana, is in keeping with this fortuitous
name-symbolism. Lorca's characterization accords with the notes of an
eye-witness, José Francisco de Luque, who says: 'This official's manner was
polite, but false; he was callous and hypocritical' (Antonina Rodrigo,
op.cit., 74). An account of his historical role in Mariana's execution is
given in the Introduction.

PEDROSA [*Mirándola fijamente, y con intención también*]:
                          ¡Sí! Muy tarde.
        El reloj de la Audiencia ya hace rato
        que dio las once.
MARIANA [*Serena e indicando asiento a Pedrosa*]:
                          No las he sentido.   45(
PEDROSA [*Sentándose*]:
        Yo las sentí lejanas. Ahora vengo
        de recorrer las calles silenciosas,
        calado hasta los huesos por la lluvia,
        resistiendo ese gris fino y glacial
        que viene de la Alhambra.
MARIANA [*Con intención y rehaciéndose*]:
                          El aire helado   455
        que clava agujas sobre los pulmones
        y para el corazón.
PEDROSA [*Devolviéndole la ironía*]:
                          Pues ese mismo.
        Cumplo deberes de mi duro cargo.
        Mientras que usted, espléndida Mariana,
        en su casa, al abrigo de los vientos,   46(
        hace encajes... o borda...
        [*Como recordando.*]
                          ¿Quién me ha dicho
        que bordaba muy bien?
MARIANA [*Aterrada, pero con cierta serenidad*]:
                          ¿Es un pecado?
PEDROSA [*Haciendo una seña negativa*]:
        El Rey nuestro Señor, que Dios proteja,
        [*Se inclina.*]

---

451 from the other side of town: Pedrosa may well have come directly from
the Albaicín district upon discovering the flag.

454 rain that picks like darts/when it comes off the Alhambra: since the
Alhambra overlooks Granada from a vantage point in the Sierra Nevada
foothills, the rain that blows from its direction has an icy bite in winter.
From his comment it seems Pedrosa is less likely to praise Granada's
beauty than he had been, according to Mariana, on a previous occasion
(line 244 of this act). The Alhambra is, of course, the famous fortified
palace built by the Moors and finally lost to Ferdinand and Isabel in 1492
when Moorish dominion in Spain ended. Alhambra comes from *Cala
al-hamra*, meaning 'red fortress', the baked clay stones of its walls having
a reddish tone. Richard Ford says, 'Alhambra, that magical word, which in
the minds of Englishmen is the sum and substance of Granada' (*op.cit.*,
545). The magnificence of the palace and the reluctance of the Moors to
surrender it are caught in a famous traditional ballad, 'Abenámar,
Abenámar', in which a Christian king asks the Moor Abenámar about the
buildings he can see in the distance, and receives the following reply:

126

PEDROSA [*studying her intently and likewise with double
        meaning*]:
            Late indeed! The Audiencia clock struck eleven
            quite a while ago.
MARIANA [*calmly, offering Pedrosa a chair*]: Oh? I didn't hear.450
PEDROSA [*sitting down*]:
            I heard it from the other side of town
            as I came stalking through these silent streets.
            I'm soaked to the skin and my bones are frozen
            from that unholy rain that picks like darts
            when it comes off the Alhambra.
MARIANA [*recovering her composure and again with some intent*]:
                                    That icy wind   455
            can pierce one's lungs with a thousand needles
            and rip one's heart in two.
PEDROSA [*returning her irony*]:   Precisely, madame.
            But I must meet my responsibilities,
            while you, my splendid Mariana, stay home
            and, safely sheltered from winds, pass your time   460
            making lace... or embroidering...
            [*As if trying to remember.*]
                                    Who was it
            told me you sewed divinely?
MARIANA [*unnerved, but maintaining a certain serenity*]:
                                    That's a sin?
PEDROSA [*shaking his head in reply*]:
            Our King and Saviour, whom God protect,
            [*He bows.*]

That is the Alhambra, sir,
and the other is the mosque;
elsewhere you see the Alexares,
so wondrously worked;
the Moor that fashioned them
earned a hundred ducats a day...
The King then speaks:
'Granada, if you are willing,
I will marry you:
for a dowry I will bring you
Cordova and Seville'
only to receive the reply:
But I am married, King Don Juan,
married, not a widow yet;
and the Moor whose wife I am
has a great love for me.
C.C. Smith, *op.cit.*, 126.

<pre>
                    se entretuvo bordando en Valençay
                    con su tío el infante don Antonio.   465
                    Ocupación bellísima.
MARIANA [Entre dientes]:   ¡Dios mío!
PEDROSA: ¿Le extraña mi visita?
MARIANA [Tratando de sonreír]: ¡No!
PEDROSA [Serio]: ·   ¡Mariana!
                    [Pausa.]
                    Una mujer tan bella como usted,
                    ¿no siente miedo de vivir tan sola?
MARIANA: ¿Miedo? ¡Ninguno!
PEDROSA [Con intención]:   Hay tantos liberales   470
                    y tantos anarquistas por Granada,
                    que la gente no vive muy segura.
                    [Firme.]
                    ¡Usted ya lo sabrá!
MARIANA [Digna]:   ¡Señor Pedrosa!
                    ¡Soy mujer de mi casa y nada más!
PEDROSA [Sonriendo]:
                    Y yo soy juez. Por eso me preocupo   475
                    de estas cuestiones. Perdonad, Mariana.
                    Pero hace ya tres meses que ando loco
                    sin poder capturar a un cabecilla...
[Pausa. Mariana trata de escuchar y juega con su sortija,
conteniendo su angustia y su indignación.]
PEDROSA [Como recordando, con frialdad]:
                    Un tal don Pedro de Sotomayor.
MARIANA: Es probable que esté fuera de España.   480
PEDROSA: No; yo espero que pronto será mío.
[Al oír eso Mariana tiene un ligero desvanecimiento nervioso;
lo suficiente para que se le escape la sortija de la mano, o
mas bien, la arroja ella para evitar la conversación.]
</pre>

---

464 Valençay: a village in central France near the Loire, between
Chateauroux and Blois. Ferdinand VII was held captive in its
Renaissance-style chateau from 1808 until Napoleon's defeat in 1814. He
apparently spent much of his time there doing petit point, which adds
another dimension to the play's Penelopean theme of patient waiting but
hardly gives the King a manly image.
465 Prince Don Antonio: Antonio de Borbón (1755–1817), second son of
Charles III and brother of Charles IV; he kept a low profile in affairs of
state, but was indignant at the French suppression of Madrid under Murat
in 1808 and was imprisoned with the future Ferdinand VII at Valençay.
Goya painted his portrait and he also appears in Goya's famous 'Family of
Charles IV' (1800) which is considered one of the most brilliant group
portraits in European painting. In this he stands immediately to the right
of the King.

spent his hours at Valençay embroidering
with Prince Don Antonio, his faithful uncle.   465
It's a most delightful pastime.
MARIANA [*under her breath*]:   My God!
PEDROSA: My presence alarms you?
MARIANA [*trying to smile*]:   Why, no!
PEDROSA [*seriously*]:   Mariana!
            [*Pause.*]
            Doesn't a woman as beautiful as you
            feel a little frightened living alone?
MARIANA: Me? Frightened? Not at all.
PEDROSA [*meaningfully*]:   There are so many   470
            liberal and anarchist types about;
            Granada is hardly the safest place.
            [*Forcefully.*]
            But then, you know that!
MARIANA [*indignant*]:   Señor Pedrosa!
            I'm just a woman who governs her house!
PEDROSA [*smiling*]:
            And I'm a judge. That's why my mind is always   475
            full of such things. Forgive me, please, Mariana,
            but for three months now I've run around like mad
            trying in vain to catch a certain leader...
[*Pause. Mariana plays with her ring as she struggles to contain
her anguish and indignation.*]
PEDROSA [*with a chilling voice as he remembers*]
            A certain Pedro de Sotomayor...
MARIANA: It's quite likely he's out of Spain by now.   480
PEDROSA: Oh, no; I think he'll soon be in my hands.
[*On hearing this Mariana comes close to fainting, and perhaps
from nervousness or else a deliberate ploy to change the course
of the conversation, she drops her ring from her hand to the
floor.*]

---

472 Granada is hardly the safest place: 'No other Spanish city had better
organised secret societies', according to Antonina Rodrigo (*op.cit.*, 17).
474 I'm just a woman who governs her house!: Mariana protests that she
is merely the stereotype of the honourable Spanish woman, as determined
by the infamous proverb: 'Mujer honrada, pierna quebrada, y en casa' (An
honourable woman has a broken leg and stays indoors).
477 For three months now: roughly the length of time which has elapsed
since Pedro escaped from jail in the First Engraving.
481+ Mariana...drops her ring: a melodramatic device, but again in
keeping with the play's Romantic flavour. Given the context of the dialogue,
it is not surprising that Mariana should say it is her wedding ring (line
483) which she has dropped, but, as previously mentioned (note to line
48+, First Engraving), we might well suppose the ring came from Don
Pedro. The fact that this issue remains unclear, however, is consistent
with the reservations we later have about Pedro's true intentions.

MARIANA [*Levantándose*]:
    ¡Mi sortija!
PEDROSA: ¿Cayó?
 [*Con intención.*]
      Tenga cuidado.
MARIANA [*Nerviosa*]:
    Es mi anillo de bodas; no se mueva,
    y vaya a pisarlo. [*Busca.*]
PEDROSA: Está muy bien.
MARIANA: Parece
    que una mano invisible lo arrancó.   485
PEDROSA: Tenga más calma. [*Frío.*] Mire.
[*Señala el sitio donde ve el anillo, al mismo tiempo que avanzan.*]
        ¡Ya está aquí!
[*Mariana se inclina para recogerlo antes que Pedrosa; éste queda
a su lado, y en el momento de levantarse Mariana, la enlaza
rápidamente y la besa.*]
MARIANA [*Dando un grito y retirándose*]:
    ¡Pedrosa!
 [*Pausa. Mariana rompe a llorar de furor.*]
PEDROSA [*Suave*]:
    Grite menos.
MARIANA: ¡Virgen Santa!
PEDROSA [*Sentándose*]:
    Me parece que este llanto está de más.
    Mi señora Mariana, esté serena.
MARIANA [*Arrancándose desesperada y cogiendo a Pedrosa
    por la solapa*]
    ¿Qué piensa de mí? ¡Diga!
PEDROSA [*Impasible*]:   Muchas cosas.   490
MARIANA: Pues yo sabré vencerlas. ¿Qué pretende?
    Sepa que yo no tengo miedo a nadie.
    Como el agua que nace soy de limpia,
    y me puedo manchar si usted me toca;
    pero sé defenderme. ¡Salga pronto!   495
PEDROSA [*Fuerte y lleno de ira*]:
    ¡Silencio!
 [*Pausa. Frío.*]
     Quiero ser amigo suyo.
    Me debe agradecer esta visita.
MARIANA [*Fiera*]:
    ¿Puedo yo permitir que usted me insulte?
    ¿Que penetre de noche en mi vivienda
    para que yo...? ¡Canalla! No sé cómo...   500
    [*Se contiene.*]

---

493 <u>My honour</u>: as the projection of tight-laced Christian morality in
Spanish society, honour was the *sine qua non* of traditional Spanish

MARIANA [*standing up*]:
      My ring!
PEDROSA: Has it fallen?
      [*Pointedly.*]   Be very careful!
MARIANA [*upset*]:
      It's my wedding ring. Stay just where you are;
      you might tread on it. [*She looks for it.*]
PEDROSA: Don't worry.
MARIANA: It seemed
      as if an unseen hand snatched it from me.   485
PEDROSA: There's no need to panic. [*Coldly.*] Look.
[*He points to where the ring is and the two of them move towards it.*]
                       Can you see?
[*Mariana bends to reach it before Pedrosa; he stays by her side
and, just as she gets up, embraces her quickly and kisses her.*]
MARIANA [*letting out a shriek and pulling herself away*]:
      Pedrosa!
      [*Pause. Mariana bursts into tears of anger.*]
PEDROSA [*softly*]:   Not so loud.
MARIANA: Mother of God!
PEDROSA [*sitting down*]:
      That seems a trifle excessive to me.
      My dear lady, Mariana, please keep calm!
MARIANA [*moving with sudden desperation to grasp Pedrosa
      by the lapels*]:
      What do you think of me? Say?
PEDROSA [*unperturbed*]:   Quite a lot.   490
MARIANA: If that's what you take me for, you're quite wrong.
      And let me tell you, no one frightens me.
      My honour is as clean as mountain water
      and I've no wish to be sullied by you.
      I can protect myself, you know. Now go!   495
PEDROSA [*loud and full of anger*]:
      Be quiet!
      [*Pause.*]
      [*Icily.*] My wish is to be your friend.
      You ought to thank me for this evening's visit.
MARIANA [*uncontrollably*]:
      And should I allow you to insult me?
      Should I give you free passage to my house
      at night?... that you might commit... unspeakable...
      [*She restrains herself.*]

---

drama; the plots of Golden Age and Romantic plays mostly revolve around
the repercussions that followed the loss of family honour, this being so
precariously dependent for the most part upon female caprice.

<pre>
                    ¡Usted quiere perderme!
PEDROSA [Cálido]:   ¡Lo contrario!
          Vengo a salvarla.
MARIANA [Bravía]:   ¡No lo necesito! [Pausa.]
PEDROSA [Fuerte y dominador, acercándose con una agria
sonrisa]:
          ¡Mariana! ¿Y la bandera?
MARIANA [Turbada]:   ¿Qué bandera?
PEDROSA: ¡La que bordó con esas manos blancas
          [Las coge.]
          en contra de las leyes y del Rey!   505
MARIANA: ¿Qué infame le minitió?
PEDROSA [Indiferente]:   ¡Muy bien bordada!
          De tafetán morado y verdes letras.
          Allá en el Albaicín, la recogimos,
          y ya está en mi poder como tu vida.
          Pero no temas; soy amigo tuyo.   510
          [Mariana queda ahogada.]
MARIANA [Casi desmayada]:
          Es mentira, mentira.
PEDROSA: Sé también
          que hay mucha gente complicada.
          Espero que dirás sus nombres, ¿Verdad?
          [Bajando la voz y apasionadamente.]
          Nadie sabrá lo que ha pasado. Yo te quiero
          mía, ¿lo estás oyendo? Mía o muerta.   515
          Me has despreciado siempre; pero ahora
          puedo apretar tu cuello con mis manos,
          este cuello de nardo transparente,
</pre>

504 The flag you sewed: with the consummate skill of an interrogator Pedrosa has advanced step by step from stating that Mariana is a fine seamstress (line 462), to suggesting she knows all about Granada's subversives (line 473), to mention of Don Pedro (line 479), finally to the dropping of this bombshell.

507 in purple taffeta, letters in green: Lorca strays only slightly from historical fact here, for while the flag was in purple taffeta, the green was a triangle at the flag's centre and the letters were in red. Only six of the letters had been sewn on, but the remainder found loose with the flag left no doubt that the three words to be placed at the triangle's points were Libertad, Igualdad and Ley (Freedom, Equality, Law), all of which were in capitals (Antonina Rodrigo, op.cit., 108-9).

508 We found it...: historically, as mentioned in the Introduction, the flag came into Pedrosa's hands because one of the two sisters to whom Mariana had entrusted it was attached to a young cleric who happened to be the son of a staunch royalist. The cleric, convinced of the imminent success of a liberal uprising, warned his father to moderate his views, but the latter, extracting information about the flag, went straight to the police. The poor seamstresses did not resist interrogation for long and, after informing as to who had sent them the flag, were richly rewarded with 400 reales,

```
                    You'd see me ruined!
PEDROSA [suggestively]:           Quite the opposite!
            I've come to save you.
MARIANA [angrily]:              I don't need your help! [Pause.]
PEDROSA [strong and authoritatively, with a cruel smile on his
        face as he draws closer]:
            Mariana, what about that flag?
MARIANA [disturbed]:                        What flag?
PEDROSA:    The flag you sewed with these two lovely hands,
            [He takes them in his own.]
            in contravention of the King and courts.         505
MARIANA:    Who told you such a lie?
PEDROSA:                    And sewed so well,
            in purple taffeta, letters in green.
            We found it over in the Albaicín,
            and now, just like your life, it's in my hands.
            But never fear, Mariana, I'm your friend.         510
            [Mariana is almost speechless.]
MARIANA [nearly passing out]:
            It's lies, all lies.
PEDROSA:                    I also know, of course,
            that quite a number are involved in this.
            And I'll expect you to give me their names.
            [Lowering his voice and growing passionate.]
            No one will know what's happened.  I want you
            for my own, you understand?  Mine or dead.        515
            You've always despised me, but from now on
            my hands have the power to squeeze your neck,
            your lovely neck of tuberose and gossamer;
```

---

that is, 100 pesetas, or, by today's exchange rates, about 50 English
pence. (Antonina Rodrigo, op.cit., 107-8).
515 Mine or dead: this compression of the alternatives that face Mariana is
highly effective in dramatic terms, but perhaps a little misleading; for
while Lorca follows the popular view of Pedrosa having lecherous intentions
towards Mariana, there is no doubt that both in the play and in history
her ultimate choice is between death and turning informant.
517 the power to squeeze your neck: the erotic and punitive implications
of this phrase totally conflate, suggesting sadism in Pedrosa and, of
course, tender vulnerability in Mariana.
518 tuberose: the tuberose, or nard, or spikenard, is a fragrant plant
which has been used since ancient times to make ointments to adorn
bodies. Frequently referred to in the Bible, notably in the 'Song of
Solomon' which firmly established its erotic significance, it is also often
found in Lorca, as for instance in the poems from Gypsy Ballads, 'Ballad
of the Moon, Moon', 'Martyrdom of Saint Olalla' and 'The Unfaithful Wife'
which describes the adultress's beauty in these terms:

| Ni nardos ni caracolas | Neither tuberoses nor sea shells |
| tienen el cutis tan fino... | have a skin so smooth... |

(Obras completas, I, 406)

y me querrás porque te doy la vida.

MARIANA [*Tierna y suplicante en medio de su desesperación, abrazándose a Pedrosa*]:

¡Tenga piedad de mí! ¡Si usted supiera!   520
Y déjeme escapar. Yo guardaré
su recuerdo en las niñas de mis ojos.
¡Pedrosa, por mis hijos!...

PEDROSA [*Abrazándola, sensual*]:   La bandera
no la has bordado tú, linda Mariana,
y ya eres libre porque así lo quiero...   525

[*Mariana, al ver cerca de sus labios los labios de Pedrosa, lo rechaza, reaccionando de una manera salvaje.*]

MARIANA: ¡Eso nunca! ¡Primero doy mi sangre!
Que me cueste dolor, pero con honra.
¡Salga de aquí!

PEDROSA [*Reconviniéndola*]:
          ¡Mariana!

MARIANA: ¡Salga pronto!

PEDROSA [*Frío y reservado*]:
          ¡Está muy bien! Yo seguiré el asunto
y usted misma se pierde.

MARIANA: ¡Qué me importa!   530
Yo bordé con mis manos;
con estas manos, ¡mírelas, Pedrosa!,
y conozco muy grandes caballeros
que izarla pretendían en Granada.
¡Mas no diré sus nombres!

PEDROSA: ¡Por la fuerza   535
delatará! ¡Los hierros duelen mucho,
y una mujer es siempre una mujer!
¡Cuando usted quiera me avisa!

MARIANA: ¡Cobarde!
¡Aunque en mi corazón clavaran vidrios
no hablaría! ¡Pedrosa, aquí me tiene!   540

PEDROSA: ¡Ya veremos!...

MARIANA: ¡Clavela, el candelabro!

[*Entra Clavela, aterrada, con las manos cruzadas sobre el pecho.*]

PEDROSA: No hace falta, señora. Queda usted
detenida en nombre de la ley.

MARIANA: ¿En nombre de qué ley?

PEDROSA [*Frío y ceremonioso*]:   ¡Muy buenas noches!
          [*Sale.*]

---

536 Iron has a way...: torture was still a legitimate part of the legal system under Ferdinand VII, a king who had reintroduced the Inquisition. Some of Goya's drawings illustrate the types of 'iron' used. Mariana,

MARIANA [embracing Pedrosa, soft and pleading in her
      desperation]:
        and love me you will, if I spare your life.

        Have pity on me, for the love of God!   520
        If only you'd let me escape I'd always
        keep a tender place for you in my heart ...
        Pedrosa... for my children's sake...!
PEDROSA [embracing her sensually]:   That flag
        wasn't made by you, my lovely Mariana,
        and you are free because I wish it so...   525
[Seeing Pedrosa's lips draw near her own, Mariana repulses
him in a fierce reaction.]
MARIANA: No! Never that! I'd sooner spill my blood!
        If I must suffer, let it be with honour.
        Get out of here!
PEDROSA [matching her anger]:
                     Mariana!
MARIANA: Out, at once!
PEDROSA [assuming an icy calm]:
        As you wish! But the matter will not rest,
        and this way you are lost.
MARIANA: What do I care!   530
        I chose to sew that flag with my own hands,
        with these two hands; you see them here, Pedrosa?
        And I know all the honourable men
        whose dream it was to hoist it in Granada.
        But I will never say their names!
PEDROSA: We'll see   535
        about that! Iron has a way of loosening
        the tongue, especially when it comes to women!
        Let me know when you're ready to talk.
MARIANA: Coward!
        Not even under torture will I talk!
        Rip out my heart, Pedrosa, it won't help!   540
PEDROSA: We'll see.
MARIANA: Clavela, bring the candlestick!
[Clavela enters terrified, her hands crossed over her chest.]
PEDROSA: I can find my way. As for you, Señora,
        I arrest you in the name of the Law.
MARIANA: In the name of what law?
PEDROSA [with chilling politeness]:   Good night to you!
        [He leaves.]

---

however, was spared that test.
543 I arrest you: true to history, since Mariana was initially placed under
house arrest.

135

CLAVELA [*Dramática*]:
        ¡Ay, señora; mi niña, clavelito,   545
        prenda de mis entrañas!
MARIANA [*Llena de angustia y terror*]:
                      Isabel,
        yo me voy. Dame el chal.
CLAVELA: ¡Sálvese pronto!
[*Se asoma a la ventana. Fuera se oye otra vez la fuerte lluvia.*]
MARIANA: ¡Me iré a casa de don Luis! ¡Cuida los niños!
CLAVELA: ¡Se han quedado en la puerta! ¡No se puede!
MARIANA: Claro está.
[*Señalando al sitio por donde han salido los Conspiradores.*]
              ¡Por aquí!
CLAVELA: ¡Es imposible!   550
[*Al cruzar Mariana, por la puerta aparece Doña Angustias.*]
ANGUSTIAS: ¡Mariana! ¿Dónde vas? Tu niña llora.
        Tiene miedo del aire y de la lluvia.
MARIANA: ¡Estoy presa! ¡Estoy presa, Clavela!
ANGUSTIAS [*Abrazándola*]:
        ¡Marianita!
MARIANA [*Arrojándose en el sofá*]:
           ¡Ahora empiezo a morir!
[*Las dos mujeres la abrazan.*]
        Mírame y llora. ¡Ahora empiezo a morir!   555
           Télon rápido

A drawing of Lorca's for Mariana

---

551 <u>Your daughter/is crying</u>: once again the act closes with a reminder of Mariana's responsibility towards her children, it being patently clear that she has not heeded the warning Angustias gave her at the end of the First Engraving.

136

CLAVELA [*tragically*]:
>Señora, my dearest, my precious angel,   545
>light of my eyes, my only jov!

MARIANA [*full of anguish and fear*]:   Isabel,
>I'll have to leave. Bring my shawl.

CLAVELA: You must run!

[*She looks out of the window. Once again a heavy rain is heard outside.*]

MARIANA: I'll go to Don Luis! Look after the children!

CLAVELA: Some men are at the door. There's no way out!

MARIANA: Of course.
>[*Pointing to where the Conspirators left.*]
>There is one way!

CLAVELA: That's impossible!   550

[*As Mariana crosses the stage Angustias appears at the door.*]

ANGUSTIAS: Mariana! Where are you going? Your daughter
>is crying. The rainstorm frightened her.

MARIANA: I'm trapped, Clavela, trapped! There's no way out!

ANGUSTIAS [*embracing her*]:
>Marianita!

MARIANA [*throwing herself on the sofa*]:
>My time has come already!
>[*The two women embrace her.*]
>Take pity on me, for my time has come!   555
>*The curtain falls quickly*

A drawing of Lorca's for Mariana

---

555 my time has come: the theme of being inexorably fated to die and, therefore, of being already dead when alive, is central to the mood of the act which follows. It is a typically Lorquian theme which finds its clearest poetic expression in the 'Ballad of the Doomed Man' in *Gypsy Ballads, Obras completas*, I, 423.

Convento de Santa María Egipcíaca, de Granada. Rasgos árabes.
Arcos, cipreses, fuentecillas y arrayanes. Hay unos bancos y
unas viejas sillas de cuero. Al levantarse el telón está la escena
solitaria. Suenan el órgano y las lejanas voces de las monjas. Por
el fondo vienen corriendo de puntillas y mirando a todos lados para
que no las vean dos Novicias. Visten toquitas blancas y trajes
azules. Se acercan con mucho sigilo a una puerta de la izquierda
y miran por el ojo de la cerradura.

NOVICIA 1.   :
                     ¿Qué hace?
NOVICIA 2.   [*En la cerradura*] :
                              ¡Habla más bajito!
                     Está rezando.
NOVICIA 1.   :
                     ¡Deja!
                     [*Se pone a mirar.*]
                     ¡Qué blanca está, qué blanca!
                     Reluce su cabeza
                     en la sombra del cuarto.   5
NOVICIA 2.   :
                     ¿Reluce su cabeza?
                     Yo no comprendo nada.
                     Es una mujer buena,
                     y la quieren matar,
                     ¿Tú qué dices?
NOVICIA 1.   :   Quisiera   10
                     mirar su corazón
                     largo rato y muy cerca.

Convent of Saint Mary of Egypt in Granada: founded in 1602, this convent
was a corrective detention centre for women, mainly prostitutes, who were
there looked after considerably by nuns. It came to be known as the
'Convent of Sheltered Women' and the street in the centre of Granada in
which it is located is today called 'Calle de la Recogidas' or 'Street of the
Sheltered', though its original meaning is not widely known (Antonina
Rodrigo, *op.cit.*, 125). Saint Mary of Egypt or 'the Pentitent', born *circa*
354, had herself been a prostitute in Alexandria before experiencing a
miraculous conversion in Jerusalem where she had travelled, plying her
trade, for the festivities of the Holy Cross. Inspired to enter the desert
on the other side of the River Jordan, she spent forty-seven years in
complete solitude until discovered by Saint Zosino who gave her the
Blessed Sacrament and, one year later, a Christian burial.
      Mariana Pineda entered the convent on March 27, 1831, and spent the
last two months of her life there. Lorca condenses this into the final act's
time scale of one day, Mariana's last day at the convent, but in so doing

THIRD ENGRAVING

*The Convent of Saint Mary of Egypt in Granada, Moorish
architectural features. Archways, cypress trees, myrtles
and small fountains. Some benches and old leather seats.
When the curtain rises the stage is empty. An organ plays
and nuns' voices are heard distantly. Two Novice Nuns
enter upstage, running on tiptoe and looking all around to
make sure they are not being watched. They are dressed
in blue with a white headdress. They make their way
secretively to a door on the left where they peep through
the keyhole.*

FIRST NOVICE:
    What's she doing?

SECOND NOVICE [*looking through the keyhole*]:
        Quiet!
    She's praying.

FIRST NOVICE: Let me look!
    [*She looks through the keyhole.*]
    How white she is! So white!
    Her whole face seems to shine
    in the room's deep shadow.   5

SECOND NOVICE:
    Her whole face is lit up.
    I can't understand it:
    an innocent woman
    and they want to kill her.
    What do you make of it?   10

FIRST NOVICE:
    I'd like to take a good
    long look into her heart.

---

he loses nothing in terms of atmosphere and tension as the fateful moment
of execution draws near. In setting the act in the convent's patio-garden
Lorca achieves both a sense of physical confinement and spiritual freedom:
the white walls clearly imprison Mariana, but the space is embellished with
trees and fountains, and, in marked contrast to the previous scenes, is
open to the sky, a lovely springtime sky whose lighting is of special
interest to the playwright later on.

Novice Nuns: young girls who have entered a religious order but who have
yet to make a solemn profession of their vows.

they peep through the keyhole: this recalls Angustias's remark at the
beginning of the First Engraving, line 2; but whereas Angustias spied on
Mariana sewing, the nuns see her praying, a telling juxtaposition.

3 How white she is! So white!: the colour white, predominant in Salvador
Dalí's original scenography, is immediately associated with Mariana and it
evidently suggests her spiritual purity as she prepares to make the
ultimate sacrifice.

```
NOVICIA 2.  :
                ¡Qué mujer tan valiente!
                Cuando ayer vinieron
                a leerle la sentencia                              15
                de muerte, no ocultó
                su sonrisa.
NOVICIA 1.  :            En la iglesia
                la vi después llorando
                y me pareció que ella
                tenía el corazón en la garganta.                   20
                ¿Qué es lo que ha hecho?
NOVICIA 2.  :
                Bordó una bandera.
NOVICIA 1.  :
                ¿Bordar es malo?
NOVICIA 2.  :
                Dicen que es masona.
NOVICIA 1.  :
                ¿Qué es eso?
NOVICIA 2.  :            Pues... ¡no sé!                            25
NOVICIA 1.  :
                ¿Por qué está presa?
NOVICIA 2.  :
                Porque no quiere al rey.
NOVICIA 1.  :
                ¿Qué más da? ¿Se habrá visto?
NOVICIA 2.  :
                ¡Ni a la reina!
NOVICIA 1.  :
                Yo tampoco los quiero.                             30
                [Mirando.]
                ¡Ay Mariana Pineda!
                Ya están abriendo flores
                que irán contigo muerta.
[Aparece por la puerta del foro la Madre Sor Carmen Borja.]
CARMEN:         Pero, niñas, ¿qué miráis?
NOVICIA 1.  [Asustada]:
                Hermana...
CARMEN:              ¿No os da verguenza?                          35
```

---

16 her smile: the smile which appears so often on Mariana's face in this act is highly evocative and ambiguous: at times it suggests her irrational conviction that she will be saved at the last moment, but more consistently it conveys the inner serenity and quasi-mystical state of one who scarcely seems to belong to this world any longer.

29 the Queen: María Cristina of Naples, whom Ferdinand VII had taken as his fourth wife in December 1830. She was to be queen regent, 1834-1840, but was an unpopular figure.

SECOND NOVICE:
        She's such a brave woman!
        Yesterday when they came
        to read out her sentence   15
        of death, her smile never
        flickered.
FIRST NOVICE: But afterwards
        in church I saw her cry
        and it seemed like her heart
        was bursting in her throat.   20
        So what can she have done?
SECOND NOVICE:
        She embroidered a flag.
FIRST NOVICE:
        Is that so bad to do?
SECOND NOVICE:
        They say she's a mason.
FIRST NOVICE:
        What's that?
SECOND NOVICE: Oh, don't ask me!   25
FIRST NOVICE:
        Why is she held captive?
SECOND NOVICE:
        Because she doesn't like
        the King.
FIRST NOVICE: Well, I'll be blowed!
        And so what?
SECOND NOVICE: Nor the Queen!
FIRST NOVICE:
        Nor do I, come to that.   30
        [*Looking again.*]
        Oh, Mariana Pineda!
        The flowers now in bloom
        will lie on your coffin.
[*The Mother Superior, Sister Carmen de Borja, appears at the door upstage.*]
CARMEN: Come, girls! What are you looking at?
FIRST NOVICE [*startled*]:
        Oh, Sister...
CARMEN: Aren't you both ashamed?   35

32-3 The flowers now in bloom...: an image which suggests the imminence of Mariana's death. Such images are important insofar as they help to create a temporal illusion in this act which seems to cover an extended period of confinement and yet all happens within the space of one day.
33+ The Mother Superior, Sister Carmen de Borja: the governess of the convent-prison whose name is presumably fictitious.

Ahora mismo, al obrador.
¿Quién os enseño esa fea
costumbre? ¡Ya nos veremos!

NOVICIA 1.	:
¡Con licencia!

NOVICIA 2.	:	¡Con licencia!

[*Se van. Cuando la Madre Carmen se ha convencido de que las
otras se han marchado, se acerca tambien con sigilo y mira por
el ojo de la llave.*]

CARMEN :	¡Es inocente! ¡No hay duda!	40
¡Calla con una firmeza!
¿Por qué? Yo no me lo explico.
[*Sobresaltada.*]
¡Viene!
[*Sale corriendo.*]

[*Mariana aparece con un espléndido traje blanco. Está palidísima.*]

MARIANA :	¡Hermana!

CARMEN [*Volviéndose*]:¿Qué desea?

MARIANA :
¡Nada!

CARMEN :	¡Decidlo, señora!

MARIANA :	Pensaba...

CARMEN :	¿Qué?

MARIANA :	Si pudiera	45
quedarme aquí, en el Beaterio,
para siempre.

CARMEN :	¡Qué contentas
nos pondríamos!

MARIANA :	¡No puedo!

CARMEN :	¿Por qué?

MARIANA [*Sonriendo*]: Porque ya estoy muerta.

CARMEN [*Asustada*]:
¡Doña Mariana, por Dios!	50

MARIANA :
Pero el mundo se me acerca,
las piedras, el agua, el aire,
¡comprendo que estaba ciega!

CARMEN :	¡La indultarán!

MARIANA [*Con sangre fría*]:¡Ya veremos!
Este silencio me pesa	55

39+ goes to look secretively through the keyhole: a humorous and very
human touch which neatly rounds off the playful-cum-tragic scene with the
novices. It is noticeable that Lorca provides a brief moment of gaiety at
the beginning of all three acts.

43 a splendid white costume: the costume matches Mariana's other-worldly
complexion and gives her a striking aura on stage.

49 For I'm already dead: Mariana's mental state hovers precariously
between the visionary and the deranged, and it is Lorca's poeticisation of
her psyche and of her neurosis which holds the final act together.

<pre>
                 To the workroom with you, at once.
                 Who taught you such frightful habits?
                 Look out! I'll speak to you later!
FIRST NOVICE:
                 Please excuse me!
SECOND NOVICE: Please excuse me!
[They leave. When Mother Carmen is sure they have gone she
too goes to look secretively through the keyhole.]
CARMEN: She's innocent! Who can doubt it?   40
                 And so determined not to speak!
                 But why? I can't understand it.
                 [Alarmed.]
                 She's coming!
                 [She runs off.]
[Mariana appears in a splendid white costume. She is extremely pale.]
MARIANA: Sister!
CARMEN [turning round]:   What is it?
MARIANA: Oh, nothing...
CARMENT: Please tell me, Señora.
MARIANA: I was thinking...
CARMEN: What?
MARIANA: If only   45
                 I could stay here in the convent
                 for ever.
CARMEN: Yes! How happy that
                 would make us all!
MARIANA: But I cannot!
CARMEN: Why not?
MARIANA [smiling]:   For I'm already dead.
CARMEN [startled]:
                 Doña Mariana, God save you!   50
MARIANA: The world is pressing in on me
                 with all its stones, water and air.
                 I know full well how blind I was!
CARMEN: You will be pardoned!
MARIANA [chillingly]:   I doubt it!
                 This silence casts a magic spell   55
</pre>

51-2 **The world is pressing in on me...**: the images which come from
Mariana's lips now seem imbued with religious meaning and they evoke not
only the sense of being buried alive but also a mystical perception that all
things of the bodily world are dross.
53 **I know full well how blind I was!**: again this line, which is later
repeated, seems to suggest more than the simple realisation that she has
been mistaken in the practical aspects of her life; rather, one senses in it
a new awareness of deeper, spiritual values.
55-9 **This silence**: the silence of the convent links also with the silence of
the grave, thus the seductive images of violets and locks of silky hair

```
                    mágicamente.  Se agranda
                    como un techo de violetas,
                    [Apasionada.]
                    y otras veces finge en mí
                    una larga cabellera.
                    ¡Ay, qué buen soñar!
CARMEN [Cogiéndole la mano]:      ¡Mariana!                    6(
MARIANA:            ¿Cómo soy yo?
CARMEN:                          Eres muy buena.
MARIANA:            Soy una gran pecadora;
                    pero amé de una manera
                    que Dios me perdonará
                    como a Santa Magdalena.                    6!
CARMEN:             Fuera del mundo y en él
                    perdona.
MARIANA:                    ¡Si usted supiera!
                    ¡Estoy muy herida, hermana,
                    por las cosas de la tierra!
CARMEN:             Dios está lleno de heridas                7(
                    de amor, que nunca se cierran.
MARIANA:            Nace el que muere sufriendo,
                    ¡comprendo que estaba ciega!
CARMEN [Apenada al ver el estado de Mariana]:
                    ¡Hasta luego!  ¿Asistirá
                    esta tarde a la novena?                    7!
MARIANA:            Como siempre.  ¡Adiós, hermana!
                    [Se va Carmen.]
[Mariana se dirige al fondo rápidamente, con todo género de
precauciones, y allí aparece Alegrito, jardinero del convento.
Ríe constantemente, con una sonrisa suave y sana.  Viste
traje de cazador de la época.]
MARIANA:            ¡Alegrito!  ¿Qué?
ALEGRITO:                          ¡Paciencia
                    para lo que vais a oír!
MARIANA:            ¡Habla pronto, no vos vean!
                    ¿Fuiste a casa de don Luis?                80
ALEGRITO:           Y me han dicho que les era
                    imposible pretender
                    salvarla.  Que ni lo intentan,
```

---

suggest that Mariana has already surrendered psychologically to the notion
of rest and release.
65 Saint Magdalen: Mary Magdalen, or Magdaleine, from whom Jesus cast
out seven evil spirits. She had been a sinner, but repented and wiped
Jesus' feet with her own hair, which is one of the favourite topics by
which she appears in Renaissance art. She was possibly also the same
Mary who was the first to see Jesus after he had risen.
68-9 how sorely grieved I am...: the lines again seem to point towards
religious enlightenment as much as worldly disillusion.

```
                    on me and soothes my soul.  At times
                    it seems to spread like violets
                    on the earth, [passionately] and then it's smooth
                    like locks of silky hair combed high.
                    How nice it is to dream!
CARMEN [taking her by the hand]:    Mariana!                       60
MARIANA:        How am I, then?
CARMEN:                            Your soul is good.
MARIANA:        No, I'm a terrible sinner;
                    but I have loved with such a force
                    that God will surely pardon me,
                    as Saint Magdalen was pardoned.                 65
CARMEN:         Outside as well as in this world
                    we find forgiveness.
MARIANA:                            If you knew,
                    Sister, how sorely grieved I am
                    by everything I find on earth!
CARMEN:         God too is full of love's harsh wounds,            70
                    and they are wounds that never heal.
MARIANA:        Reborn is he who dies in pain.
                    I know full well how blind I was!
CARMEN [deeply troubled by Mariana's state]:
                    Goodbye for now.  Will you be coming
                    to this afternoon's novena?                     75
MARIANA:        Yes, of course.  We'll talk then, Sister.
                    [Carmen leaves.]
[Mariana goes quickly upstage, very circumspect in her movements,
and there the convent gardener, Alegrito, appears.  He is a very
cheerful person, with a good-natured laugh and almost permanent
smile.  He is dressed in the hunting clothes of the period.]
MARIANA:        Alegrito!  What news have you?
ALEGRITO:      My lady, prepare for the worst!
MARIANA:        Speak quickly, in case they see us!
                    Did you go to Don Luis's house?                 80
ALEGRITO:      I did, and I've been told it was
                    impossible for them to try
                    to save you.  Nor do they plan to,
```

---

73 I know full well...: repeating line 53, but in a more markedly religious
context.
75 novena: a religious service held, literally, for nine consecutive days
and which usually implores the protection or divine intercession of Christ
or a saint.
76+ Alegrito: the name itself means cheerful in Spanish, being the
diminutive of 'alegre', happy.
80 Don Luis's house: we remember Don Pedro had sheltered there
following his escape from prison (line 389, First Engraving).

```
                porque todos morirían;
                pero que harán lo que puedan.                    85
MARIANA [Valiente]:
                ¡Lo harán todo! ¡Estoy segura!
                Son gentes de la nobleza,
                y yo soy noble, Alegrito.
                ¿No ves cómo estoy serena?
ALEGRITO:       Hay un miedo que da miedo.                       90
                Las calles están desiertas.
                Solo el viento viene y va;
                pero la gente se encierra.
                No encontré más que una niña
                llorando sobre la puerta                         95
                de la antigua Alcaicería.
MARIANA:        ¿Crees que van a dejar que muera
                la que tiene menos culpa?
ALEGRITO:       Yo no sé lo que ellos piensan.
MARIANA:        ¿Y de lo demás?
ALEGRITO [Turbado]:             ¡Señora!...                      100
MARIANA:        Sigue hablando.
ALEGRITO:                       No quisiera.
                [Mariana hace un gesto de impaciencia.]
                El caballero don Pedro
                de Sotomayor se aleja
                de España, según me han dicho.
                Dicen que marcha a Inglaterra.                   105
                Don Luis lo sabe de cierto.
MARIANA [Sonríe incrédula y dramática, porque en el fondo
                sabe que es verdad]:
                Quien te lo dijo desea
                aumentar mi sufrimiento.
                ¡Alegrito, no lo creas!
```

---

85 they'll do what they can: in view of the fact that no attempt is made to save Mariana, one wonders what indeed the conspirators did do on her behalf.

94-5 just one girl...outside the old Alcaicería: the image of a single girl in the deserted streets is a lyrical echo of the Prologue. It reminds us too of Mariana's own children and prepares us for the theme, soon to be developed, that Mariana's sacrifice is for the wellbeing of future generations. Finally, the image echoes a poignant moment in the ancient epic ballad, *Poem of the Cid*: when the Cid was banished from Burgos by King Alfonso VI, only one nine year old girl dared to defy the royal order by going out into the deserted streets to speak to the great warrior.

The Alcaicería was located in the centre of Granada, near the Cathedral and Bibarrambla Square. Richard Ford: 'On leaving the Cathedral enter the Zacatín, the "shopping street" of now decayed Granada; to the left is the *Alcaiseria* (sic), which previously to the sad

```
                    since all would surely die in vain.
                    But they say they'll do what they can.          85
MARIANA [bravely]:
                    They will do all they can, I'm sure!
                    For they are high nobility,
                    as I, too, am noble, Alegrito.
                    You see how calm I keep myself?
ALEGRITO:           Fear has a way of spreading fear.              90
                    The streets are all deserted now,
                    with only the wind passing through,
                    and every living soul indoors.
                    I saw just one girl all alone
                    outside the old Alcaicería,                    95
                    sobbing her eyes out by its door.
MARIANA:            And do you think they'd kill someone
                    who is not guilty of a crime?
ALEGRITO:           I don't know what they plan to do.
MARIANA:            What about the rest?
ALEGRITO [distressed]:              Señora...!                     100
MARIANA:            Come on, tell me.
ALEGRITO:                           I'd rather not.
                    [Mariana shows her impatience.]
                    According to what I've been told,
                    Don Pedro de Sotomayor
                    is now leaving Spain. Señora.
                    They say he's sailing for England.             105
                    Don Luis knows this for definite.
MARIANA [smiling dramatically and incredulously, though in her
          heart she knows it is true]:
                    Whoever told you such a lie
                    wished only to double my grief.
                    Alegrito, don't believe it!
```

---

fire in 1843, was an identical Moorish bazar, with small Tetuan-like shops, and closed at night by doors' (op.cit., 583).
102-3 Don Pedro de Sotomayor/is now leaving Spain: this flat announcement of Don Pedro's name in full is very apt; not only does it leave Mariana no room for doubt on receiving the devastating news, it also lends bitter irony by contrasting the noble ring of his appellations with his ungallant flight. Speculation as to a possible rescue attempt virtually ends with this news; that Lorca should have introduced it at such an early point in the act is itself an indication that his dramatic focus falls increasingly on his heroine's psychic make-up as opposed to plot.
107 Whoever told you such a lie: Mariana's rejection of undisputable truth and her subsequent recourse to delusion are psychologically convincing features which conform to well known patterns of neurotic behaviour, notably the self-defensive mechanism of fleeing from reality. The so-called Ganser syndrome, typically illustrated in the prisoner who awaits trial or execution, is characterised by the abrupt loss of the ability to reason.

	¿Verdad que tú no lo crees?	110

[*Angustiada.*]

ALEGRITO [*Turbado*]:
Señora, lo que usted quiera.

MARIANA: Don Pedro vendrá a caballo
como loco cuando sepa
que yo estoy encarcelada
por bordarle su bandera.   115
Y, si me matan, vendrá
para morir a mi vera,
que me lo dijo una noche
besándome la cabeza.
El vendrá como un San Jorge   120
de diamantes y agua negra,
al aire la deslumbrante
flor de su capa bermeja.
Y porque es noble y modesto,
para que nadie lo vea,   125
vendrá por la madrugada,
por la madrugada fresca,
cuando sobre el cielo oscuro
brilla el limonar apenas
y el alba finge en las olas   130
fragatas de sombra y seda.
¿Tú qué sabes? ¡Qué alegría!
No tengo miedo, ¿te enteras?

ALEGRITO: ¡Señora!

MARIANA: ¿Quién te lo ha dicho?

ALEGRITO: Don Luis.

MARIANA: ¿Sabe la sentencia?   135

ALEGRITO: Dijo que no la creía.

MARIANA [*Angustiada*]:
Pues es muy verdad.

ALEGRITO: Me apena
darle tan malas noticias.

MARIANA: ¡Volverás!

ALEGRITO: Lo que usted quiera.

MARIANA: Volverás para decirles   140
que yo estoy muy satisfecha
porque sé que vendrán todos,
¡y son muchos!, cuando deban.

---

120 <u>Like a Saint George of old</u>: this hyperbolic and mythical image
epitomises the extravagant tenor of the speech and is indicative of
Mariana's surrender to dream and delusion, which is to say, of her
dissociation from reality.
125-6 <u>he'll come at daybreak...</u>: Mariana even manages to protect and

	Tell me now: you don't believe it!	110
	[*Distressed.*]	
ALEGRITO [*confused*]:		
	Whatever you say, Señora.	
MARIANA:	When he finds out I'm imprisoned	
	for sewing his flag of freedom,	
	Pedro won't spare his horse the whip	
	as he gallops to my rescue.	115
	And if they should kill me, he'll come	
	gallantly to die at my side,	
	for that's what he told me one night,	
	his lips soft upon my forehead.	
	Like a Saint George of old he'll come,	120
	dressed up in brilliant finery,	
	the flower of his flowing cloak	
	a bright vermillion in the air.	
	And just because he is so noble	
	and modest, he'll come at daybreak,	125
	at a time when no one sees him,	
	when dawn is fresh upon the earth	
	and lemon trees scarcely glimmer	
	in the cold of the morning breeze,	
	when tall ships of shadowy sails	130
	float on the silken waves of light.	
	You see what joy he'll bring me then?	
	You see why I'm so unafraid?	
ALEGRITO:	Señora!	
MARIANA:	Who told you this news?	
ALEGRITO:	Don Luis.	
MARIANA:	Does he know my sentence?	135
ALEGRITO:	He said he couldn't believe it.	
MARIANA [*distressed*]:		
	Well, it's true enough.	
ALEGRITO:	I'm sorry	
	it was I who had to tell you.	
MARIANA:	Go back to them!	
ALEGRITO:	If you say so.	
MARIANA:	Go back and tell them I am well,	140
	moreover very satisfied,	
	because I know they'll all come soon,	
	- hordes of them! - as soon as they can.	

---

personalise her dream, for the implication is that only she will know when
Don Pedro comes.

127-31 <u>when dawn is fresh...silken waves of light:</u> here the ethereal
quality of Lorca's images beautifully matches Mariana's wishful
hallucinations, while the negative associations of <u>lemon trees,</u> <u>cold</u> and
<u>shadowy sails</u> forecast the unlikelihood of realisation.

	¡Dios te lo pague!	
ALEGRITO:	Hasta luego.	

[*Sale.*]

MARIANA [*En voz baja*]:
Y me quedo sola mientras   145
que, bajo la acacia en flor
del jardín, mi muerte acecha.
[*En voz alta y dirigiéndose al huerto.*]
Pero mi vida está aquí.
Mi sangre se agita y tiembla,
como un árbol de coral   150
con la marejada tierna.
Y aunque tu caballo pone
cuatro lunas en las piedras
y fuego en la verde brisa
débil de la primavera,   155
¡corre más! ¡Ven a buscarme!
Mira que siento muy cerca
dedos de hueso y de musgo
acariciar mi cabeza.
[*Se dirige al jardín como si hablara con alguien.*]
No puedes entrar. ¡No puedes!   160
¡Ay Pedro! Por ti no entra;
pero sentada en la fuente
toca una blanca vihuela.

[*Se sienta en un banco y apoya la cabeza sobre sus manos. En el jardín se oye una guitarra.*]

VOZ:
A la vera del agua,
sin que nadie la viera,   165
se murió mi esperanza.

---

146 the budding locust tree: in Spain the most common form of 'acacia' or locust tree has white blossoms. Symbolically locusts represent the forces of destruction, though that meaning does not apply in the Spanish. What does, of course, is the union of two opposites – Spring's budding and death (line 147) – which relate to Mariana's youth and imminent execution.

147+ Speaking more loudly, as she goes towards the garden: Mariana's abstracted wandering and the raising of her voice – as though speaking to the garden or the absent Pedro – are clear signs of her developing neurosis and eccentricity.

153-4 sparking its moonlight hooves...silver in the Spring's green breeze: the first image of hooves, crescent moons and sparks on cobble stones has a synthetic power which Lorca developed in several different variations, for instance in '*Rider's Song (1860)*':

La noche espolea	The night digs spurs
sus negros ijares	into her black flanks
clavándose estrellas.	pricking herself with stars.

The second image possibly suggests a flash of lightning, but certainly the

```
                    May God reward you!
ALEGRITO:                          Farewell, then.
            [He leaves.]
MARIANA [quietly]:
            You leave me to my solitude                    145
            under the budding locust tree
            where death is setting snares for me.
            [Speaking more loudly as she goes towards the
              garden.]
            And so my life has come to this.
            The blood in my heart is trembling
            like coral branches slowly stirred              150
            by gentle surges in the sea.
            As fast as your horse rides, Pedro,
            sparking its moonlight hooves on stone,
            flashing its silver in the Spring's
            green breeze, you must gallop faster!           155
            Come save me now!  Come quickly my love!
            For surely you must see how close
            to caressing my head and neck
            are those mossy fingers of bone.
            [Gesturing towards the garden, as though speaking
              to someone.]
            Stay away!  Keep clear!  Out of here!           160
            Oh, Pedro!  You keep death at bay;
            but sitting still by my fountain
            it plucks the strings of its white lute.
[She sits down on a bench with her head in her hands.  A
guitar is heard to play in the garden.]
VOICE:      At the cool water side,
            where no one's eyes could see,                  165
            all hope left in me died.
```

mixture of silver and green is again ominous.
157   For..see how close: in this unmistakably hallucinatory sequence death
is seen as a horrific seducer. Such necrophobia again recalls Romantic
models, from José Cadalso's *Noches lúgubres* (1790) to José de
Espronceda's *El estudiante de Salamanca* (1840). The culminating sequence
in the latter is the marriage of the donjuanesque Montemar to the corpse of
a woman he once seduced, and there we find many such macabre images as
that of the bride reaching out her skeleton hand to embrace her lover.
162-3 sitting...by my fountain...: the Moorish flavour of this image –
notably in its mention of the lute or *vihuela*, an early form of guitar in
fact – returns us once again to the more lyrically seductive powers of
death.
164-6 At the cool water side...: this wistful song, which Mariana repeats
in traditional vein, has a function not unlike that of the chorus in classical
drama which was essentially informative of unseen action, or, as here, of
inner mood.

MARIANA [*Repitiendo exquisitamente la canción*]:
        A la vera del agua,
        sin que nadie la viera,
        se murió mi esperanza.
[*Por el foro aparecen dos Monjas, seguidas de Pedrosa. Mariana no los ve.*]

MARIANA: Esta copla está diciendo   170
        lo que saber no quisiera.
        Corazón sin esperanza,
        ¡que se lo trague la tierra!
CARMEN: Aquí está, señor Pedrosa.
MARIANA [*Asustada, levantándose y como saliendo de un sueño*]:
        ¿Quién es?
PEDROSA: ¡Señora!
[*Mariana queda sorprendida y deja escapar una exclamación. Las Monjas inician el mutis.*]
MARIANA [*A las monjas*]:   ¿Nos dejan?   175
CARMEN: Tenemos que trabajar...
[*Se van. Hay en estos momentos una gran inquietud en escena. Pedrosa, frío y correcto, mira intensamente a Mariana, y ésta, melancólica, pero valiente, recoge sus miradas. Pedrosa viste de negro, con capa. Su aire frío debe hacerse notar.*]
MARIANA: Me lo dio el corazón: ¡Pedrosa!
PEDROSA: El mismo
        que aguarda, como siempre, sus noticias.
        Ya es hora. ¿No os parece?
MARIANA: Siempre es hora
        de callar y vivir con alegría.   180
[*Se sienta en un banco. En este momento, y durante todo el acto, Mariana tendrá un delirio delicadísimo, que estallará al final.*]
PEDROSA: ¿Conoce la sentencia?
MARIANA: La conozco.
PEDROSA: ¿Y bien?
MARIANA [*Radiante*]: Pero yo pienso que es mentira.
        Tengo el cuello muy corto para ser
        ajusticiada. Ya ve. No podrían.
        Además, es hermoso y blanco; nadie   185
        querrá tocarlo.
PEDROSA [*Completando*]:   ¡Mariana!
MARIANA [*Fiera*]:   Se olvida

176+ dressed in black: Pedrosa's unchanging colour of clothing now contrasts starkly ·with Mariana's white costume and clearly evokes his role as executioner.

180+ muted delirium: though Mariana's mood is predominantly unreal and dissociative, from time to time she shows rational awareness of her predicament.

MARIANA [*repeating the song with exquisite delicacy*]:
         At the cool water side,
         where no one's eyes could see,
         all hope left in me died.
[*Upstage two nuns appear, followed by Pedrosa. Mariana is unaware of them.*]
MARIANA: That ditty is saying something   170
         that I would never wish to know.
         A heart that can no longer hope
         has nowhere but the grave to go.
CARMEN: Here she is, Señor Pedrosa.
MARIANA [*startled, getting up as though waking from a dream.*]
         Who is it?
PEDROSA: Señora!
[*Mariana, still surprised, gasps. The nuns begin to leave.*]
MARIANA [*to the nuns*]:   Why leave?   175
CARMEN: We have things to do, Mariana.
[*They leave. There is a great sense of uneasiness. Pedrosa, correct and austere in his manner, looks at Mariana intently, while she, downcast but still brave, returns his stare. Pedrosa is dressed in black and wears a cloak. His icy manner is most apparent.*]
MARIANA: Pedrosa! I might have guessed it was you.
PEDROSA: Once again I await your testimony.
         It's time for talking, don't you think?
MARIANA: It's time
         to keep one's peace, I think, and peace of mind.   180
[*She sits down on a bench. Here, as throughout the act, Mariana's mood is one of muted delirium which will increase to breaking point by the end.*]
PEDROSA: Are you aware of your sentence?
MARIANA: I am.
PEDROSA: Well then?
MARIANA [*radiantly*]: But I refuse to believe it.
         Can't you see that my neck is far too short
         for execution? Look! It can't be done.
         Besides, my neck is white and beautiful;   185
         and no one will want to harm it.
PEDROSA [*stopping her*]:   Mariana!
MARIANA [*angrily*]:
         You forget that if I die all Granada

183-4 my neck is far too short/for execution: this is a verbatim account of what Mariana herself said on hearing the news of her death sentence, according to the report of her first biographer of 1836, José de la Peña y Aguayo (Antonina Rodrigo, *op.cit.*, 134). Clearly, then, Lorca had researched Peña y Aguayo.

que para que yo muera tiene toda
Granada que morir. Y que saldrían
muy grandes caballeros a salvarme,
porque soy noble. Porque yo soy hija   190
de un capitán de navío, Caballero
de Calatrava. ¡Déjeme tranquila!

PEDROSA: No habrá nadie en Granada que se asome
cuando usted pase con su comitiva.
Los andaluces hablan; pero luego...   195

MARIANA: Me dejan sola; ¿y qué? Uno vendría
para morir conmigo, y esto basta.
¡Pero vendrá para salvar mi vida!

[*Sonríe y respira fuertemente, llevándose las manos al pecho.*]

PEDROSA [*En un arranque*]:
Yo no quiero que mueras tú, ¡no quiero!
Ni morirás, porque darás noticias   200
de la conjuración. Estoy seguro.

MARIANA [*Fiera*]:
No diré nada, como usted querría,
a pesar de tener un corazón
en el que ya no caben más heridas.
Fuerte y sorda seré a vuestros halagos.   205
Antes me daban miedo sus pupilas.
Ahora le estoy mirando cara a cara
[*Se acerca.*]
y puedo con sus ojos que vigilan
el sitio donde guardo este secreto
que por nada del mundo contaría.   210
¡Soy valiente. Pedrosa, soy valiente!

PEDROSA: Está muy bien.
[*Pausa.*]
Ya sabe, con mi firma
puedo borrar la lumbre de sus ojos.
Con una pluma y un poco de tinta
puedo hacerla dormir un largo sueño.   215

MARIANA [*Elevada*]:
¡Ojalá fuese pronto por mi dicha!

PEDROSA [*Frío*]:
Esta tarde vendrán.

MARIANA [*Aterrada y dándose cuenta*]:
¿Cómo?

PEDROSA: Esta tarde;

190-2 <u>My father was</u>...: while Mariano de Pineda was indeed a ship's
captain, Mariana's claim that he was a Knight of Spain's most prestigious
Order, Calatrava, is a measure of her need to fantasise.
195 <u>Andalusians talk a lot</u>...: Pedrosa, a Castilian, voices a common
enough prejudice held against Andalusians, namely that they are all talk
and no action.

```
                    must die too.  And that the finest grandees
                    in all the land will rush to rescue me,
                    for I too am noble.  My father was                       190
                    captain of a ship and also a knight
                    of Calatrava.  So leave me in peace!
PEDROSA:            The people in Granada will not dare
                    to leave their homes when you head for the gallows.
                    Andalusians talk a lot, but as for...                    195
MARIANA:            They'll let me rot.  Who cares?  As long as one
                    is there to die with me, that's all I need.
                    But see, he'll even come to rescue me!
```

[*She smiles, breathing deeply, raising her hands to her breast.*]
PEDROSA [*in a sudden outburst*]:

```
                    You must not die, for I won't allow it!
                    Nor will you, because first you'll give the names    200
                    of those conspirators.  Of that I'm sure.
```

MARIANA [*vigorously*]:

```
                    I'll speak not a word to satisfy you.
                    My heart is now so brimful of sorrow
                    it has no room for any other wounds.
                    Your fawning words will fall on deaf ears.           205
                    There was a time your eyes struck fear in me,
                    but now I face you, cool and unafraid,
                    [she draws closer]
                    eyeball to eyeball, in the sure knowledge
                    that you can never see into my world
                    and read that secret I will never tell.              210
                    No, you won't break me, Pedrosa.  You can't!
PEDROSA:            Very well, then.
                    [Pause.]
                                    You know my signature
                    is all it takes to close your eyes for good.
                    With just a pen and some small drops of ink
                    I'll make you sleep the deepest sleep of all.        215
```

MARIANA [*spiritedly*]:

```
                    My only wish is that it could be soon!
```

PEDROSA [*chillingly*]:

```
                    They'll come this evening.
```

MARIANA [*terrified on fully realising her predicament*]:

```
                                    What!  When?
PEDROSA:                                        This evening.
```

---

199 I won't allow it!: Pedrosa had the absolute power to pardon Mariana,
if she informed of the conspirators' names.
206-8 There was a time your eyes...: compare with Mariana's comments in
the First Engraving (lines 250-4) and especially the Second Engraving
(lines 246-50).

ya se ha ordenado que entres en capilla.
MARIANA [*Exaltada y protestando fieramente de su muerte*]:
        ¡No puede ser! ¡Cobardes! ¿Y quién manda
        dentro de España tales villanías?   220
        ¿Qué crimen cometí? ¿Por qué me matan?
        ¿Dónde está la razón de la Justicia?
        En la bandera de la Libertad
        bordé el amor más grande de mi vida.
        ¿Y he de permanecer aquí encerrada?   225
        ¡Quién tuviera unas alas cristalinas
        para salir volando en busca tuya!
[*Pedrosa ha visto con satisfacción esta súbita desesperación de Mariana y se dirige a ella. La luz empieza a tomar el tono del crepúsculo.*]
PEDROSA [*Muy cerca de Mariana*]:
        Hable pronto, que el rey la indultaría.
        Mariana, ¿quiénes son los conjurados?
        Yo sé que usted de todos es amiga.   230
        Cada segundo aumenta su peligro.
        Antes que se haya disipado el día
        ya vendrán por la calle a recogerla.
        ¿Quiénes son? Y sus nombres. ¡Vamos pronto!
        Que no se juega así con la Justicia,   235
        y luego será tarde.
MARIANA [*Fiera*]:   ¡No hablaré!
PEDROSA [*Fiero, cogiéndole las manos*]:
        ¿Quiénes son?
MARIANA: Ahora menos lo diría.
        [*Con desprecio.*]
        Suelta, Pedrosa; vete. ¡Madre Carmen!
PEDROSA [*Terrible*]:
        ¡Quieres morir!
[*Aparece, llena de miedo, la Madre Carmen; dos monjas cruzan al fondo como dos fantasmas.*]
CARMEN: ¿Qué pasa, Marianita?
MARIANA: Nada.

---

218 The priest...at the chapel: Lorca condenses history by suggesting that Mariana will spend her last moments at a chapel in the convent, attended by a priest. In fact Mariana left the convent on May 24 and spent her last three days in the less salubrious *Cárcel Baja* (Low Prison) where the Brothers of Peace and Charity – who customarily attended the condemned – and her own priest, Father Juan de la Hinojosa, all implored her to seek pardon through informing.
219 It can't be true! You cowards!...: this outburst is the nearest Mariana comes to losing her serenity. It conforms historically to the moment when, upon arriving at the Low Prison, she was told that the King had approved her death sentence and, fleetingly, she lost her self-control

                    The priest is waiting for you at the chapel.
MARIANA [*impassioned, protesting fiercely*]:
                    It can't be true! You cowards! Who says so?
                    What Spaniard could permit such villainy?   220
                    What crime did I commit to merit this?
                    And what respect has Justice in our land?
                    It's true that on the dear flag of Liberty
                    I sewed the one real love of my poor life.
                    And just for that you keep me locked up here?   225
                    If only I had glistening wings to fly,
                    how quickly they would speed me to your side!
[*Having noted Mariana's new desperation with some satisfaction,
Pedrosa draws closer to her. The light begins to take on the
hue of dusk.*]
PEDROSA [*very close to Mariana*]:
                    If you speak now the King will pardon you.
                    Mariana, who were the conspirators?
                    I know you are friend to all of them.   230
                    Each second you delay can only make
                    your peril worse. Before the day is out
                    they'll be coming down the street to get you.
                    Who were they? I want their names! Quickly, now!
                    The Law has no more patience for your games.   235
                    Your time has just run out.
MARIANA [*proudly*]:   I will not speak!
PEDROSA [*fiercely taking her by the hands*]:
                    Who were they?
MARIANA: That's no way to make me talk!
                    [*Scornfully.*]
                    Let go, Pedrosa, and be off! Carmen!
PEDROSA [*aghast*]:
                    You want death!
[*Mother Carmen, struck with terror, appears; two nuns cross
the scene upstage like two phantoms.*]
CARMEN: Marianita, what is it?
MARIANA: Oh, nothing.

(Antonina Rodrigo, *op.cit.*, 147-8).

225 And just for that...: the case against Mariana was, in legal terms,
extremely flimsy. Apart from the flag being in an unfinished state, it is
also apparent, as Mariana's lawyer argued in court, that the flag could
only indicate the intention to commit a crime, as opposed to constituting a
criminal act in itself.

227+ The light begins to take on the hue of dusk: this indicates a
foreshortened process of darkening which contributes greatly to the
lyricism and anxiety of the play's final moments. It also counterbalances
the mood of the opening act when night's dark cover came all too slowly
for Mariana: 'The lights of evening persist...' (line 168 *et seq.*).

CARMEN: Señor, no es justo...
PEDROSA [*Frío, sereno y autoritario, dirige una severa mirada
a la monja, e inicia el mutis*]:
                        Buenas tardes.   240
            [*A Mariana.*]
            Tendré un placer muy grande si me avisa.
CARMEN: ¡Es muy buena, señor!
PEDROSA [*Altivo*]:   No os pregunté.
            [*Sale, seguido de Sor Carmen.*]
MARIANA [*En el banco, con dramática y tierna entonación
andaluza*]:
            Recuerdo aquella copla que decía
            cruzando los olivos de Granada:
            "¡Ay, qué fragatita,   245
            real corsaria! ¿Dónde está
            tu valentía?
            Que un velero bergantín
            te ha puesto la puntería."
            [*Como soñando y nebulosamente.*]
            Entre el mar y las estrellas   250
            ¡con qué gusto pasearía
            apoyada sobre una
            larga baranda de brisa!
            [*Con pasión y llena de angustia.*]
            Pedro, coge tu caballo
            o ven montado en el día.   255
            ¡Pero pronto! ¡Que ya vienen
            para quitarme la vida!
            Clava las duras espuelas.
            [*Llorando.*]
            "¡Ay, qué fragatita,
            real corsaria! ¿Dónde está   260
            tu valentía?
            Que un famoso bergantín
            te ha puesto la puntería."
[*Vienen dos monjas.*]
MONJA 1. : Sé fuerte, que Dios te ayuda.
CARMEN: Marianita, hija, descansa.   265
            [*Se llevan a Mariana.*]

---

240 Sir, it's not right: it is important to the play's final spiritual
emphasis that Mother Carmen and the Church should be seen as
sympathetic to Mariana and not mere upholders of authority.

CARMEN: Sir, it's not right...
PEDROSA [*austere, calm and fully aware of his authority; he looks
          threateningly at the nun and then begins to leave*]:
                                        Good evening.   240
          [*To Mariana.*]
          I trust you'll wish to speak to me later.
CARMEN: But sir, she's... good!
PEDROSA [*haughtily*]:   I was speaking to her!
          [*He leaves, followed by Mother Carmen.*]
MARIANA [*on the bench, speaking in the tender and yet intense
          Andalusian manner*]:
          I remember that song I used to sing
          when strolling through Granada's olive groves:
          "Oh, fine ship,   245
          fine pirate ship,
          show us how brave you are!
          You see that brig, that speedy brig,
          it's shooting at you from afar."
          [*Lost in a cloud of dreams.*]
          How I used to love to sail   250
          between the sea and a star,
          the breeze fresh upon my face
          as I leaned over the bar.
          [*Overcome with anguish.*]
          Oh, Pedro, lash your horse,
          rip through the dawn like a scar.   255
          Come quick! Come quick!
          for they're taking my life,
          so give your spurs a jar!
          [*Sobbing.*]
          "Oh, fine ship,
          fine pirate ship,   260
          show us how brave you are!
          You see that brig, that speedy brig,
          it's shooting at you from afar."
[*Two nuns enter.*]
FIRST NUN: Be strong, my child. God will help you.
CARMEN: Mariana, my dearest, keep calm.   265
          [*They lead Mariana off.*]

---

245 <u>Oh, fine ship</u>: another song in popular style which has the Romantic
theme of freedom at its core. But while the song implicitly challenges
Pedro - <u>show us how brave you are</u> (line 247) - its poignant irony lies in
the fact that Pedro is at this moment speeding away towards England and
enjoying the very freedom which the song depicts.

159

[Suena el esquilón de las monjas. Por el fondo aparecen varias de ellas, que cruzan la escena y se santiguan al pasar ante una Virgen de los Dolores que con el corazón atravesado de puñales, llora en el muro, cobijada por un inmenso arco de rosas amarillas y plateadas de papel. Entre ellas se destacan las Novicias 1. y 2. . Los cipreses comienzan a teñirse de luz dorada.]

NOVICIA 1. :
　　　　　　¡Qué gritos!　¿Tú los sentiste?
NOVICIA 2. :
　　　　　　Desde el jardín; y sonaban
　　　　　　como si estuvieran lejos
　　　　　　¡Inés, yo estoy asustada!
NOVICIA 1. :
　　　　　　¿Dónde estará Marianita,　　　　　　　　　　270
　　　　　　rosa y jazmín de Granada?
NOVICIA 2. :
　　　　　　Está esperando a su novio.
NOVICIA 1. :
　　　　　　Pero su novio ya tarda.
　　　　　　¡Si la vieras cómo mira
　　　　　　por una y otra ventana!　　　　　　　　　　275
　　　　　　Dice: "Si no hubiera sierras,
　　　　　　lo vería en la distancia."
NOVICIA 2. :
　　　　　　Ella lo espera segura.
NOVICIA 1. :
　　　　　　¡No vendrá por su desgracia!
NOVICIA 2. :
　　　　　　¡Marianita va a morir!　　　　　　　　　　280
　　　　　　¡Hay otra luz en la casa!
NOVICIA 1. :
　　　　　　¡Y cuánto pájaro!　¿Has visto?
　　　　　　Ya no caben en las ramas
　　　　　　del jardín ni en los aleros;
　　　　　　nunca vi tantos, y al alba,　　　　　　　　285

265+ A convent bell rings...: the ringing of the bell, the bustle of nuns crossing the stage and the darkening of the set as the cypress trees begin to take on a golden hue are all signs of the fatal moment's imminence. The nun's movements draw attention to the martyred image of Our Lady with her heart pierced by daggers, which is itself a religious correlation of Mariana's sacrifice.

268-303 In this sequence the function of the two Novices as a chorus is particularly evident. They comment, with ever increasing lyricism, on the mood and actions of Mariana off-stage, reminding us at the same time of her inexorable fate: And Mariana will die! (line 280). The sequence also serves as a kind of temporal glide, suggesting that a greater span of time elapses during Mariana's relatively short absence.

[*A convent bell rings. Several nuns appear upstage. They cross the stage and make the sign of the Cross as they pass in front of an image of Our Lady of Sorrows. The latter, her heart pierced by daggers, is crying; she is set into the wall, while above her there is a large arch of paper roses in yellow and silver. Prominent amongst the nuns are the First and Second Novices. The cypress trees begin to take on a golden hue.*]

FIRST NOVICE:
>What shrieks! Did you hear them?

SECOND NOVICE:
>They came from the garden,
>though they seemed further off.
>Oh Inés, I'm so frightened!

FIRST NOVICE:
>And where is Marianita,   270
>rose, jasmine of Granada?

SECOND NOVICE:
>She's waiting for her love.

FIRST NOVICE:
>But he's so slow to come.
>Her eyes move from window
>to window and back again!   275
>She says: "If there were no
>mountains, I'd see him coming."

SECOND NOVICE:
>She's so sure he will come.

FIRST NOVICE:
>But the truth is he won't!

SECOND NOVICE:
>And Mariana will die!   280
>Another light appears!

FIRST NOVICE:
>And so many birds! See?
>They perch on every branch
>and at the rooftops throng.
>I never heard so many   285

282-285 And so many birds!: while a greenfinch alighted on the Duke of Lucena's coffin in the ballad at the beginning of the Second Engraving (line 53), it is, if anything, more typical of traditional poetry to remark on the attendance of birds in advance of a tragedy, for they are of course harbingers of sorrow. This preternatural gathering of birds is found for instance in the ancient ballad of Count Arnaldos (mentioned in the note to line 29 of the Second Engraving) and in a ballad by the contemporary writer Ramón Sender:

>las cotovias se paran | the skylarks perch
>en la cruz del camposanto. | on the cemetery cross.

R. Sender, *Réquiem por un campesino español* (Barcelona: Destinolibro, 1980), 95.

                    cuando se siente la Vela,
                    cantan y cantan y cantan...
NOVICIA 2.   :
                    ... y al alba
                    despiertan brisas y nubes
                    desde el frescor de las ramas.   290
NOVICIA 1.   :
                    ... y al alba
                    por cada estrella que muere
                    nace diminuta flauta.
NOVICIA 2.   :
                    ¿Y ella?... ¿Tú la has visto? Ella
                    me parece amortajada   295
                    cuando cruza el coro bajo
                    con esa ropa tan blanca.
NOVICIA 1.   :
                    ¡Qué injusticia! Esta mujer
                    de seguro fue engañada.
NOVICIA 2.   :
                    ¡Su cuello es maravilloso!   300
NOVICIA 1.   [*Llevándose instintivamente las manos al cuello*]:
                    Sí, pero...
NOVICIA 2.   :   Cuando lloraba
                    me pareció que se le iba
                    a deshojar en la falda.
                    [*Se acercan las monjas.*]
MONJA 1.   :   ¿Vamos a ensayar la Salve?
NOVICIA 1.   :
                    ¿Muy bien!
NOVICIA 2.   :   Yo no tengo gana.   305
MONJA 1.   :   Es muy bonita.
NOVICIA 1.   [*Hace una señal a las demás y se dirigen
rápidamente al foro*]:   ¡Y dificil!
[*Aparece Mariana por la puerta de la izquierda, y al verla se
retiran todas con disimulo.*]
MARIANA [*Sonriendo*]:
                    ¿Huyen de mí?
NOVICIA 1.   [*Temblando*]: ¡Vamos a la...!

---

286 Vela: the *Torre de la Vela*, or 'Watch Tower', is the best known of all
the Alhambra's towers. Sometimes called the 'Bell Tower', its bell was
installed by Ferdinand after the defeat of the last Moorish king, Boabdil,
in 1492, and its purpose was to warn of coming dangers. In his 'symbolic
fantasy', *Impressions*, of 1917, Lorca writes: 'The Vela bell speaks such a
solemn and stately melody that the cypress trees and the rose groves
tremble nervously'. Then the bell itself speaks: 'When I ring out so sad
and mournfully it is because I am crying for something that is gone
forever... I am the poet's heart and my peals are his heartbeat' (*Obras
completas*, I, 929).

```
                    singing at the dawn Vela
                    when the bells go ding-dong...
SECOND NOVICE:
                    ... at dawn,
                    waking flowers and clouds
                    with the music of their song.                    290
FIRST NOVICE:
                    ... at dawn,
                    for every star that dies
                    a tiny flute is born.
SECOND NOVICE:
                    And she...? Did you see her?
                    Passing through the choir stalls              295
                    she seemed wrapped in a shroud
                    with that white vestment on.
FIRST NOVICE:
                    It's a terrible mistake,
                    she was surely led on.
SECOND NOVICE:
                    Her neck is pure as dawn!                      300
```
FIRST NOVICE [*lifting her hands instinctively to her neck*]:
```
                    Yes, but...
SECOND NOVICE:          I saw her crying
                    and it seemed her neck fell
                    in petals to her lap.
```
                    [*Two nuns approach them.*]
FIRST NUN: Let's practise the Salve.
FIRST NOVICE:
```
                    Very well.
```
SECOND NOVICE: I'd rather not.   305
FIRST NUN: It's pretty!
FIRST NOVICE [*she gestures to the others and they make off
                    quickly towards the choir room*]:
```
                    But very hard!
```
[*Mariana appears through the door on the left, and on seeing her
all the nuns surreptitiously withdraw.*]
MARIANA [*smiling*]:
```
                    Are you afraid of me?
```
FIRST NOVICE [*trembling*]:   We were...

---

293 a tiny flute is born: the images suggests that a bird takes the place
of each disappearing star at dawn.
294 Did you see her?: The *Obras completas*, in error, gives '¿Tú las has
visto?' While the other editors give 'Tú la has visto?'
304 the Salve: the Latin salutation, "Salve Regina", a prayer to the
Virgin Mary which asks for her protection.
306 But very hard!: once again the Novices' schoolgirl innocence provides
a softening touch of humour.

                              163

NOVICIA 2. [*Turbada*]:
   Nos íbamos... Yo decía...
   Es muy tarde.
MARIANA [*Con bondad irónica*]:
                     ¿Soy tan mala?
NOVICIA 1. [*Exaltada*]:
   ¡No, señora! ¿Quién lo dice?   310
MARIANA: ¿Qué sabes tú, niña?
NOVICIA 2. [*Señalando a la primera*]:
                     ¡Nada!
NOVICIA 1. :
   ¡Pero la queremos todas!
   [*Nerviosa.*]
   ¿No lo está usted viendo?
MARIANA [*Con amargura*]:   ¡Gracias!
[*Mariana se sienta en el banco, con las manos cruzadas y la
cabeza caída, en una divina actitud de tránsito.*]
NOVICIA 1. :
   ¡Vámonos!
NOVICIA 2. :   ¡Ay, Marianita,
   rosa y jazmín de Granada,   315
   que está esperando a su novio,
   pero su novio se tarda!...
   [*Se van.*]
MARIANA: ¡Quién me hubiera dicho a mí!...
   Pero... ¡paciencia!
CARMEN [*Que entra*]:   ¡Mariana!
   Un señor, que trae permiso   320
   del juez, viene a visitarla.
MARIANA [*Levantándose, radiante*]:
   ¡Que pase! ¡Por fin, Dios mío!
[*Sale la monja. Mariana se dirige a una cornucopia que hay
en la pared y, llena de su delicado delirio, se arregla los
bucles y el escote.*]
   Pronto..., ¡qué segura estaba!
   Tendré que cambiarme el traje:
   me hace demasiado pálida.   325
[*Se sienta en el banco, en actitud amorosa, vuelta al sitio
donde tienen que entrar. Aparece la Madre Carmen. Y
Mariana, no pudiendo resistir, se vuelve. En el silencio de
la escena entra Fernando, pálido. Mariana queda estupefacta.*]

323-6 At last... Oh no!: a sequence of extreme pathos in which Mariana is
disillusioned to find that her visitor is the young Fernando and not Don
Pedro. Though it borders dangerously on sentimental melodrama, the

SECOND NOVICE [*embarrassed*]:
>> We were going... I was saying...
>> It's very late,
MARIANA [*kindly, but with irony*]:
>> Am I so bad?
FIRST NOVICE [*roused*]:
>> Oh no, Señora! Who said so?   310
MARIANA: And what do you know, child?
SECOND NOVICE [*speaking for the First Novice*]:
>> Nothing!
FIRST NOVICE:
>> But every one of us loves you!
>> [*Nervously.*]
>> As I'm sure you know full well.
MARIANA [*bitterly*]:   Thanks!
[*Mariana sits down on the bench, her hands crossed and her
head leaning forward in an other-worldly pose.*]
FIRST NOVICE:
>> Come on, let's go!
SECOND NOVICE: Oh, Marianita,
>> rose and jasmine of Granada,   315
>> for her lover she lies in wait,
>> but he has left it very late!...
>> [*They leave.*]
MARIANA: If only someone had told me!...
>> But then... I must keep calm!
CARMEN [*entering*]:   Mariana!
>> A gentleman, with the Judge's   320
>> permission, has come to see you.
MARIANA [*getting up, radiant*]:
>> Let him in! Oh, thank God! At last!
[*The nun leaves. Mariana goes over to a cornucopia mirror which
is fixed to the wall, and there, in a mixture of fantasy and ecstasy,
she arranges her hair and the neckline of her dress.*]
>> At last ... Oh how my heart knew it!
>> But I'll need to get a new dress:
>> this one makes me look too pale.   325
[*She sits down on the bench, her mind full of amorous thoughts,
her back towards the place where the visitor will enter. Mother
Carmen appears, and Mariana, unable to contain herself, turns
round. When the stage is silent, Fernando enters; he is very pale.
Mariana looks stupefied.*]

---

depiction of Mariana's futile cosmetic preparations and of her nervous,
exultant state of mind is perfectly consistent with the compulsive and
neurotic behaviour of one who lives in an unreal dream.

MARIANA [*Desesperada, como no queriéndolo creer*]:
       ¡No!
FERNANDO [*Triste*]:
       ¡Mariana!, ¿No quieres
       que hable contigo? ¡Dime!
MARIANA:
       ¡Pedro! ¿Dónde está Pedro?
       ¡Dejadlo entrar, por Dios!
       ¡Está abajo, en la puerta!   330
       ¡Tiene que estar! ¡Que suba!
       Tú viniste con él,
       ¿verdad? Tú eres muy bueno.
       El vendrá muy cansado, pero entrará en seguida.
FERNANDO: ¡Vengo solo, Mariana. ¿Qué sé yo de don Pedro? 335
MARIANA: ¡Todos deben saber, pero ninguno sabe!
       Entonces, ¿cuándo viene para salvar mi vida?
       ¿Cuándo viene a morir, si la muerte me acecha?
       ¿Vendrá? Dime, Fernando. ¡Aún es hora!
FERNANDO [*Enérgico y desesperado, al ver la actitud de Mariana*]:
                                   Don Pedro
       no vendrá, porque nunca te quiso, Marianita.   340
       Ya estará en Inglaterra, con otros liberales.
       Te abandonaron todos tus antiguos amigos.
       Solamente mi joven corazón te acompaña.
       ¡Mariana! ¡Aprende y mira cómo te estoy queriendo!
MARIANA [*Exaltada*]:
       ¿Por qué me lo dijiste? Yo bien que lo sabia;   345
       pero nunca lo quise decir a mi esperanza.
       Ahora ya no me importa. Mi esperanza lo ha oído
       y se ha muerto mirando los ojos de mi Pedro.
       Yo bordé la bandera por él. Yo he conspirado
       para vivir y amar su pensamiento propio.   350
       Más que a mis propios hijos y a mí misma le quise.
       ¿Amas la Libertad más que a tu Marianita?
       ¡Pues yo seré la misma Libertad que tú adoras!
FERNANDO:
       ¡Sé que vas a morir! Dentro de unos instantes
       vendrán por ti, Mariana. ¡Sálvate y di los nombres!
       ¡Por tus hijos! ¡Por mí, que te ofrezco la vida!

330-34 <u>He's right outside...he'll see me soon</u>: Mariana invents a complete
scenario to protect her dream-reality to the end; this is psychologically
convincing in that a dissociated mind tends to follow through logically on
its illogical premise.
339-40 <u>Don Pedro...never loved you</u>: for Mariana this is the most
devastating news of all, and the pin that bursts the fragile bubble of her
dream.
345-8 <u>I knew very well...when once I looked in Pedro's eyes</u>: that her
delirium was a defensive mechanism is now all too plain, and it appears to

MARIANA [*in desperation, as though not wanting to believe
          her eyes*]:
                 Oh no!
FERNANDO [*sadly*]: Mariana! Would you prefer
                 me not to speak to you? Please say!
MARIANA: But Pedro! Tell me! Where is he?
                 For the love of God let him in!
                 He's right outside! Yes, at the door!   330
                 Of course he is! So ask him in!
                 You brought him here, naturally,
                 since you're a very good young man.
                 He must be tired; he'll see me soon; of course he will!
FERNANDO: I came alone, Mariana, without news of Pedro.   335
MARIANA: No one knows anything of him; though they all should!
                 Tell me, then: when do you think he'll come to save me?
                 Since death is stalking me, won't he come to my side?
                 He'll come. Tell me, Fernando. There's still time.
FERNANDO [*forceful and desperate because of Mariana's attitude*]:
                                          Don Pedro
                 will not come, Mariana, for he never loved you.   340
                 He's bound for England now, with other liberals.
                 All those you called your friends have now deserted you.
                 Just one young heart is left to keep you company. 340
                 Oh Mariana! Can't you see the one who loves you?
MARIANA [*intensely*]:
                 Why did you have to tell me? I knew very well,   345
                 though I had hoped to keep it secret from my heart.
                 Now I no longer care. Your words have ravaged me;
                 for my hope died when once I looked in Pedro's eyes.
                 I sewed that flag for him, and my conspiracy
                 was just to live and love his own most cherished dream.
                 I loved him, more than my children, more than myself.
                 If you love Liberty more than your own Mariana,
                 then I will be the Liberty that you adore!
FERNANDO: But you are going to die! In no time at all
                 they'll come for you, Mariana. Speak up! Give the names!
                 For your children's sake! For me, who can give you life!

---

be one she began to cultivate even in Pedro's presence in the Second
Engraving. As a mechanism it recalls, among others, Don Quixote's
'madness', Hamlet's 'antic disposition' and Lorca's crazy María Josefa in
The House of Bernarda Alba. The latter's madness, which stemmed from a
wish to have more children, led to her nursing a lamb on stage, but,
typically, when told it was just a lamb, she replied: 'I know very well it's
a lamb. But... it's better to have a lamb than not have anything' (*Obras
completas*, II, 874).
352-53 If you love Liberty...then I will be the Liberty: Mariana's final
resolution − to incarnate liberty in her sacrifice and therefore be the very
ideal that Pedro loves − is a persuasive mixture of dream and rationality, a
mathematical equation based on the tenuous logic of poetic metaphor.

MARIANA: ¡No quiero que mis hijos me desprecien! ¡Mis hijos
tendrán un nombre claro como la luna llena!
¡Mis hijos llevarán resplandor en el rostro,
que no podrán borrar los años ni los aires!   360
Si delato, por todas las calles de Granada
este nombre sería pronunciado con miedo.

FERNANDO [*Dramático y desesperado*]:
¡No puede ser! ¡No quiero que esto pase! ¡No quiero!
¡Tú tienes que vivir! ¡Mariana, por mi amor!

MARIANA [*Loca y delirante, en un estado agudo de pasión y angustia*]
¿Y qué es amor, Fernando? ¡Yo no sé qué es amor!

FERNANDO [*Cerca*]:
¡Pero nadie te quiso como yo, Marianita!

MARIANA [*Reaccionando*]:
¡A ti debí quererte más que a nadie en el mundo,
si el corazón no fuera nuestro gran enemigo!
Corazón, ¿por qué mandas en mí si yo no quiero?

FERNANDO [*Se arrodilla y ella le coge la cabeza sobre el pecho*]:
¡Ay, te abandonan todos! ¡Habla, quiéreme y vive!

MARIANA [*Retirándolo*]:
¡Ya estoy muerta, Fernando! Tus palabras me llegan
a través del gran río del mundo que abandono.
Ya soy como la estrella sobre el agua profunda,
última débil brisa que se pierde en los álamos.

[*Por el fondo pasa una monja, con las manos cruzadas, que
mira llena de zozobra al grupo.*]

FERNANDO: ¡No sé qué hacer! ¡Qué angustia! ¡Ya vendrán a busca
¡Quién pudiera morir para que tú vivieras!

MARIANA: ¡Morir! ¡Qué largo sueño sin ensueños ni sombras!
Pedro, quiero morir por lo que tú no mueres,
por el puro ideal que iluminó tus ojos:
¡¡Libertad!! Porque nunca se apague tu alta lumbre
me ofrezco toda entera. ¡¡Arriba, corazón!!
¡Pedro, mira tu amor a lo que me ha llevado!
Me querrás, muerta, tanto, que no podrás vivir.

[*Dos monjas entran, con las manos cruzadas, en la misma expresión
de angustia, y no se atreven a acercarse.*]
Y ahora ya no te quiero, ¡sombra de mi locura!

CARMEN [*Entrando, casi ahogada*]:
¡Mariana!
[*A Fernando.*]
¡Caballero! ¡Salga pronto!

FERNANDO [*Angustiado*]:   ¡Dejadme!   385

---

371 for I'm already dead!: repeating line 49 and developing the idea of a
transitional other worldly reality which is Lorca's ambitious theme in this
act.
384 My love for you is gone: following on from the previous note's point
about Mariana being in an intermediary state, after death, it could be said

168

MARIANA: I have no wish for my children to despise me!
                Their name will be luminous as the moon when full.
                My children will hold up their faces to the sky,
                and neither time nor tongues will tarnish their pure light.
                If I betray my friends, this name of mine would then
                be uttered with terror in all Granada's streets.
FERNANDO [*intense and desperate*]:
                But it can't be! I won't let you! No. It can't be!
                You must live, Mariana, if only for my love!
MARIANA [*sad and delirious, acutely passionate and anguished*]:
                And what is love, Fernando? Do you know? I don't! 365
FERNANDO [*near her*]:
                But no one has loved you as much as I, Mariana!
MARIANA [*responding*]:
                I should have loved you more than anyone on earth,
                if only our hearts were not our own worst enemy.
                But heart, why do you rule my head against my will?
FERNANDO [*kneels down and Mariana holds his head to her breast*]:
                They've all abandoned you! Speak now, live and love me!
MARIANA [*pulling back*]:
                It's too late, Fernando, for I'm already dead!
                Your words reach me across the world's river, from shores
                left far behind. I'm like a star above deep water,
                the last breath of evening that fades in poplar trees.
[*A nun passes upstage, crossing her hands on her chest and looking
anxiously at the two of them.*]
FERNANDO: What can I do? Soon they'll be here! And this anguish!
                Oh God, if only I could die instead of you!
MARIANA: To die: what's that? A long and peaceful rest from care!
                Pedro, I'm ready to give my life for something
                you'd not die for; the only dream that fired your eyes:
                Liberty! I sacrifice myself that its light   380
                might never be extinguished. Hold steady! Be brave!
                Perhaps your love will see how far it's driven me!
                Once I am dead, you'll love me and not want to live.
[*Two nuns enter, their hands crossed, their faces full of anguish, and
both too afraid to draw near.*]
                My love for you is gone, shadow of my madness!
CARMEN [*entering breathlessly*]:
                Mariana! [*To Fernando.*] Young man, please go at once!
FERNANDO [*tormentedly*]:   Let me be! 385

---

that this purging of her love for Pedro conforms to the Catholic notion of
expiatory purification in Purgatory.
shadow of my madness!: the *Obras completas* gives 'porque soy una
sombra' (because I am a shadow), but the Rivadeneyra, Losada and Harrap
variant which I follow is more forceful in terms of Mariana's renunciation of
the world.

MARIANA: ¡Vete! ¿Quién eres tú? ¡Ya no conozco a nadie!
¡Voy a dormir tranquila!
[*Entra otra monja rápidamente, casi ahogada por el miedo y la emoción. Al fondo cruza otra con gran rapidez, con una mano sobre la frente.*]
FERNANDO [*Emocionadísimo*]: ¡Adiós, Mariana!
MARIANA: ¡Vete!
Ya vienen a buscarme.
[*Sale Fernando, llevado por dos monjas.*]
Como un grano de arena
[*Viene otra monja.*]
siento al mundo en los dedos. ¡Muerte! Pero ¿qué es mu‹
[*A las monjas.*]
Y vosotras, ¿qué hacéis? ¡Qué lejanas os siento! 390
CARMEN [*Que llega llorando*]:
¡Mariana!
MARIANA: ¿Por qué llora?
CARMEN: ¡Están abajo, niña!
MONJA 1. : ¡Ya suben la escalera!
[*Entran por el foro todas las monjas. Tienen la tristeza reflejada en los rostros. Las Novicias 1. y 2. están en primer término, Sor Carmer digna y traspasada de pena, está cerca de Mariana. Toda la escena irá adquiriendo, hasta el final una gran luz extrañísima de crepúsculo granadino. Luz rosa y verde entra por los arcos, y los cipreses se matizan exquísitamente, hasta parecer piedras preciosas. Del techo desciende una suave luz naranja, que se va intensificando hasta el final.*]
MARIANA: ¡Corazón, no me dejes! ¡Silencio! Con un ala,
¿dónde vas? Es preciso que tú también descanses.
Nos espera una larga locura de luceros 395
que hay detrás de la muerte. ¡Corazón, no desmayes!
CARMEN: ¡Olvídate del mundo, preciosa Marianita!
MARIANA: ¡Qué lejano lo siento!‑
CARMEN: ¡Ya vienen a buscarte!
MARIANA: Pero ¡qué bien entiendo lo que dice esta luz!
¡Amor, amor, amor, y eternas soledades! 400

392+ the whole scene increasingly acquires that strangely sharp light of a Granada sunset: this infusion of light is of vital importance to the profoundly spiritual mood of the play's last moments. In contrast to the darkening process which has prevailed for most of the act - indeed, most of the play - the rose, green and orange tones which Lorca's scenography describes in remarkable detail suggest now a sense of beauty, triumph and complete transcendence, for the light itself has meaning, as line 399

MARIANA: Go now! I no longer know you! I know no one!
I wish to sleep in peace!
[*Another nun enters quickly, almost choking with fear and grief.
Upstage another crosses quickly, one hand on her forehead.*]
FERNANDO [*greatly moved*]:   Farewell, Mariana!
MARIANA: Go!
They're coming for me now!
[*Fernando leaves, led away by two nuns.*]
                                The world is like a grain
of sand between my fingers.
[*Another nun enters.*]
                            And death! What is death?
[*To the nuns.*]
What are you doing there? You seem so far away! 390
CARMEN [*crying as she approaches*]:
            Mariana!
MARIANA: Why are you crying?
CARMEN: My child, they're here!
FIRST NOVICE:
They're coming up the stairs...
[*A number of nuns enter upstage, all with sorrowful faces. The First
and Second Novices are to the front. Sister Carmen, dignified though
deeply grieving, stands near Mariana. Right through to its end the
whole scene increasingly acquires that strangely sharp light of a
Granada sunset. A rose and green light comes in through the archways,
while the cypress trees take on exquisitely subtle tones which make them
seem almost like precious stones. A soft orange light comes down from
above, which increases in intensity as the scene draws to a close.*]
MARIANA: Oh heart, do not betray me! Be still now! If you
had wings, where would you go? You too must rest a while.
A fantasy of shooting stars now waits for us   395
behind the silent cloak of death. Oh heart, stand firm!
CARMEN: Forget the world, Marianita, forget the world!
MARIANA: How far from me it seems already.
CARMEN: They have come!
MARIANA: How well I understand the meaning of that light!
It speaks of love, love and eternal solitude!   400

---

indicates, 'Granada', Lorca wrote, 'has complicated sunsets, filled always
with hitherto unknown lights, which seem as if they will never end' (*Obras
completas*, I, 938).

    The attention given to lighting and stage effects reminds us of the
atmospheric scenographies of Romantic playwrights such as the Duque de
Rivas and José de Zorrilla, but it also anticipates Lorca's later use of light
in such surreal sequences as the Moon's appearance on stage in *Blood
Wedding*.

171

[*Entra el Juez por la puerta de la izquierda.*]

NOVICIA 1. :
¡Es el juez!

NOVICIA 2. : ¡Se la llevan!

JUEZ: Señora, a sus órdenes;
hay un coche en la puerta.

MARIANA: Mil gracias. Madre Carmen,
salvo a muchas criaturas que llorarán mi muerte.
No olviden a mis hijos.

CARMEN: ¡Que la Virgen te ampare!

MARIANA: ¡Os doy mi corazón! ¡Dadme un ramo de flores!   405
En mis últimas horas yo quiero engalanarme.
Quiero sentir la dura caricia de mi anillo
y prenderme en el pelo mi mantilla de encaje.
Amas la Libertad por encima de todo,
pero yo soy la misma Libertad. Doy mi sangre,   410
que es tu sangre y la sangre de todas las criaturas.
¡No se podrá comprar el corazón de nadie!

[*Una monja le ayuda a ponerse la mantilla. Mariana se dirige al fondo, gritando.*]

Ahora sé lo que dicen el ruiseñor y el árbol.
El hombre es un cautivo y no puede librarse.
¡Libertad de lo alto! Libertad verdadera,   415
enciende para mí tus estrellas distantes.
¡Adiós! ¡Secad el llanto!

[*Al Juez.*] ¡Vamos pronto!

CARMEN: ¡Adiós, hija!

MARIANA: Contad mi triste historia a los niños que pasen.

400+ The Judge enters: Mariana was in fact visited by Rafael Ansaldo, the deputy mayor of Granada, who took her by berlin coach to the Low Prison on May 24, 1831 (Antonina Rodrigo, *op.cit.*, 146–7).

404 please care for my children: Mariana's last three days at the Low Prison – omitted by Lorca for greater dramatic unity – were largely spent worrying about her children's future. Since Mariana's own possessions had been confiscated, her children were totally destitute. All Mariana had left was her ring, which she was anxious to leave to her daughter. In the event, Mariana's son José María was taken into care by the priest José Garzón, and her daughter Luisa went to her natural father, Mariana's first biographer, José de la Peña y Aguayo (Antonina Rodrigo, *op.cit.*, 149, 154).

407-8 I wish to wear a lace mantilla...my engagement ring: Mariana prepares herself as a bride for her final encounter with death. In this lyrical transformation of defeat into triumph she seems to be at once the bride of spiritual love and of liberty.

414 Man is a prisoner who can never be free: this forceful declaration comes as a visionary insight to the human condition and it puts the play's political idealism in an absolute and negative perspective. Furthermore, as

[*The Judge enters through the door on the left.*]
FIRST NOVICE:
    The Judge!
SECOND NOVICE: He's come for her!
JUDGE: Señora, are you ready?
    A coach awaits outside.
MARIANA: I'm grateful. Mother Carmen,
    many young children will be saved in mourning me;
    please care for my children.
CARMEN: May the Virgin save you!
MARIANA: My heart I give to you! Give me a spray of flowers! 405
    I wish to leave this world adorned and beautiful.
    I wish to wear a lace mantilla in my hair
    while my hand feels the weight of my engagement ring.
    If you love liberty more than anything else,
    I am that self same Liberty. I give my blood,   410
    which is your blood and the blood of all living things,
    so no one's heart might ever more be bought or sold.
[*A nun helps her to put on her mantilla. Mariana goes upstage, her voice sounding out loudly.*]
    Now I know what the oak and the nightingale say:
    Man is a prisoner who can never be free.
    Oh, noble Liberty! Beloved Liberty,   415
    light up the sky for me with your radiant stars.
    Farewell! Dry your tears!
    [*To the Judge.*]   Let's go, quickly!
CARMEN: Farewell, child!
MARIANA: Tell my sad story to the children who pass by.

---

mentioned in the Introduction, it is a striking reminder of the concurrence of the Romantic ethos with that of twentieth-century thought as it was to crystallise in Surrealism. On the one hand, liberal-Romanticism, which took as its archetype the tormented hero,

el hombre que en fin que en su	the man who finally in his
ansiedad quebranta	anxiety breaks
su límite a la cárcel de la vida	the bounds of life's prison

(José de Espronceda, *op.cit.*, 139)

- a man who tragically found that his ambition could only be realised in death. On the other hand, Surrealism, the political affiliation of which was Marxist and the ethos of which is given by one of Spain's foremost surrealists, a close friend of Lorca, the film-maker Luis Buñuel: 'Through Surrealism I also discovered for the first time that man is not free' (*The World of Luis Buñuel*, edited by Joan Mellen (New York: Oxford U.P., 1978), 252.) This parallel is argued further in my forthcoming book, *From Romanticism to Surrealism* (University of Wales Press), which includes a chapter on Lorca; but my point at the moment is simply to suggest that *Mariana Pineda*, for all its period flavour, is not conceptually far removed from Lorca's own time.

CARMEN:	Porque has amado mucho, Dios te abrirá su puerta.
	¡Ay triste Marianita! ¡Rosa de los rosales! 420
NOVICIA 1.	[*Arrodillándose*]:
	Ya no verán tus ojos las naranjas de luz
	que pondrá en los tejados de Granada la tarde.
	[*Fuera empieza un lejano campaneo.*]
MONJA 1.	[*Arrodillándose*]:
	Ni sentirás la dulce brisa de primavera
	pasar de madrugada tocando tus cristales.
NOVICIA 2.	[*Arrodillándose y besando la orla del vestido de Mariana*
	¡Clavellina de mayo! ¡Luna de Andalucía! 425
	que en las altas barandas tu novio está esperándote.
CARMEN:	¡Marianita, Marianita, de bello y triste nombre,
	que los niños lamenten tu dolor por la calle!
MARIANA [*Saliendo*]:	
	¡Yo soy la Libertad porque el amor lo quiso!
	¡Pedro! La Libertad, por la cual me dejaste. 430
	¡Yo soy la Libertad, herida por los hombres!
	¡Amor, amor, amor, y eternas soledades!

[*Un campaneo vivo y solemne invade la escena, y un coro de niños empieza, lejano, el romance. Mariana se va, saliendo lentamente, apoyada en Sor Carmen. Todas las demás monjas están arrodilladas. Una luz maravillosa y delirante invade la escena. Al fondo, los niños cantan.*]

                ¡Oh, qué día tan triste en Granada,
                que a las piedras hacía llorar,
                al ver que Marianita se muere 435
                en cadalso por no declarar!
                [*No cesa el campaneo.*]
                        Telón lento

419-28 The verse couplets of the Novices, the First Nun and Mother Carmen lend a suitably formal and incantatory tone to Mariana's departure.
426 on the high. verandah!: the verandah or high railing is a fairly frequent symbol in Lorca, as J.M. Aguirre shows in his article 'Apostillas a "El sonambulismo de Federico Garcia Lorca"', *Bulletin of Hispanic Studies*, 53 (1976), 127-32. Aguirre argues convincingly that the verandah's basic symbolic value, by association with the moon, is death. Certainly the present context bears that out. The Spanish word *baranda* had occurred earlier in this act (line 253), where, for syllabication requirements, I translated it as *bar*.

CARMEN: Oh Marianita! Oh tender petal of rose!
              Having loved so truly, in God's arms you'll repose.   420
FIRST NOVICE [*kneeling*]:
              Never again will your eyes see this orange light
              that falls in blossoms on Granada's roofs at night.
              [*Offstage there sounds a distant ringing of bells.*]
FIRST NUN [*kneeling*]:
              Never again will you hear the sweet breeze of spring
              come touching your window at dawn with its soft wing.
SECOND NOVICE [*kneeling and kissing the hem of Mariana's dress.*]
              Oh springtime carnation, moon of Andalusia!   425
              Your beloved awaits you on the high verandah!
CARMEN: Mariana, Marianita, how sad is your name,
              the children in the street will always sing your tale!
MARIANA [*leaving*]:
              Now I am Liberty itself. Love made me so!
              That self-same Liberty for which you left me, Pedro.430
              I am Liberty, Liberty by man abused!
              And oh, love, love: love and eternal solitude!
[*A sharp and solemn peal of bells breaks upon the scene, and a
distant children's choir begins to sing the ballad. Mariana leaves
the stage slowly, leaning on Sister Carmen. All the other nuns are
kneeling. A splendrous, joyful light invades the scene. Offstage
the children sing*]:
              How sad was that day in Granada,
              when all the stones were made to cry,
              when on the scaffold stood Mariana   435
              who would not talk and had to die!
              [*The bells continue.*]
                   The curtain falls slowly

432+ <u>A sharp and solemn peal of bells:</u> the bells, the choir, the kneeling
nuns and the new infusion of light bring the play to a resounding spiritual
climax in what is perhaps the most positive and orthodox religious
sequence in the whole of Lorca's work.
433 <u>How sad was that day in Granada:</u> by repeating the opening sequence
of the Prologue Lorca encloses the entire drama within the parentheses of
the ballad. In addition to lending an appealing symmetry, this epilogue
reinforces our awareness of the play's fatalistic projection, while the past
tenses of the ballad serve to distance the audience once more from the
historical reality of Mariana's execution.

OTHER NEW AND FORTHCOMING BOOKS IN THE HISPANIC CLASSICS SERIES

All you need in one volume: introduction, original text, new Engli. translation, notes and commentary

Vicente BLASCO IBAÑEZ(1867-1928)
LA BARRACA (1898) translated into English by Lester Clark and Er Farrington Birchall, with Introduction by Pat McDermott

Antonio BUERO VALLEJO (b. Madrid 1916)
THE SHOT *(La Detonacion)* translated and edited by David Johnston
A DREAMER FOR THE PEOPLE *(Un Soñador para un Puebl* translated and edited by Michael Thompson

Federico GARCIA LORCA (1898-1936)
GYPSY BALLADS *(Romancero Gitano)* translated and edited by R. Havard
YERMA translated and edited by I. R.Macpherson, J. Minett & J.E.Lyc

Ramón María del VALLE-INCLÁN (1866-1936)
LIGHTS OF BOHEMIA,*(Luces de Bohemia)* translated and edited John Lyon
MR PUNCH THE CUCKOLD *(Los cuernos de Don Friolera esperpento)* translated and edited by R. Warner & D. Keown

For a full descriptive catalogue of these and other works, you a cordially invited to write to the publisher:

ARIS & PHILLIPS Ltd,
Teddington House, Warminster, Wiltshire BA12 8PQ, England

Printed and bound by CPI Group (UK) Ltd, Croydon, CR0 4YY

13/04/2025

14656566-0005